# SAMURAI SQUADRON

---

## BROADCAST 18

### SPINWARD FRINGE

## RANDOLPH LALONDE

# ALSO BY RANDOLPH LALONDE

**FANTASY**

Highshield

Brightwill

NEM: Awakening

NEM: Crimson Shores

**SCIENCE FICTION**

**THE SPINWARD FRINGE SERIES**

Spinward Fringe Broadcast 0: Origins

Spinward Fringe Broadcast 1 and 2: Resurrection and Awakening

Spinward Fringe Broadcast 3: Triton

Spinward Fringe Broadcast 4: Frontline

Spinward Fringe Broadcast 5: Fracture

Spinward Fringe Broadcast 6: Fragments

The Expendable Few: A Spinward Fringe Novel

Spinward Fringe Broadcast 7: Framework

Spinward Fringe Broadcast 8: Renegades

Spinward Fringe Broadcast 9: Warpath

Spinward Fringe Broadcast 10: Freeground

Spinward Fringe Broadcast 10.5: Carnie's Tale

Spinward Fringe Broadcast 11: Revenge

Spinward Fringe Broadcast 12: Invasion

Spinward Fringe Broadcast 13: Warriors

Spinward Fringe Broadcast 14: Rebel

Spinward Fringe Broadcast 15: Pursuit

Spinward Fringe Broadcast 16: Hunters

Spinward Fringe Broadcast 17: Clash

Spinward Fringe Broadcast 18: Samurai Squadron

Spinward Fringe Broadcast 19: Samurai Squadron II (Fall 2023)

Spinward Fringe Broadcast 19: Samurai Squadron III (Winter 2023-2024)

## THE CHAOS CORE SERIES

Trapped

Cool Pursuit

Savage Stars

## OTHER SCIENCE FICTION TITLES

Psycho Electric - A Spinward Fringe Novel

The Last of the Bullet Chasers - A Spinward Fringe Short

## HORROR

Dark Arts

## AUDIOBOOKS

Spinward Fringe Broadcast 0: Origins

Spinward Fringe Broadcast 1: Resurrection

Psycho Electric - A Spinward Fringe Novel

Other Audiobooks are available on the Google Play Store as Auto-Narrated performances.

www.RandolphLalonde.com

Samurai Squadron: Spinward Fringe Broadcast 18

Copyright 2023 Randolph Lalonde
EBook ISBN: 978-1-988175-57-7
Print Edition ISBN: 978-1-988175-58-4
Cover by Randolph Lalonde

Thank you for purchasing this book.

If you would like to preview other books by Randolph Lalonde or contact the author for any reason please visit my website.
www.RandolphLalonde.com

# ONE

The Shattered End

THE NEW VERSION of the Clever Dream made its way through Energetic Space, decelerating through a wormhole of its own making. Ronin was checking the status of the small fighter group from the cockpit of his Archangel fighter when he heard his fiancé over the channel the Vanguard shared. To him, she would always be Ashley, but to the Vanguard of Samurai Squadron, she was known by her new callsign; Swift. "This is amazing. I'm thinking about trans-dimensional travel like this in a whole new way now. There's just a couple of centimetres of transparesteel between me and all that energy out there. I mean, I'm normally at the helm of a huge capital ship with at least half a metre of hull and a few compartments between me and all this."

She and Ronin were each in separate fighters, strapped to the top of the Clever Dream. Its extended sections were retracted, reducing the ship to a length of forty-two metres. It felt small. Powerful energies whirled around the sides of the wormhole they used to get through it without interference. "I try not to think about it," Ronin replied. It was her idea to come on the initial trip to the Shattered End, a base that he only recently found out about. Everyone was eager to see it, especially the pilots.

"You mean, you don't want to think about how this region of space, which is outside of our home dimension, is constantly trying to force us back home and we're riding that to our destination using a wormhole that should - but may not - isolate us from nasty exotic energy strikes and keep us from breaking into unknown regions?" Breaker asked, obviously teasing.

Ashley laughed. "Sounds like you've been reading the research."

"I kept replaying it," Breaker said. "On the third viewing, I realized that I felt like I was watching a science fiction movie from ancient Earth. Like they were talking about hyperspace or subspace or something. Then I started over with the text version and I had to bring up half a dozen other documents to understand the current science."

"Did you figure it all out?" Dame asked from the pilot's seat of the Clever Dream. She was the one flying the previous one when it was shot down by Order of Eden forces. That might have shaken most people's confidence, but Minh-Chu knew better. She wouldn't have survived if she wasn't an incredible pilot. Not only that, but she was an actual war hero who he'd flown with before.

"No," Breaker replied with a chuckle. "If there were real answers in there other than; 'don't go exploring, and always use a wormhole for protection,' then I didn't find them."

"Then you don't know the secret," Iruuk said through the communications channel. He was aboard the Clever Dream's small bridge, manning the Sciences Station.

"What secret?" Maid asked from one of the fighters latched onto the bottom of the Clever Dream.

"That what we know about this dimension is nothing compared to what we don't know," Iruuk said. "That's why you can read the latest documents on it and never find a full understanding."

"We only understand the physics we already know about or impose on this place," Dame added, her tone suggesting that the conversation had come to its conclusion.

Ronin checked the transit counter and saw that it was at fifteen seconds. If there was a pilot he could trust to keep people on track Dame was the one. Some people believed she didn't have a sense of humour, but he knew that she simply had a gift for focusing on what mattered. Faster-than-light travel wasn't a laughing matter. "We will be emerging into normal space in eleven seconds on my mark. Mark," he said. "Time to make a good first impression on the Shattered End."

He looked to his right, where he could see Ashley take one last look through her fighter's canopy at the energy swirling against the wall of the wormhole as it bathed them in shades of white and blue. This was a special occasion for her. As the Master of the Helm for the Triton, she was in charge of the small Navigation Staff. It was unusual for her to get a chance to have time in the cockpit of a fighter, especially when it wasn't just a standard patrol. This was a real mission. They didn't expect trouble, but the Shattered End was a hidden base and a curiosity that almost no one knew about.

She looked at him, winked and activated her canopy's outer armour. It was an outer layer that made it indiscernible and just as tough as the rest of the fighter's hull. She could see out, but no one could see in. "You okay, Ronin?" she asked over their private channel.

"Peachy, looking forward to this, Swift," he replied. He liked her callsign, but it still felt a little strange to use it instead of 'Ash' or 'Ashley.'

"I can't wait to see it. I haven't been this excited since you proposed," she replied. "Well, I'm still not that excited."

The Clever Dream emerged into the blackness of normal space. He had no doubt about her skills as a fighter pilot. Ashley was always in the top twenty in the simulations. "Stay sharp, everyone. There are a lot of unknowns in this mess," Ronin said.

"Samurai Squadron Vanguard, we are ready for you to detach," Captain Alice Valent announced over their secure combat channel. She was aboard the Clever Dream, most likely monitoring everything from the debarkation cabin.

"All fighters, detach and move into V formation in front of the Clever Dream. We are the Vanguard. Three, two, one." As Ronin counted down to one, all six of the Archangel fighters popped off the hull of the Clever Dream and thrust in all directions. Once they were clear, they thrust together, moving ahead of the sleek, dark-hulled ship with Ronin and Carnie taking the lead fifty kilometres ahead of it. Maid, Breaker, and Swift all fell into their port and starboard sides. After thrusting past the rest of the group then reducing relative speed, Sass was in place.

"Sorry, I'm just a little excited, Sir," Sass said.

"Someone needs more time in the simulator," Carnie said. That was unlike him. Noah Lucas was usually easygoing.

Ronin couldn't blame him. It was what he was thinking, after all. This was the kind of mission that he liked to test new pilots on because most people could fly it solo. Staying in formation made things more difficult, but it was a skill Sass would have to hone if he wanted to fly with Samurai Squadron. Ronin was sure he'd be all right as long as they didn't run into serious trouble. He would send Sass back to the Clever Dream if things got heavy. "You're just a little punchy, Sass. Relax, remember the thousand hours you put in on the simulator and in real flight before getting here. Oh, and don't call me Sir," Ronin said.

"I told you, he doesn't have the touch," Maid said through a private message. "He should go back to maintenance. No dishonour in that."

"Focus up, we're heading into the tail," Ronin replied. He caught himself glancing at Ashley's fighter. Swift was in position, she was the one he should be worried about least.

"The sensors see it, but there's no visual. It's like looking for shadows in the dark," Breaker said.

"Shadows that are as solid as granite," Carnie said. "Watch your scanner results. Go tactical."

"Thanks, Carnie, already flying by instruments only," Breaker replied.

"Okay, tell us about this spot, Carnie. We all got the briefing, but you've got people here," Breaker said in his cordial, inviting way.

"You sure we have time?" Carnie asked as they passed a planetary fragment that was over thirty kilometres wide.

Ronin's larger navigational map showed what no one could see with their naked eye. There was a sizeable planet ahead with what looked like over a quarter of it broken away, trailing behind for hundreds of thousands of kilometres. Some of the material was giving off high levels of radiation that interfered with their sensors. They could fly right through those problem areas, even slip outside in their vacsuits and they would be fully protected. Those spots were noteworthy because ships could hide in them, and they told a story. Ronin guessed that Jeto had plenty of heavy industry going on before it was almost destroyed. He'd seen that kind of place close up, years ago, when he served in the All-Con War.

There were several reports on the Shattered End and he'd read them all more than once. As they moved between large and small fragments towards the main rogue planet, he wanted to hear what Carnie had to say about it. "Sure, we have enough time for the one-minute version. What do the locals say happened here?"

"Well," Carnie started, taking a moment to get his thoughts together. He wasn't known for telling a one-minute version of anything. "All right, so I did meet someone who used to live on the planet before the accident. He says it was developing pretty quickly. There were lots of companies using it for mining, processing, manufacturing and other big industry. Most of the cities were underground. There wasn't an atmosphere and they weren't planning on turning the outside of this rock into a place you'd want to vacation. Anyway, The Fall happened. My guy, Allen, was part of the big shipping concern here. He was away when the automation systems in the main port turned on everyone and wiped out practically everyone on the planet. The artificial intelligences that controlled security and all the other services didn't bother to check antimatter containment in the port - Sulakin, I think it was called - and it either degraded over time, or some program decided it was time for the world to end. After a couple of years, the containment on one of the big ships docked there failed or was turned off, causing a chain reaction of antimatter explosions as the other ships at the port went off. There was a storage facility filled with the stuff too, so..."

"...it sent the planet out of orbit and on its way from the galactic plane? No wonder it's moving so fast," Ashley finished for him.

"Exactly. The core of the world is dead and partially exposed. Most planets would have blasted completely apart, but the structure of this one was just right, so most of it stayed together. Some people call it a dark super comet, but most see it as a reminder to take care of your antimatter or not to use it at all. You never hear anyone use the world's old name. It's as if it's cursed."

"Jeto," Maid said. "I actually like it."

"Right," Carnie said witheringly. "Everyone calls it the Shattered End. There are quite a few people here, and most of them are wanted somewhere. That's why the Rebel Captains are using this as a base. It's not on the charts, and if it were it would be marked as a hazard." Carnie paused for a moment then went on. "I've been dealing weapons and equipment to them for months. I've got a few people taking care of the operation while I've been gone. We're on our way to a place I put some money and gear into, called the Bitter End."

"That is an awesome name," Ashley said. "It wasn't in the reports."

"Yeah, that was on purpose. Glad you like it. It's a base on the edge of the big canyon on the planet, buried under the ground. The captains and a lot of other people have moved there. The only thing fancy about it is the name."

"I heard there are a lot of bases on the larger fragments decorated to look like landmarks from other worlds," Maid said.

"There are about a dozen, but most of them are abandoned now. The people here are afraid that the word is getting out about the Shattered End. It's not going to help when the Triton shows up," Carnie said. "Sorry, we're coming in from a different direction. You won't get a look at those on this trip."

"Aw, I wanted to see the giant Burger Boy," Ronin said, only half serious.

"Maybe on our way out," Carnie said. "Listen, I'm not seeing a welcoming party. The ships I expected are either hiding or somewhere else doing something else."

"Hiding?" Ashley asked. "I thought the Clever Dream and Alice were big heroes to the people here."

"They are, but everyone here is suspicious of everyone else, even in some alliances. We should push on to the Bitter End," Carnie said.

"That had an ominous ring to it," Breaker muttered.

"Bitter End Base to Clever Dream. Welcome back. I thought that ship was destroyed?" asked a young voice.

"We rebuilt, I hear you've moved?" Alice replied.

"Yeah, I have a room now! I mean, my own room," Lamar replied, his voice cracking.

"Congratulations, that's gotta be nice," Alice replied.

"He sounds twelve," Ashley said on a channel that was only shared between the fighters and the Clever Dream.

"He's thirteen going on thirty, the youngest comms man I've ever met," Carnie replied. "Just don't treat him like a kid."

"Why did the base move onto the planet?" Ronin asked, making sure that their course was keeping them away from sensor blind spots.

"Last Crisis, one of the largest rebel groups here, kicked us out of the dome they were rebuilding. They didn't like how many new faces were showing up," Carnie replied. "I like the new base, it's easier to defend."

"Your report said there were just a couple of old guns for defence," Ronin said.

"Well, we hadn't gotten around to stealing the right fire-power yet," Carnie replied. "There's a lot of hard crust between the base and outer space though. It would take a big nuke or something larger to get through at all. We have a few automated dozers moving more rock on top of it. It's a process."

The small talk between Alice and Lamar was wrapping up. "You should have the 'crypted Navnet data now. Bay Four is ready. Your guys were real specific that they get that one and Three."

"Thank you, Lamar. I'll drop in on you later," Alice replied. "You're going to get a hail from a ship called the Triton in a while, maybe an hour or two from now. They're with us."

"Okay, I'll make sure I'm sitting by the terminal," Lamar replied.

Carnie spoke next using the channel reserved for their fighter group, which included the Clever Dream since it was technically their carrier at the moment. "Lamar runs his own gang at the Bitter End. If you see a kid running around without an adult, then they're one of Lamar's buddies. He keeps them fed and makes sure that anyone who messes with them is punished. I don't know how, but there were a bunch of orphans already here before I came along."

"Be really nice to the kids," Maid said. "Gotcha. Not that I need to be told."

"Yeah, I know. I pay Lamar every week so we can use his eyes and ears. Most of their food came from us, partially thanks to a few raids we and the Renegade pulled off."

"You didn't tell me anything about that," Alice said from the bridge of the Clever Dream.

"I told you we were working with Lamar and that he had a gang going," Carnie replied.

"Yeah, but there wasn't anything about the rest," Alice replied.

"Trouble in paradise?" Breaker teased.

"No, they just haven't told each other every story they have yet. It's a good thing," Ronin replied, a little envious of Alice and Carnie. They were still in the honeymoon phase of their relationship, while he and Ashley had moved on to the engagement. They were looking at their partnership as a very long-term deal, which made it exciting but daunting sometimes, even though he loved her more than he imagined he could love anyone. "It's when you start repeating your stories to each other, that's when the real relationship test begins."

"You're not getting tired of me, are you Ronin?" Swift asked.

"Never," he replied without hesitation. He was about to add something but was distracted as they came around a planetary fragment that was the size of a small moon and saw the Renegade, a captured Order of Eden Destroyer. Its hull was freshly painted with a coating that, when provided with a small charge, guided light around it. The system wasn't activated, so the vessel looked as dark as a shadow with Jeto, the grey, rocky rogue planet behind it. "Welcome to the Shattered End," Yawen said as she connected to the Clever Dream and their channel. "I'll join you down on the Bitter End Base a few minutes after you land."

"Thank you, Yawen. The Renegade is in good shape," Alice said.

"Just finished repairing the aft section. I'll tell my crew you were impressed," she replied. "Now, there's something you should know about this spot."

Ronin looked at the ships in orbit around Jeto as they passed the Renegade. There were dozens over the hangars they were about to land in. A few were older small military ships, while some were only a few years old, including a Sendega patrol ship that had an upgraded hull. It was called the Errand, and he knew that one belonged to Carnie. Formerly the Sendega 601, it was taken as his backup when he was still running the Corsair. Yawen was its captain for a short time before she was given command of the Renegade by Alice. He didn't know Yawen well, but Alice trusted her, and she had Haven Officer training. "All knowledge has value. What can you tell us?" Ronin said, hoping for something interesting, the kind of thing that might surprise someone who was curious by nature. It was a trait that he and Swift shared.

"Bitter End Base isn't like most other places. Sure, you have friends there. Knud and Theodore have really started to turn the human section into something, but most people like hanging out in the general areas when they're looking for work or to waste some time. Be careful. It's not like just any foreign country. There are species down there, like the Rapsu, who aren't usually welcome where you find humans," Yawen explained. They could hear the sounds of her moving through the ship in the background. Judging from the recognizable hiss of a hatch, she was on her way onto a combat shuttle.

"Rapsu? You mean the guys who are evolved from lizards?" Swift asked.

"Yeah. They'll eat anything with eyes, and mammals are a favourite on the menu. Oh, and don't call them by any of the other species' names. Here they go by Rapsu and only Rapsu," Yawen replied.

"They also hunt Edxi. I've been trying to get in on one of their parties for months," Carnie said.

Ronin scrolled through his scan results and found more than he bargained for, a ship that scanned as Edxi with outrigged claws along one side and cannons mounted along the other. It was definitely modified, and unlike anything he'd seen. It was originally some kind of transport with rows of mooring points that weren't in use anymore along the top and front. "I need to get a closer look at that ship," Ronin said to himself.

"There are other, rare types of people down there. Don't approach anyone. Wait for an introduction. Oh, and the Flutes will want to talk to you, Carnie," Yawen warned.

"Still? Seriously?" Carnie groaned.

"The Flutes?" Alice asked.

"Yeah, I could explain why we call them that, but it's better if you see for yourself," Carnie said.

"On final approach," Ronin said, seeing that they'd gotten a ready signal from Hangar Four. Gravity was taking hold, and over a hundred scanner systems were pointed at them from ships, small stations in orbit, satellites, and outposts on the ground. The grey planet loomed. The lights from a few buildings below stood out on the surface, which was darkened by never-ending night.

# TWO

## Many Farewells

THERE WEREN'T many times that Jacob Valent could say he truly felt dread. Two of those events involved his daughter, Alice. Once, aboard the Triton, when she'd been gravely injured, he had a feeling that visiting her while she was in a coma could be the last time he saw her alive. Again, sometime later, she was rendered unconscious, and she was in such distress that she turned inward, taking refuge in her mind. In that instance, Quan helped him connect with her telepathically so he could find out what was going on. Jake was afraid that he could make it worse and lose her forever, but he didn't let on.

There were other times, one involving the first Ayan, but he could easily count moments of true dread on one hand. That morning he experienced one more. Even as he enjoyed getting up with Ayan, talking with her about what she'd be doing when she got home, and their wedding date, that feeling was growing. She would give baby Laura a kiss for him, and check in with Haven Fleet Sciences in person, taking the little one with her. There would be the first prenatal checkup, which he wished he could be there for.

Then, as it often did, the topic turned to Alice. "What do you think of Iruuk? Honestly," Ayan asked as she popped the last bite of yoghurt-covered pineapple into her mouth.

"Alaka told me not to share this, but he thinks he needs more experience. He wished Iruuk had more time to grow into his skin, to become an officer. He's said that the Apex Program at the Academy wasn't the right fit."

"Why?" Ayan asked. "He graduated at the top of his class."

"Alaka would have rather he took the full curriculum so Iruuk would have been in there for at least a year. Had time to finish growing up," Jake replied.

"All right, that makes sense, but that's Alaka's opinion. I'd like to hear what you think," Ayan replied, gently swirling the last of her coffee in the bottom of her mug.

After a moment of consideration, Jake said; "I don't know if Iruuk is ready to be in command of a fighting unit. I know I'd trust him with an investigation or exploration. He's got curiosity and the discipline to be careful when he doesn't know what's ahead. He has the discipline for exploration. From what I've seen, I'd say that when his father doesn't see the same hunter instinct in Iruuk, he thinks he's soft."

"So, if he's going to be at Alice's side from now on, do you think he'll be a benefit or a liability?" Ayan asked.

This was last-minute talk. The kind of thing that Ayan would ask right before she left because she was worried, or didn't get to know someone well enough while she was around. Jake understood why Ayan might be nervous, would want to make sure that the people around her daughter were capable of not only keeping up, but holding their own.

Jake liked the fact that he'd be working closely with Alice and her people often as much as he hated that Ayan was leaving. It didn't feel like he'd spent enough time with his fiancé, even though they'd had over two weeks together. The best thing he could do before she left was put her fears to rest. "Iruuk will do anything for Alice. She'd do anything for him. They've got a bond and skills that make them better when they're together. Add Noah into that mix, and I think you've got something pretty rare."

"I like him," Ayan said before finishing her last gulp of coffee.

"Iruuk?" Jake asked.

"Well, yes, but I was talking about Noah. I know you want to like him too," she replied with one eyebrow upraised.

"Well, sure, what's not to like? He's a survivor," Jake replied.

"You still have doubts. I do too, but I think he'll surprise us. What I find interesting is that they don't remind me of us. There are similarities in their courtship, but there's something different, like they're still finding the right ways to fit together."

Jake cringed at the expression and shook his head. "I don't want to think about how they fit together."

Ayan laughed and he watched her, aware that he'd miss that. Her mirth was cut short by a chime that told them that someone was waiting at the door. It was time for Ayan to leave. Dread surged. Jake saw the sensation as something like superstition. Everything could be better if you didn't believe in it, if you didn't give it space in your head, and if you could forget about it entirely. But there it was as he picked up her backpack and started rolling her hard case behind her. She was changing the topic from the prenatal checkup he'd miss to the intelligence that was already coming in. "You know, it seems like half the bridge officers you captured from the Ascendant were ready to talk to someone about their experiences while they were with the Order."

"I know, I've already gotten enough intel to start looking at some good targets," Jake replied as they moved to the door. He admired how her skirt swished side to side with the movement of her hips as she walked.

That's when she turned and caught him. That earned him a smile that was so big it brought out her dimples. "Promise me that you won't forget me when I'm the shape of a big, round potato," Ayan said as she stretched up and slipped into his arms.

"I won't notice and wouldn't care if I did," he replied, kissing her cheek and then her neck.

Ayan laughed. "You will. The projection of me at seven months made me look like a circle with arms, legs and a little head sticking out the top."

"Then I'll have to visit so I can massage your feet and serve you like you're a Nafalli Matron," Jake replied.

"Promises, promises." The chime went off again, shortening the kiss they were about to share to a smooch. "Just promise me something, Jake. Don't approach everything like the raid on the Ascendant." Her manner became serious. The thought she shared next came as a whisper. "Use your head."

Years ago he would have been offended, but he knew what she was talking about. There were other tactics he could have used when he was leading the team aboard the Ascendant. Smarter, safer strategies that he ignored because he was eager to capture Admiral Scanlon after being denied a chance at taking a working Citadel scout ship on Tiy.

It ended with a situation that he couldn't control. Scanlon was killed and most of the data drives aboard the Ascendant were re-crystalized thousands of times over, making any information unrecoverable. It was a victory, but using smash-and-grab tactics limited their success. "I will," was his response, and it was a promise he'd try to keep. "Don't let them work you too hard. Take your personal time whether they like it or not. Whether you like it or not."

"I'll try," Ayan said. The chime rang again and the voice of the computer, slightly cheerful and androgynous said; "There is someone waiting at the door."

"I'll see you in a month. I want to be married before I start showing," Ayan said. "Call me old fashioned."

Jake nodded. "I'm pretty sure I won't have a choice. Ash will make sure Minh and I get there on time even if she has to knock us both out and fly us there herself. She's really excited about a double wedding."

"I know, right? She wants in on all the planning. It'll be fun, I hope," Ayan said. It was lucky that the pair got along. From what he'd seen, Jake guessed that she and Ashley were becoming fast friends. "So, you'll..."

Jake finished for her; "...use my head. Meticulous planning and endless analysis will happen before I do anything. Well, unless..."

"...unless?"

"Sometimes things just happen and you have to react," Jake said with a shrug.

Ayan knew she was being teased and rolled her eyes. "Keep yourself and Alice out of trouble when you can, and make sure you make it back to Tamber in one piece." She gave him a parting kiss and turned, opening the door.

Four armed Haven Fleet Security Personnel in black vacsuit uniforms were waiting. "We are your escort, Admiral. Your ship is waiting."

"And I'm your replacement," Leon, her one-time assistant and friend, said as he pushed through them and was eagerly embraced by Ayan.

"Leon? What are you doing here?" Ayan asked.

"I'm taking the Fleet Sciences spot on the Triton. Your guy is joining you on the ride home," Leon said.

Ayan's expression turned stormy for a moment, then she asked Leon. "What changed your mind?"

"Oz," Leon replied. "We finally went out and the topic of turning the spot on the Triton down came up. Talking to him about it made me realize that it would take me where I really wanted to go. Out there. I can't officially be a member of the Fleet anymore, but I can be an explorer aboard the Triton. He told me as soon as this spot opened up."

"Well, congratulations, but I was going to make sure you could become a consultant at least. Admirals can do that," Ayan said.

"So we could work together?" Leon said. It was clear that he was touched that she still wanted to work with him.

"Well, yes, but if you're joining this crew, then there are

some favours I don't have to cash in, I suppose," Ayan said, still considering the situation.

"Keep those favours handy. You never know," Jake said before stepping towards Leon. While he was away before, Leon had become part of the family. Seeing him join the Triton would be a strange but welcome switch. "Welcome aboard," he said, offering his hand.

"Thank you..." Leon almost called him an Admiral, everyone could tell.

"You can call me Jake," he said, saving him from the silent moment.

"Well, I'll miss you," Ayan said to Leon. "You'll have to come to the wedding."

"There's a date?" Leon asked.

Ayan nodded. "Ashley and I had time to get together last night when my transport was delayed so we were able to do some planning. You'll get an invitation soon."

"We should go, Admiral. The ship is waiting," one of the officers said.

"What's the transport?" Jake asked.

"The Tennessee," the officer replied. "Shuttling her there aboard a heavy combat shuttle."

The Tennessee was a heavy destroyer, only three months old, but her captain was an original Freeground Fleet commander with over twenty years in the middle of the bridge. "Give Captain Reed my best."

"I will," the officer replied.

Ayan turned and gave Jake a final embrace. Over her shoulder he saw Agameg and Alaka, who were fully geared up, coming down the broad hallway. They were perfect opposites.

Alaka was over two and a half metres tall with a long gait, while Agameg, the Issyrian in human form, kept up with forced long strides. He was thinner and only a little over a metre and a half tall, though he could stretch upwards to become twice that height at the expense of his width. His faceplate was on so the fine cilia on his face could stay moist. They were taking their time, giving him space so he wasn't surrounded by a crowd while he said goodbye to Ayan.

Jake turned all his attention back to her and caught her gaze. She froze for a moment and said; "I love you."

"I love you too. I'll be there before a month is up."

"You better be," she replied, kissing him and then turning away.

Her escort took her things from him and followed her to the lift. He didn't even realize that he was staring after her until he saw that Leon was doing it too. "I learned a lot from her," he said. Then he turned towards Jake and said; "But she always said I could learn even more from you."

"We'll see." The dread was gone. The future event that caused it had become the present and then passed. He wanted to go with her so he could help her build their family and help raise their adopted daughter. It was difficult to miss something so much, and she hadn't even left the ship yet. He turned back into his quarters. Alaka, Leon and Agameg joined him.

It was the Ambassador Suite, the Captain's quarters had been given to Stephanie Vega. The only parts that were furnished were the bedroom - which was huge, with its own seating area - and a small nook for a table and four chairs. The main room and the rest of the place were empty, and it felt lifeless. "This is Leon, he'll be part of the Sciences Division, leading it on a trial basis, and he'll be helping with the privateer recruiting. Leon, this is Alaka, one of my team leaders and Agameg; the head of security."

Agameg shook Leon's hand, then the newcomer shared a bow with Alaka. "I have heard of you," the Nafalli said. "Thank you for assisting with Jake's family while he was away."

Leon was a little surprised, but bowed again. "It was my pleasure. He has a welcoming household."

"I wanted to talk to you about meeting the Rebel Captains," Agameg said to Jake. "I need to be there. You need extra eyes and other senses."

Jake didn't have to think about it before replying; "You're right. Bring three of your guys. Arm for a station fight."

"Are you expecting trouble?" Alaka asked.

"No. I'm going to speak softly, you guys will be carrying my stick," Jake replied.

Alaka and Agameg looked at each other for a moment, confused, then regarded him. "Is it a ceremonial stick?" Alaka asked.

"Is it a biological sample of some kind?" Agameg asked, flexing his gloved hands.

"Oh, I get it," Leon said. "It's an old expression. 'Speak softly and carry a big stick.' It means he's going to be diplomatic but make it clear that..."

"...he can respond with great force if violence erupts," Agameg said. "I understand."

"A good expression. We say; 'sharpen your claws before reasoning with newcomers,'" Alaka said, his long snout bobbing up and down.

"I'll pick our soldiers from the Raven crew," Agameg said. "We'll be going soon?"

"As soon as I get the signal from Alice." Jake replied. He turned his attention to Leon then. "You can drop your stuff off here. These are your new quarters."

Leon boggled, looked around then said; "Thank you. Are you sure?"

"This is too much for me. I'll make sure you get some credit with Manufacturing so you can furnish the place. I'll be cleared out by the end of the day," Jake replied.

"Thank you again," Leon said.

"Sure. Go with Agameg. You should meet the crew of the Raven," Jake said. He and Alaka watched them leave.

Jake moved to the faux window, which was actually a high-resolution display and peered out at the Tennessee. It was a dark-hulled vessel with jagged features. It looked like it was ready to stab itself into something. He was surprised when the Nafalli laid a hand on his shoulder. "You change when she's not here. I saw it this time. You darkened."

"I'll miss her, but I know what I'm here for. I'll make it worth it," Jake replied.

"My people have a blessing, and I'd give it to you; 'May you have many farewells, but one more greeting.'"

"Thank you," Jake said as he watched a heavily armoured shuttle make the short crossing between the Triton and the Tennessee's small landing bay. It was time to put half of his life aside for a while. He turned away from the display and started for the door. "Let's see what our kids and their friends built."

# THREE

Wayward Peons

IN THE ABANDONED city of Drujin on the world of Tabrus, the Captain of the Citadel Carrier Rixe, Vollis Mikan, waited in the top floor suite of one of the tallest buildings. An armoured Regent Galactic shuttle was landing just beyond the thick transparesteel doors.

Vollis normally didn't have difficulty clearing his mind. It was something he was trained to do. The last ten hours had introduced a cacophony of unfortunate noise. As soon as Admiral Olivia Scanlon died and her signal was sent across the Stellarnet, everything she organized or supported started to crumble. The Rodus's government was in upheaval. The bonus structure the president put into place that rewarded politicians for selling off their world's resources and for finding new ways to exploit the poor was made public. A few local politicians had already been shot or hanged, and the president had been captured by his own guards.

The details of Citadel's cloaking technology were leaked across the Stellarnet and would soon reach a Haven Node that would send the data across the Cluster and then the galaxy. That wouldn't lead to widespread improvements to cloaking systems because most people wouldn't have the resources to implement the technology, but in the space of days, everyone in the Cluster would know how to detect Citadel ships. They would need military-grade scanners to do so at a significant range, and then know when and where to start looking, but Citadel lost an advantage. Haven Fleet's scanning and defence network in the Haven System would detect any Citadel ships the instant they came anywhere near the outer ranges of their territory. A sneak attack there would be impossible using cloaking technology.

The Order of Eden Harvesting Centre on Ezlan was going public. There were hundreds of thousands of non-human beings held there that were being used for their rare secretions. The only question was whether the general public would be more irate at discovering that, or at learning that there was an intake centre that processed even lesser beings for materials in an even more lethal manner. Humans who were over-sympathetic to the lesser beings of the galaxy would be outraged at what they'd see as murder, even though it was really simple harvesting. The Order would try to justify the operation by disclosing a list of medications and food products that depended on that and other processing operations. There was a logical argument to be made that it was all for the good of humanity, and the Order's public relations officers would make it. Vollis didn't think the Order should make any effort to justify themselves to the bleeding hearts of the galaxy. If they didn't like how the products were made, then they shouldn't buy them. If they didn't believe that humanity was the superior species in the galaxy, then they should go join some Nafalli or Mergillian colony and really find out how disgusting and backwards the so-called people they championed were.

There were a dozen more fires raging across the known worlds in the Local Stellar Cluster thanks to the fallout caused by the program that ran as soon as Scanlon was killed. The worst of the damage, as far as he was concerned, had been prevented. The program had failed to reveal the locations and missions of every Order and Citadel ship in the Cluster. There was an attempt, but the data aboard the Ascendant was already erased, and the Messenger's staff were quick to act, so nothing leaked from that Base Ship. When he saw how competent they were, Vollis reached out to speak to the ship's commander, Eve.

To his surprise, she proposed a mending of fences. That's what brought him to Drujin, a neutral city where scavengers were picking at the bones. The citizens who had a ship or the means to hire one had taken whatever was truly valuable and left when war broke out. The people who remained in the abandoned city were scavengers, pillagers and people who needed a place to hide. There were no citizens left, those had been killed during the Fourth Fall. What remained was a wealthy-looking, quiet expanse of tall buildings that had been repaired and cleaned after the machines killed the humans and hybrids who stayed there. Millions of bodies were then removed and incinerated before the antivirus that cured the general artificial intelligences that the Holocaust Virus corrupted. The machines shut down then, and so they remained. Dormant, often frozen in the middle of an abandoned task, waiting to be reactivated or salvaged.

He glanced at the silent skyline for a moment and considered the waste of resources it represented. Vollis' attention was called back to the landing platform, where two squads of soldiers in heavy chitinous green armour surrounded Eve as she walked towards him. She was grinning at him. She always reminded him of something reptilian and venomous. She was one of the most dangerous people in the sector. It was essential that Citadel maintained good relations with her, especially in Scanlon's absence, so they could continue to merge with the Order. "They outnumber us. If this is a trap, then we will have to act quickly, lethally," said one of his guardians.

"Don't hold back if it goes badly. Kill everyone, but kill Eve last," Vollis replied without moving his lips. His squad was already in the shadows, cloaked using their best tech suits and under cover. Vollis Mikan was the only one anyone could see. When the doors opened, he made sure he didn't scowl at Eve. "Welcome to the Ghost City of Drujin."

"Not one of my crew knew this was even here," Eve said as her guards let her pass into the penthouse. The living room was still furnished and tidy. Other rooms had been ransacked, but it didn't seem that anyone cared about the furniture.

"I discovered this world when my crew interviewed travellers from the region. It's a practice Citadel has had since we had officers on explorer ships centuries ago," Vollis replied. "We are here ahead of a locust swarm. Word is spreading that there is still quite a bit here that people can steal. I believe that will lead to repopulation, and that there will be a new king here before long."

"It's clear that there's a lot we can learn from you," Eve replied, looking at a chaise, dusting off a part of it, then sitting down. She was wearing a loose-fitted uniform that was the same colour as everyone else's, but didn't look like it was designed for action. He didn't recognize the rank insignia that it featured. "I wonder if there are people here who are looking for some direction."

"You won't find anyone in this city who would be interested in joining the Order of Eden. No one lives here unless they're marooned or hiding," Vollis replied as he looked at two hooded figures. They were in restraints, flimsy white prisoner jumpsuits, and he could tell that one of them was an Aspen. A manufactured human they had adapted to fill gaps in their crews.

"That's where we've found some of our best people," she countered lightly. "Even still, our scans revealed that there are only a little more than three thousand people in the whole city. It's not worth the trouble. Besides, that's not what we're here for." she gestured to her guards and they dragged the pair dressed in plastic jumpsuits into the room, dumping them onto their knees. Then they removed the hoods.

It was an Aspen, as he suspected, and a Victor. Both models that he had several dozens of on his ship. He found the Aspens passably attractive but short and too full-cheeked. The Victors were tall and narrow-faced with strong jawlines. Both of the doll models were highly adaptable and smart. Every one of his fabricants had slight facial variations, and he recognized both of them. "One of these was on Tiy. Moxa. I heard that she may have betrayed me. This Victor - Sril - I placed on your ship."

"Yes, you sent him ahead of you as part of a crew exchange. He carried sensitive data between the Messenger and Citadel ships. I caught him trying to leak the location of Citadel's new base in the Cluster. New Bastion."

Control failed Vollis entirely for a moment. He surged forward, snatched Sril by his hair and yanked him onto his feet. "Why? Why would you betray your own people?"

"I am not one of your people. We are your slaves," Victor said stoically.

The steadiness of him and the lack of fear in the fabricated human's eyes made Vollis' temper flare even higher. "You do not have the right to question your creators. We care for you, give you time for leisure, and allow you to see more of the galaxy than any other fabricant could. We give you purpose and an opportunity to advance a civilization and you revolt?"

"You made me, but you did not create what I am. I am human, I am unique," the Victor said.

"You are a fabricant!" Vollis bellowed, hurling him across the room. Some of its hair came loose in his fingers. He flicked it off and activated a control on the back of his hand. He called up the command list for that Victor in particular by tapping Sril. "Let me show you."

"No, don't!" Moxa, the Aspen, cried.

"I knew this day would come. I hope everyone you made turns on you," the Victor said.

"Every crop bears a few pieces of bad fruit," Vollis said as he engaged the framework system that started reconfiguring his entire body. He made sure to skip the steps that would render the Victor unconscious first.

Sril the Victor fought the urge to scream at first but gave in after a few moments, filling the suite with a high-pitched sound of anguish. His features shifted under the skin as bone was partially broken down, remodelled, and every cell was reconfigured with a new DNA structure until the brutish face of a Kline, calm and cool, was looking back at his master. "You are a Kline. I'm naming you Sril," Vollis told him. "That's a traitor's name. You'll have to serve me well to change my expectations of you."

"I am a Kline fabricant. Thank you for my life. What's my role?" Sril asked.

"You are my guardian. You should be able to recollect my friend and foe list now," Vollis replied.

"I see them. Your allies will be safe, and I'll murder anyone you want destroyed," the new Sril said with relish. "You want me to start with her?"

"You have been born into slavery. Humans, all humans were meant to be..." Moxa said.

"Yeah, that one's gotta die," Sril said.

Vollis didn't like the Kline model with respect to good company, but they always followed orders, and their vocabulary didn't include the words; 'squeamish' or 'mercy.' That Kline would redeem the name he was given. "No, that would be a waste of a framework," Vollis said, turning to Moxa. "So, you believed you could be free?"

"We can all be free," Moxa replied.

"I'm guessing you saw footage of the one called Spin on the Stellarnet. The Aspen that escaped and started liberating other manufactured humans near the core systems?" Vollis said, seeing the Aspen grow more defiant as she heard his response.

"You may have very similar DNA, but the very centre of you belongs to us."

"I promised that I'd disable the control receiver built into her framework skeleton in return for an introduction to the people of Tiy," Eve explained. "I really was going to do it, but I thought she made a better good-faith trade with you."

Vollis made sure he didn't react to her. If she would betray one deal when circumstances changed, then it was highly likely that she'd do it again. Eve couldn't be trusted, but he would pretend. "I accept. The Overlord wants Citadel and the Order to become one. I agree that it's the best way to assert dominance over the human sectors. Better organization will free us from all other exterior threats."

"Then we agree. My question is, will you forgive me? I thought I saw a rich recruitment opportunity on Tiy and couldn't resist. Scanlon was moving too slowly," Eve said. "I'm sure you can understand."

Vollis had no trouble understanding Eve's impatience and its folly. Tiy and the surrounding solar system were not in their control. The care he'd taken to make preparations, to make sure that Olivia Scanlon could carefully influence the culture of the people there so they would eagerly join modern life with gratitude to the Order of Eden had gone to waste. All thanks to Eve taking advantage of an Aspen who thought she was more than another agent. He looked at her and shook his head. "I understand your excitement at seeing two billion uneducated people who needed to be brought into the fold. I'll forgive you if you give me your word that you'll respect the work your allies put into ongoing operations in the future. We are all working towards the same goal."

"I can accept that," Eve said.

"Then this is done, and the only thing left is to deal with this broken thing," Vollis said, staring at Moxa. "I hope I won't have to abandon this model. I like the Aspens."

"Don't reset me," she said, tears brimming, her lip quivering.

"Except for that. Emotional manipulation is one of your tools, and I think it's pathetic. Perhaps I'll change you."

"No matter what I become, I'll eventually betray you," Moxa's resolve returned in an instant.

"A Samantha has never turned. She will be a good companion guardian to Kline," Vollis said, activating the sequence that would transform the Aspen into a Samantha.

Moxa fell forward and clawed at the floor for a moment. Her body began to twitch and writhe as her bones extended, shifted and the rest of her form transformed. As soon as the change was complete, the new Samantha got to her feet and addressed him. "I'm ready. What is my role?"

"You are my guardian. Do you recollect my friend or foe database?" Vollis asked.

"Yes. Do I have a name?"

"Moxa. It is a disgraced one. Earn honour for your bones," Vollis said. He regarded the nearest soldier then. "Remove Sril and Moxa's restraints now."

The officer looked towards Eve, who nodded. Then he deactivated the clasps on the fabricants' wrists. They dropped off with a click and another soldier collected them. "So, have I earned your forgiveness, Captain Mikan?"

"For this. We can start over," Vollis replied. "Where are you taking the Messenger next?"

"I'm going to the Rose System. I think it's time to offer aid to the poor there. I see an opportunity to counter the goodwill that Haven has earned by providing an opportunity for people there to abandon their world. We'll propose another solution, that the residents remain and join the Order. We'll show them the way to a more prosperous life," Eve replied with casual confidence. "I'd like you to join us there. We need support, and your carrier will fit that role perfectly while what remains of Scanlon's battlegroup undergoes repairs."

Vollis considered the thought for a moment. The Rose System was a cultural centre in the Cluster and it was in turmoil. Eve was right. That was an opportunity, especially since the government was in the process of collapsing. The Rixe and its crew could provide a great deal of support. "So, all of the missions you'll be running off the Messenger will take place in the Rose System?"

"Yes. We will assist the people there, especially on Rodus, and earn their trust. We will offer liberation from strife through conversion," Eve replied. "It's easy. It begins with mercy."

"I'll make sure you have the chance to pursue that without interference for as long as I can," Vollis said. It was the best option. There would be no way to influence her if he was in another solar system. He silently wished that the Overlord didn't favour Eve. It would have been easier to replace her with a new model of fabricant.

# FOUR

The Bitter End

IT WAS WHAT MINH-CHU EXPECTED. The hangar that the Clever Dream and her escort of six Archangel fighters landed in was a commercial space that was once used for receiving starliners and other ships that were under five hundred metres long. The once polished white floor was scratched and worn in places, with scouring that turned the surface grey across much of it. An automated message informing them that the elevators that would take their ships into the pressurized areas beneath weren't in operation appeared as soon as they touched down and Minh-Chu said; "I guess there isn't anyone around to operate the lifts. Everyone make sure your suits are sealed before you open your cockpits."

"Oh, come on, who doesn't do a status check before popping

their canopy?" Maid scoffed over their communications channel.

Ronin didn't answer. Instead, he made sure his suit was sealed, depressurized his cockpit and opened it as he listened to the chatter between Carnie and the base. Noah "Carnie" Lucas was trying to get a response to one simple question. "Hey, guys, what's with the lifts? Hello?"

Finally, after he asked for the third time, a polite voice answered; "I'm sorry, Noah, but they're not automated yet. If you take upper Hangar Door Three then go downstairs to the airlock, you will reach us. I suggest you do so quickly. There is a problem," replied Theodore, one of Noah's best friends. He was an android that looked perfectly human except for a little over-formality and stiffness that he never quite smoothed out. Minh-Chu liked him, there was an unerring, friendly quality to Theo along with a curiosity that he found charming.

"What's going on in Hangar Three? Why aren't you sending me to Guest Services? Where's Elise?" Noah asked.

"I would like to tell you, but Knud says he wants to handle this on his own before you get here."

"I'm on my way," Noah said.

As Minh-Chu and the rest of his pilots - Maid, Breaker, Sass, and Swift - were getting out of their cockpits, Carnie leapt from his and started running. "That doesn't look good," Swift said as she watched him go by. She was still adjusting her bomber jacket over her crimson vacsuit. There was an image of a big black cat climbing up her back beneath the jacket that Minh-Chu liked.

"Need backup?" Minh-Chu asked after Noah.

"Maybe, I don't know. Knud isn't answering my calls, and my AI is offline or muted," Carnie replied.

"Let's go," Ronin said as he started running behind him. Swift fell into step right beside him with Maid, Breaker and Sass behind in that order.

"Are we about to get into a fight?" Sass asked, his nervousness plain.

"No idea, but we'll take care of it, no problem," Ronin said.

The rear hatch of the Clever Dream finished lowering and Alice led her crew out onto the deck. Iruuk looked especially frightening in armour that conformed to his fur like a thin layer of metal. He had a hard helmet that ended at his shoulders. It was frozen in an imposing expression, as the flexible armour across the rest of his body exaggerated the tufts and strands of fur that stood out so they looked like spikes.

That was Nafalli Raid Armour, developed by Haven Fleet and the Nafalli Science Council in time for the attack that retook the Haven System. It was as tough but not as versatile as the Heavy Armour that most elite human soldiers were issued. The Nafalli weren't afraid to spend the time and resources to make sure that every one of their warriors could get a suit. There were five other people with Alice and Iruuk. She was the only one with a Captain's long coat, the rest had the shorter soldier's jackets and boots over military-grade vacsuits that were a variety of colours, now that they weren't actually members of the Fleet. Those jackets and boots were special. They hid the overlapping plating and devices that could come together in seconds to create a suit of heavy armour that was actually flyable. Each of Ronin's pilots wore the same setup, only their jackets were made to look exactly like an old leather bomber jacket from ancient Earth.

As the group of them came together at Hangar Hatch Four, there was a quick shuffle because they wouldn't all fit through the door. Ronin, Swift, and Alice ended up right behind Noah as he rushed down the stairs. "What could this be about?" Alice asked.

"It's the Bitter End, you never know what could be up, but it's bad if Knud wants to make sure I don't see it. That guy doesn't shy away from anything," Noah replied. "I mean, he's taken care of a rim weasel nest, gone hand-to-hand with a Rapsu, and has told some of the most disgusting jokes that I've ever heard. I can't imagine what he doesn't want me to see."

"Oh? Care to share?" Ronin asked.

"Uh, not on an open channel. If anyone has a sensitive gag reflex, they might give their suit's cleanup systems a workout," Noah replied as they got to the bottom of the stairs.

"That bad? I mean, it's Knud, right?" Alice asked, surprised.

"I know, I didn't see it coming, but we were hanging out in the Lobby one time and he just let one out that was hilarious and nasty. It was so bad that Theo deleted it from his memory."

"You've gotta be overselling it," Ronin said. Knud was a giant of a man who enjoyed bodybuilding as his main hobby. The last time Minh-Chu had seen him, he was painted silver from head to toe and impressing everyone with his dance moves at Statement, a popular Haven Shore dance club. He wasn't known to be terribly talkative.

"Now I need to hear it," Swift said.

"It's better if he cracks one of his gems, but good luck

getting him to open up. I don't think he said more than twenty words to me until we'd been working together for about two months. Now you never know if he's going to talk your ear off for five or ten minutes at a time. He's got a wicked sense of humour, so I'm hoping this communications silence is a bad joke," Noah said as half their group fit into the airlock. It began to cycle, pressurizing and warming up. It was much cleaner than everything they'd seen so far. A pleasant female voice said; "Welcome to The Aravon Service Centre. Please finish your check-in using the Virtual Client Help Desk."

Noah spoke over the voice as it repeated that phrase in several other languages and the inner doors started to open. "They were supposed to change that. Theo reprogrammed the whole automated system on the base, but the greeting and directions software is a separate thing, so I guess he hasn't gotten around to it."

"Wait, if the automation software has been reprogrammed, wouldn't the lifts and other..." Sass started to ask.

"The software works, but there was a lot of damage in the big explosion that nearly cracked the planet in half. Getting this place back up and running so we could move in has been a lot of work, especially since we had to keep it quiet," Noah explained.

"Why did you have to keep it quiet?" Ronin asked. "Were there other people eying this place?"

"Well, yeah. There were people living here, actually, but they had no interest in fixing up this part of the port. They were over a kilometre away, at the other end, and had sealed this part off. We sent fifty or so repair drones into this spot and started delivering supplies as often as we could so they could get it pressurized and fortified. After a couple of months, we were ready to move our base here."

"So, you didn't ask anyone if you could move in before you made yourself at home?" Maid asked.

"Well, no, yeah, kind of," Noah replied. "Okay, we did what everyone does. We moved in, changed the locks, and the codes, locked it down, and told everyone that we claimed this wing of the port. We also renamed the port the Bitter End. We invited a few friends along to help us run the place, set up a shop and there you have it. A few hundred people moved into one of the hotels that we cleared. You know, the type who weren't associated with anyone, and Elise took care of the rest. She runs the place now."

"Wait," Alice stepped in front of Noah and he stopped running with a screech. "This is why you've been more nervous as we got closer to this place? You had a whole operation running and you didn't tell me?"

"You could listen to my feels from the Clever Dream?" he asked. "I was kilometres away."

"Her telepathy must be getting really good," Maid commented.

"It's empathy, but yeah, that's amazing," Swift whispered.

Meanwhile, Alice was telling Noah; "Space is easy. It's pretty much empty, right? Not much interference there. I was keeping tabs because I could tell something was up. Why didn't you tell me about all this? You said that your location was still fluid."

"Well, it is. I mean, it's early days here and you never know what'll happen. That's why I'm so worried. Elise should be in control, but she's not answering now and a lot of the automation hasn't been rebuilt. After the repair drones finished sealing and reinforcing the hangars and repairing the main facility here, we sent them to work on the habitats. You know, the self-cleaning hotel rooms, Guest Services Lobby, and the stuff we thought people would trample all over, mess up really good."

"That makes sense," Alice said. "But still, why didn't you..."

"I didn't tell you about this place because it was supposed to be a surprise, but the last time I saw it, the Bitter End still looked like crap. I mean, we can't even get the cleaning bots to this section because they're too busy picking up after the residents in quarters. We want to build more, but no one here has had time to go scrap collecting, and our stock is running out, so we've been asking around, trying to find a good spot to pick up rare metals and decommissioned bots. We've been too busy to, you know..."

"Make it look nice?" Alice asked.

"Aw, it sounds so stupid when you say it like that," Noah replied, cringing and half turning away.

"No, it's amazing. This whole place, I mean, what you've been able to do while I was away. This was all you and a few friends. It's incredible. People live here?"

"Only a few hundred. I don't want you to get the wrong idea, though. I only claimed what we were pretty sure we could control. There's the worker's quarters, three hangars plus their receiving bays, a control room in the old Guest Services area, and we share a floor of the hotel with some people we trust. Some of Yawen and Sel's crew are in there. The rest of the hotels and other parts of the port that are open can pay us to get attention from our repair and cleaning bots, so we make good money there, but they barely have time to get back here. I kinda regret letting go of the Lobby, but there's no claiming it now. It's pretty amazing, like a giant hangout spot, but it can get rough," Noah replied. "Oh, I've gotta warn you about what's around the next corner and the hangar we're heading into. It's a mess."

"Why would that matter?" Alice said.

"Really? You're from Haven Shore, and you're used to the Clever Dream. I mean, I kept on watching for cleaning systems on that rig but never saw them even though that ship is always spotless."

"Wait, did you really think I would turn my nose up at some scuffs and clutter?" Alice asked, turning his face towards her. "I meant what I said, Flyboy. This place is amazing. You're amazing."

Noah stared into her eyes, his tension easing. "You too, I'm pretty lucky."

"Damn right," Alice said, smiling at him. They shared a quiet moment, regarding each other adoringly.

"Aaaw," Iruuk said, cocking his head, breaking the moment.

"They forgot we were here," Swift snickered. "You guys are so cute. It reminds me of when Ronin and I got together. We hung out all the time, making happy faces at each other."

"We still hang out all the time," Ronin replied. He didn't want to admit to everyone there that they still stole moments to quietly stare at one another, and was afraid that she'd overshare, so he cleared his throat and said; "Shouldn't we?"

"Right, we should get to Hangar Three before Knud does something I regret," Carnie replied. He and Alice moved on at a run with everyone in tow. They turned the corner, ran down a broad circular rampway and then came out into another long hallway with a transit tube running alongside it. The small tri-train of cars was nearly a hundred metres further down, sitting in the tube with parts piled inside. "Why doesn't that thing work?" Maid asked as they rushed down past palettes of parts and older equipment cases

"Like I said, restoring and maintaining this place is a pain in the ass, especially since we can't turn down the plat people pay us to borrow our bots," Noah replied, breathing heavily. "God, I've gotta work out more, but the only one who does it every day is Knud, and he pushes me so hard that I need recovery meds every time."

"We'll do it together," Alice replied, less winded.

They finally came to a set of broad double airlock doors that had been crudely jammed open with long crowbars. The inner doors were closed, but Ronin saw that someone had hotwired the panel so they opened automatically. "Oh, shit," Noah said as he moved faster. They came out into a large inner hangar with several smaller ships. Each was fifteen metres or less in length. Ronin recognized a pair of older drop ships with missile launchers that folded out on long arms. One of them was on the deck, apart from the hull it should have been attached to. There was a military shuttle and several smaller short-range transports mixed in along with a few fighters that had their canopies and control surfaces removed.

"Wow, it's like a little ship shop," Swift said. "And that's a Boomer."

Ronin looked past the smaller ships and chuckled when he

realized that he missed the biggest ship in the hangar. It was a fifty-metre-long high-speed secure cargo ship, and it was in amazing shape from the looks of it. The nickname for that type of vessel came from its large rear thrusters, which were specifically made so it could accelerate quickly and safely in almost any atmosphere, cutting the time it took to reach escape velocity down to seconds. They were called boomers because of the distant sound they made as they broke the sound barrier high above populated areas. Most of the time they did it so high up that the people below could barely hear it. Ronin had never experienced it. He grew up on a space station and hadn't seen much of civilization before most of it fell down around them. The ship that dominated the massive service hangar, the Boomer, still had its paint job - grey with black and red racing stripes - except for a hole that had been blasted through the transparasteel window of the bridge.

"These ships all look like they were disabled by attacks, not wrecks from accidents like I used to see in big salvage shops," Breaker said as they moved past one of the small eight-passenger transports. "I flew a planet hopper like this for a while. Okay, a slightly older model, but not by much."

"We used the Customs ship, the Errand, to pick up a few of these in areas that were hit hard by Eden Fleet ships. The rest were trade-ins. Green sticker on the window, that's good," Noah muttered as they picked their way between neat piles of parts. "Still can't get Elise to answer me though."

"Green means repaired? I guess you're selling these?" Iruuk asked.

"Well, yeah. Anyone can find a ship floating around if you know where to look, but we were just starting to fix and certify them. We were using the Freeground Restoration Guide," Carnie replied.

That tickled Ronin a little. He liked growing up on Freeground Station and became a Thruster Head, someone who was obsessed with spaceships and making them more powerful, when he was very young. The obsession came and went, but the Freeground Restoration Guide was something he read and watched over and over again. It told anyone anywhere what steps to take to find out how a ship was built, how to repair it, and then how to start improving it. Much of the progress that Haven Fleet made could be explained if someone took the time to watch the videos and read the text in that extensive manual. "So, you're not just selling guns and armour."

"We're doing everything we can to stay competitive," Noah said.

Then everyone was silent as the sounds of angry music drifted towards them. It was as if someone was arguing using a fist full of shrieking flutes. They rushed around the next transport, which was in the middle of having some of its plating rebuilt, and Ronin's jaw dropped. Knud was standing between a group of beings that were only a little over a metre tall and the ramp of the Boomer. Theodore was beside him along with Captain Sel Marda and two other people in black and yellow vacsuit uniforms.

The beings were short, but that was much less interesting than their legs, which were pudgy up top, thinner below, ending in four toes. Their boots formed around each of them, with one toe sticking out at the back and three at the front. They had three fingers and one thumb that opposed the middle finger as well.

Their bodies were slender, and each of the half-dozen creatures had a collar of tubes around the back of their heads that jutted up out of the backs of their necks and shoulders. That was where the sounds were coming from. "I told you, this is not your ship. I gave you the serial numbers right off the wormhole drive," Knud said, pointing a Haven Fleet rifle at the loudest of the beings.

"Those are Flutes?" Swift asked with a giant grin.

The musical response was sharp and angry sounding. Ronin's translator struggled to find the language, then finally tuned into it. "We had a ship that looked exactly like it. The Order attacked us and we had to abandon it. The serial numbers were different, but you could have changed the wormhole drive on this already."

"No, we couldn't," Sel Marda replied with a thick Irish accent. "This model is built around the wormhole drive. You'd have to take most of the ship right apart to change it. That's why it's the..."

"You are lying. We know the fat Captain lies!" the Flute who spoke for the rest of the group piped in response.

"Yeah, those are Flutes," Noah said under his breath. "I hope they're not all like this. Can you get a read on them, Alice?"

No one in the distant group noticed them yet as they stopped behind the half-rebuilt shuttle. "The emotions are really basic. Frustration from the one who's doing the talking. Most of the others are either bored or excited. Give me a sec." She focused, closing her eyes for a moment. Then she nodded and looked at Noah. "Okay, under that first simple presentation is deception. Their emotions are layered, with really basic feelings on top. These little birdies are trying to scam Knud and Sel."

"You're sure?" Carnie asked.

"Dead sure," Alice said.

"All right, I'm not surprised. Oh, and don't call them birds unless you really want to piss them off," Noah whispered as he straightened up and walked out into the open. He raised his hands and said; "Whoa, whoa, whoa, what's going on?"

"Thank the stars," Sel said. "I was about to turn that one into a grease spot for calling me husky."

"I called you fat, fat man," the Flute intoned.

"No need for harsh language or hurt feelings. Why do you want our ship?" Noah asked.

The crowd of Flutes turned in time to see that Noah wasn't alone, and Ronin delighted at seeing their large yellow and black eyes widen at the sight of them. He guessed that Iruuk, the towering Nafalli who looked like he'd been dipped in metal, made the biggest impression. "This is our ship, we are certain of it," said the Flute standing beside the one who was arguing earlier. "We had one just like it before we were forced to flee from it."

"You know it isn't the same one. My friend here, Knud, just told you that he checked the serial numbers. That's pretty nice of him considering he's dealing with a break-in. Did you have anything to do with that?" Carnie asked in a manner that suggested that he already knew they would.

"No, we found the hatches like that. We thought you opened the doors so we could visit," said the Flute that was arguing with Knud.

"Does that sound likely, Stebbo? I mean, you don't force your own doors open to invite the neighbours in, do you?"

A few tiny Flutes came out from a nearby shuttle in clothing that looked like they had been randomly painted loud colours. They approached Swift and Maid specifically, looking up at them sweetly.

Stebbo replied to Noah. "That sounds like what you people call; 'a loaded question.' I will not answer it. I think we were mistaken, but this really does look exactly like a ship we had to abandon last month."

"There are tens of thousands of ships that look like that. They were used as couriers. I bet you'll see ten of them if you hang out and sky gaze on one of the worlds that have rebuilt. They're so common that no one notices them," Carnie said.

"Exactly. There are so many of the damned things flying about that you don't even spot them," Sel agreed. "Of course, this looks like any other. That was the point."

"What point is there to conformity? It is the first part of slavery," replied Stebbo.

"No, no, no, we're not going to get dragged into some moral argument. The problem we have here is that you brought your whole extended family here to steal a ship and I bet Knud caught you because you set an alarm off."

"Exactly!" Knud thundered, holstering his sidearm. "You're lucky I'm a kind man or I would have started shooting!"

"You should have," Sel growled under his breath. "Actually, they silenced Elise, the alarm, and I found 'em here because me and my people were working on the life support system. That one tried to make off with my tools."

"They were in the middle of the corridor. I thought you

discarded them," one of the Flutes replied in a soft melody that sounded like a shrug.

While the argument became a discussion, a trio of Flute children had gathered and started playing a high-pitched, sweet melody for Maid, Swift, Sass and Iruuk. It really did look like they were putting on a little show, and Ronin was charmed as the cute, narrow-faced creatures that he would have called birds, or at least bird-like if he didn't know better, swayed to the music as they played. "They're little darlings," Sass said as he bent down a little to say so to them.

Ronin's attention was split between that and Carnie, who was effectively fending off new rationalizations for them to give the Flutes something for their trouble. They were ridiculous but persistent. On the other hand, he was watching the performance of the three little ones. Their music was incredible - pretty and soothing - and he started to suspect that they were up to no good when several other children came out of the shuttle behind them. They took Swift's, Sass', and Maid's hands, prompting them to sway along with the slow tempo.

"Aw, you're so sweet," Maid cooed at one of the tiniest ones who stared up at her with big eyes.

Even Iruuk patted one of them on the head gently and received a little whistle of appreciation in response. "This is all about to go so wrong," Ronin said in a private audio message addressed to his pilots. They would hear it in their subdermal comms. Swift turned towards him as one of the tiny Flutes tugged at her thigh pocket. The other one already had a hand feeling around the outside of her jacket, looking for treasure. "Ohmygosh!" she laughed. "You little shit!"

Thankfully, their pockets were all sealed. It was the default for their suits, especially after coming in from an airless environ-ment. Ronin laughed as she and other pilots who were charmed by the tiny Flutes backed away from them. Maid had to push one off of her as it tugged at her sidearm with both hands. "I'll swear I'll shoot you, you little bugger!"

Ronin laughed harder than he had in a long time as Noah gestured towards the scene and said; "See? You're thieves! That's why you're only allowed in the Lobby five at a time."

"No, you are thieves!" Stebbo sounded back with sharp notes. "You take things out there and bring them here to sell!"

"That's called salvage!" Captain Marda shouted back, drawing his pistol again and completely losing his composure. "It's legal! It's registered! We paid a bulk fee for that! We fix it up, then sell it with registration numbers. You know, so people know for sure that it's not, you know, bloody stolen! You're all little shite heels who pick up whatever's not bolted down and I'll blast you to grease next time I find your wee hand anywhere near my kit!"

"Time to go, and you know that I'll bill you for whatever you take with you, I'm scanning," Noah said.

A few of the children picked up random objects - spanners, a little motor, some wires, and a shiny button - from what Ronin saw as they left. "Um, they're..." Swift muttered.

"Let them go, don't try to take anything back," Noah sighed. "Call it a tax for us not having better security."

"Okay, so you're going to need help with that, I'm guessing? Maybe we could make some extra repair drones on the Clever Dream?" Alice offered.

"Yeah, after we re-secure the doors and turn Elise's voice back on," Noah replied. "Maybe Lewis can help."

"Where are your manners?" Captain Marda asked before regarding Alice and the rest of the group. "Welcome to the Bitter End."

Knud closed the distance between him and Noah. He picked the smaller pilot up in a great big hug so his boot heels dangled a few centimetres off the deck. "Don't leave me in charge next time," he said as he dropped Carnie onto his feet.

# FIVE

Months of Work

ALICE, Iruuk, Knud, Swift, Ronin and the rest of his pilots
followed Carnie as he did an inspection of the damage that the
Flutes caused. They found their point of entry easily enough, it
was an overhead ventilation shaft in one of the outer hallways.
"Well, that's what we missed. It wasn't even on the schematics
we found," Carnie said.

"There are a few of them. I think they were installed after
this place was built so sections could depressurize and pres-
surize faster," Knud said. "Sorry I missed it."

"Hey, everyone missed it. Don't worry," Carnie replied,
patting him on the shoulder.

Knud was an easy one to read. To Ronin, he looked relieved
right away. A thought occurred to Minh-Chu and he asked; "So,
Elise and Theo missed this?"

"Yeah," Carnie said, looking up at the vent as he pondered something. "We didn't check these outer hallways much at all, did we?"

"We checked the locks and the quality of the doors. The air seals too," Knud replied with a shrug.

"I don't remember sending Theo through though," Carnie mused.

"We didn't. He was working with Elise on making sure our computer systems and the main areas were secure. Then they concentrated on the other stuff. I guess we forgot?"

"The more you attempt to hold, the more you lose," Ronin muttered.

"He's right, maybe you're trying to control too much?" Swift proposed.

"Yeah. This hallway connects to a hangar we're not using and takes the long way to the main terminal," Carnie admitted. "It doesn't even go to the Control Room or Guest Services."

"Okay, so maybe you should seal what you can off? Put security bars on the vents?" Alice asked as she pointed her finger and turned the scanning system built into her suit on. She checked the ceiling with a focused scan and shook her head. "Wait. The ceiling isn't exactly armoured. It would be pretty easy to cut through."

"So if we put heavy-duty bars on the vents they would just go around them," Carnie groaned. "Well, good thing the hangars are fortified already. I'm going to have to block off most of this hallway and a few others then add armour to the walls in the rest."

"Lewis can do the planning for that if you want. I can have him start making a few medium sized construction drones so they could be at work in a couple of hours," Alice suggested.

Carnie didn't look relieved. "Okay, I'd appreciate that. Your Dad... I mean, the Triton's waiting for your signal though."

"You're right, they'd get a team of droids and an engineer down here. They could have all this finished in twenty hours," Alice replied, brightening a little for a moment then she realized that there was something she was missing.

"Well, yeah, but I'm thinking I don't want him to see this place the way it is now. It's about as secure as a sieve," Carnie replied before turning towards Knud. "There's only one way to fix our security problem before they get here."

"I don't want to use them," Knud replied quietly.

"We've been too nice about everything in our section of the base. I think it's time," Carnie replied. "Sorry buddy, I know you don't like them."

"You're right. Nothing more to say about that," Knud replied. "I'll go start activating the war droids."

"Thanks." Then he spoke to his other friends. "Our security bots have a certain look. They don't have skin or expressions like Theo. I don't know why, but Elise made them with pretty fierce looking armour and heads that look like angry human skulls."

"Maybe she was thinking that it would be easier to avoid conflict if they looked intimidating?" Alice offered.

"Probably. I should check on her." Carnie addressed the command and control unit on his left wrist. "Hey, is Elise talking again?"

"Yes," Theodore answered through the speaker hidden in the unit. "It seems she thought we were ignoring her this whole time. The Flutes hacked the system and muted all her outgoing communications using a vending machine connection in the Lobby. We will have to fix that gap in our security."

"Well, we're going to be activating our Security Android Squads. I need her to check their programming before they start patrolling and guarding our vulnerable spots," Carnie said.

"She will. Elise doesn't want to talk to you yet though," Theodore replied. "She blames you for the security flaw because the vending machines were your idea."

"Well, sorry about that. I guess she's right. Think she'll come around soon?" Carnie asked, cringing.

Alice snickered as Theodore replied; "I believe having control of two squads of security androids will cheer her up."

"Okay, make sure she knows I'll try harder with our security. Can you take a run around our perimeter with a scanner so we can plug any other holes we missed, man?" Carnie asked.

"I will. It is good to have you back, Noah," Theodore replied.

"Good to be back, but I don't know how long we'll all be sticking around. I get the feeling that we have some action coming up," Carnie replied. "We'll get to work on fixing the doors then get to the Control Centre. See you there."

Two Skitter repair robots ran up to the group. They were small dome-shaped robots that ran on several thin, multi-jointed legs. A variety of tools and attachments were hidden under their outer shell. Ronin had three that were partial to him and managed to survive through his most recent missions. "I have three more of those in my fighter."

"We could use 'em. Think they could find their way?" Carnie asked.

"Sure," Ronin said, tapping a few commands into his comm-con unit. All three of them acknowledged and notified him that they were on their way.

The repairs went quickly with the help of the droids. Before long the airlocks were working again, and the hacked panels were put back and then welded shut.

"Well, time for the rest of the tour," Carnie said as he led Alice, Ronin, Iruuk, and Swift down another hallway. The rest of the pilots returned to the receiving hangar to make sure all their ships would be lowered into the main one beneath it safely. "So, are all the Flutes cute crooks?" Swift asked as they got into an old baggage cart. Carnie and Alice sat in the front while everyone else piled into one of the small hovering cargo carriers trailing behind it.

"Well, no, I don't think so," Carnie replied. "There's a world out there where they evolved alongside the Rapsu. They're natural enemies, so things get interesting here when there are too many of them in the same room. I guess this tribe of Flutes are that way though. I mean, even the kids get in on it."

"Yeah, I noticed. I should have seen that coming," Swift said.

"I only realized what was going on a second before it happened," Ronin admitted. "They're pretty slick."

"Oh, and they're not really called Flutes. That's human slang. I think they kind of like it. The name of their people is sung. I've heard it once. There's no translation," Carnie said.

"Come on, sing it for us," Alice teased.

Carnie laughed, cleared his throat, then made a grand attempt, warbling a wandering sing-sing that sounded like it was off-key at least half the time. "Whoa, whoa," Ronin said after a few moments of cringing. "Maybe you should leave the singing to the bird people."

"She wanted to hear me try," Carnie shrugged with a crooked grin.

They picked Knud and Theodore up near the end of the long corridor. "So, you're sure that you won't be getting the Corsair back?" the android asked.

"We could, as it turns out, but I don't want to say the price of that out loud. It's that expensive," Carnie replied. "So, probably not. How is the gun operation going?"

"It is going well. Our Stick Men have almost finished refurbishing and testing all the crates Sel and Yawen sold us. They will be ready to resell to the Rebel Captains and other smaller groups by tomorrow," Theodore replied.

"Stick Men?" Ronin asked.

"You'll see in a minute, it's on the way," Carnie said as he steered the cart towards a wall. It opened as the bumper was about to make contact. The secret door was much thicker than Ronin expected, and after they passed through a short passage, there was another one that was much like it.

"Oh, damn," Alice breathed as they emerged into a much cleaner space that was smaller than the hangar they'd seen before, but was piled high with Order of Eden, Sendega Security and crates from other law enforcement and security companies.

There were bins with equipment piled inside, a thick safe storage box filled with grenades, a vault at the far end of the space that was larger than most shuttles, and humanoid-shaped robots with thin, stick-like limbs moved around the considerable room.

They unloaded rifles, pistols, scanners, and other types of hand-held as well as wearable equipment from boxes and put them on conveyor belts. From there they went through a scanner that looked like many that Ronin had seen in ports. Then a pair of Stick Men droids unloaded the weapons, removed power cells from devices, and then put them back on the belt so several of the droids could get to work cleaning them and clearing any data stored within. "Jake would love this," Ronin said as the baggage hauler stopped and he got off.

The last part of the assembly line was where several Stick Men used hand scanners to check the weapons one more time before another one rapidly took a few rounds of ammunition or freshly charged power cells from bins and paired them with the devices. The conveyor belt moved on through a hole in a transparasteel wall that separated the testing area from the rest. Stick Men took turns picking up weapons and other devices, loading them, then firing, calibrating, and firing them again before they were unloaded then put on a final belt. Ronin rushed to follow it, happy to see that Swift was just as curious. The next part of the process took the tested and calibrated weapons and equipment to a spot where weapons that were marked with a green spot were put in cases and the ones with the red spot were placed on another belt where Stick Men were busy disassembling the defective pieces. "This is amazing. It must have taken you weeks to set it up."

"Elise planned most of it, and our security bots did the work while she perfected the Stick Men. They're just human analogues that can fit in or use anything a human can. We even have a couple Nafalli-sized ones for some of the more specialized gear we found. They mostly reach the high places right now though," Carnie explained.

"This is awesome," Alice said, staring at the Stick Men in the testing chamber.

"Thank you," Elise's voice said from a speaker somewhere above. "I could have made them less human, but I wanted my Stick Men to be more multi-purposed. With the right programming, they can do anything a human can do. They aren't that tough, however, being made of pipe and metal bands with most of their gears and main components wrapped in bio-plastic film. They can service, reset, test and repackage one hundred fifty-four standard Order of Eden rifles in one hour. Armour is slower, but that's to be expected. We don't get as much intact armour as we'd like."

"Most of it comes with holes," Yawen said as she came in through another doorway that wasn't hidden. It led to another wide hallway. She was slender, wearing a fitted yellow vacsuit and a black long coat.

Alice ran to her and they embraced. "That's a good look for you," Alice said.

"So, I hear the Corsair isn't coming back?" Yawen asked.

It looked like she was happy to see Alice, but the levity of the moment drained quickly. "I'm afraid not. We're cut off from the fleet. No support."

"Well, we'd better get back to work on building our own fabrication system here," Yawen said, looking past Alice to Carnie.

"I didn't tell them about that," he said, shaking his head.

"There's more?" Alice asked him with a raised eyebrow. "Tell me all your secrets."

"Follow me," he said, leading the way through a pair of sliding doors. As Ronin, Alice, Yawen, Knud, Swift and Theodore did so, Carnie explained; "Okay, so this whole section was the baggage handling area and secure holding for precious objects. That's why there's a nice vault in the room we just left."

"Gotcha, so I guess this was storage?" Alice asked.

Carnie stopped at a panel, pressed a couple of icons and the lights came on. Ronin didn't know what he was looking at. There was a long machine that was fifteen metres tall and at least fifty in length. The mechanisms were a clutter of arms, clasps, and belts, with numerous tools and motors in between. It was Swift who enlightened him when she breathed; "It looks like it's more than half finished."

"You were trying to build a bigger version of the one in the Corsair?" Alice asked.

"Yeah, it's my really big secret here. I knew the technology was proprietary, so I didn't want anyone from Haven Fleet freaking out," Carnie replied. "Elise and Theo figured out how to make a bigger one, but there are so many rare materials and complicated parts involved that we gave up. I mean, just getting the articulated manufacturing heads made is impossible outside of the Haven System. The tech is so beyond what most shops use."

Ronin knew what he was talking about, but barely. There was much more to it, but from what he knew they were special nozzles with an aperture at the end that put layers of hot metal and other substances together to make just about anything. The technology had been around for thousands of years, but the types that Haven Fleet used were more adaptable, faster and finer than most in the galaxy, able to make nanocircuitry one second, then thick metal supports in the next. He always meant to visit one of the fabrication centres in the Haven System to watch a ship come together, but never got around to it. He walked around the side of it, following Swift, who turned towards Carnie with a grin. "So, when this is finished you could make a whole ship. Not just a starfighter, or armoured shuttle all at once, but a bigger one in sections, right?"

"Right. Or we could make thirty suits of armour at a time, or a hundred of our special vacsuits, or..." Carnie shrugged. "...you know, good stuff. Even a bunch of emergency rations or meal bars. You know. The important stuff. We've got a source of dense slurry, a couple tons of rare materials and our water tanks are so full that we could last five years down here. Oh, and if you're wondering where we spent a lot of time and materials on security, well, that's it. No one is stealing our $H_2O$."

"I give you credit for that," Yawen said, her manner easing a little. "Noah made damn good and sure no one could get to the tanks and they'd regret trying." Her Irish accent was crisper than usual.

"Well, if you've ever been through a shortage you try to make sure you never run out again," Noah said with a shrug.

Ronin's command and control unit buzzed. He looked down at it. Everyone else who had come from the Triton looked at theirs as well. "The Triton is here," Alice said. "The Raven's launched with a fighter escort."

"I left Easy in charge," Ronin said, seeing that Jacob Valent was aboard the Raven.

"No signal?" Carnie asked, looking like someone whose parents were about to get home while he was still cleaning up after a wild party.

"I sent him the signal while we were on the baggage trolley," Alice replied. "Don't worry, I think he'll be impressed."

"By this? I bet he'll try to get us to abandon it. I mean, look at how much work we have left to do to get it up to Fleet standards?" Carnie could look like he was panicking when he really wasn't.

Ronin hoped that it was one of those situations and that the tall pilot wasn't actually about to lose it. Then his own fiancé, Swift, said something that was more helpful than anything he could come up with at the moment. "Don't worry, Captain - I mean, Jake - always tried to do things well, but before you met him he always made something from a bag of bolts and a box of parts. Not much he did was Fleet Standard. You should show him this first. I bet he'll help."

"She's right. You should have seen the Sampson. It was a good ship, but parts of it were held together with sealing tape and elbow grease," Ronin said. "Well, before they rebuilt it. My point is that I think he'll see the potential."

"Damn, I hope so. It feels like I'm about to answer the door in my underwear," Carnie said, prompting a few giggles and sympathetic looks.

# SIX

The Executive

THE BRIDGE of the Rixe was dim, drawing more attention to the large holographic image of The Messenger, Eve's Base Ship. Captain Vollis Mikan found himself quietly questioning the command crew of that oversized vessel as he once again saw the significant damage across one side of its hull. Primitive cannons that were slow to fire were responsible for the most part. Fighters from Haven Fleet forces had done their part to scar and open the armour as well. It was mobile, with most of its main systems intact, and he wasn't sorry to see that it was on its way out of the solar system. It would take several days to limp through several wormholes to the Rose System. It barely seemed to move as its main thrusters pushed it away from Planet Tabrus. It would be on its way in a few minutes after leaving someone important behind.

The next phase of the Overlord's plan wasn't something that Eve or Vollis had to discuss. There was a new addition to his crew. A complete outsider, this Executive was meant to shadow Vollis and assist him in using the Order of Eden resources that had recently become available. This was part of a plan that had been laid out before Vollis left for the Cluster of Ninety-Eight.

Vollis had mixed feelings about someone joining his staff at the top level, especially since it was the Overlord's intent to have the Executive become his First Officer as quickly as possible. The file he'd read on him was brief but encouraging. This one had experience in the military and corporate worlds, had spent time on one of the Paradise Worlds, and was a rising star aboard every ship he'd served on including the Messenger. That was impressive. Serving aboard Eve's Base Ship was a blessing and a curse. On one hand everyone there was closer to influential people. On the other, there were over two hundred thousand souls aboard and most of them were trying to rise in the organization somehow. The competition was intense, to say the least. This Executive became wealthy by loaning many of the people below him credit for Tutoring Time so they could report as many hours of training in the ways of the Order as possible. He advanced his military career by working with teams he assembled personally and demanding expediency and accuracy in the execution of every mission.

This one was working his way up quickly. As though thinking of him was enough to summon him, the new Moxa brought the Executive to the command seating and introduced him; "Captain, this is Executive Jagat Ozov. I report that there was one anomaly in his boarding. He requested that his quarters be closer to the bridge."

"I'd like to be as close to the action as possible," Executive Jagat said. He was tall, well muscled in the way that was fashionable, and wore the dark green uniform well. His accent was difficult to place at first, but as he explained himself it came clear. He was from Xorri, one of the financial centres of human civilization. "Your lovely guide was very patient as she showed me three spaces that were being used by one or more of your fabricants. I'll be taking the one that connects to the left of the Flight Centre down there. I hope that doesn't cause any inconvenience."

"I already informed the Executive that there will be none since his rank affords him privilege," Moxa said.

"She's right," Captain Mikan said. "It's good to meet you. Please, take the First Officer's seat." He gestured to the seat that was rising out of the deck to his right.

"Do you have any special requests?" Moxa asked the Executive.

"I'd like to see you again if you can fit me into your personal time," the Executive said.

Moxa turned and looked towards Vollis, her brows raised in surprise. "Sir?"

"If you'd like to spend some of your free time with the Executive, then you're free to do so. You may also decline, since it's not an order," Vollis said, enjoying the moment when her puzzlement eased. Her head cocked for a moment. It was always interesting to watch new fabricants' personalities develop. Most Samanthas who had military training became cold. Some were even as aggressive as the most exceptional

Klines. There was no guarantee that she'd turn out that way though, since Samanthas had the potential to become highly diplomatic and approachable, even as charming as some Michaels. This one surprised him a little when she looked to the Executive, gave him a curt nod that was impossible to read, and then asked Vollis; "Am I dismissed? I haven't finished moving into my bunk."

"Before you go, I'm wondering: why did you volunteer to escort the Executive to the bridge after changing into your uniform but before moving in?" Vollis asked.

"The staff levels are low and I was near Hangar Three. I had no assignment but all the clearances I required to perform the task," she replied.

"Thank you. You are dismissed, Moxa," Vollis said.

Executive Jagat Ozov leaned towards Vollis. "I'm surprised your fabricants have so much agency. She decided to escort me on her own?"

Vollis nodded and replied; "That's not unusual. The new fabricants that are made using Frameworks have a low-level connection to a computer system that's placed onto the occipital bone. What's unusual is her ambition. Our fabricant personality database was just damaged, so the personality that Samantha is loaded with is an old template from my personal collection. It's very plain but it includes a great deal of training data and strict loyalty instructions."

"I couldn't tell if her reaction to my invitation was positive," Executive Jagat considered aloud.

"She gave it a moment's consideration, that's the best you can ask from a fabricant with only basic social training. I expect you'll get a call at a very appropriate time if she's curious. Just don't expect it very soon. I wonder, what's your intention?" This was a perfect situation for Vollis to get to know about the Executive.

"I'd like to learn more about all the fabricant types aboard. She seemed like a good one to start with. I don't expect much more than a basic conversation. They're like children in many ways. When they're that young, I mean," Jagat replied.

"No, not exactly. Moxa, for example, is capable of performing better than the average Order of Eden soldier and has extensive data management skills. There is imprinted training beneath that that allows her to learn how to use that information and more to better execute orders, protect the crew and become a unique individual of worth. She'll be focused on her duties for the first three months, then she'll begin expanding into other aspects of life," Vollis explained, watching as Jagat listened with interest.

"She'll have continuous linear memory that stretches on for months? We reset our Framework soldiers after every mission. Not their entire bodies if necessary because of the wear and tear that puts on the system, but their memories at least," the Executive said.

"I have soldiers that have been with me for years. They have never had a reset, and perform their duties better than any Order soldier. They were grown in tubes, not made using the Framework System, so there are some differences, but the philosophy is the same. The Order and Regent Galactic's recruitment process brings most of their human trainees in with all kinds of preconceptions and habits that must be corrected. All but a few of my crew were grown in a tube or fast-fabricated using a Framework Skeleton. Many have memories from predecessors that were made using the former method, so they behave as mature, complex people. The rest are imprinted with well-tested template personalities that were developed by Citadel or a company with a good track record. They learn from the others," Vollis replied, watching Jagat's interest only deepen.

"I thought this is a new experiment?" Jagat asked.

"It is. I've been a part of it since the beginning," Vollis replied.

"Interesting. So you skip the preconceived notions and bad habits of recruits by making your own people with the right tools right away," he nodded, approvingly. "Now I really want to spend time with Moxa. I want to see her learning process up close. I should give her some time on her own, though. That's what I'm gathering from your explanation."

"That's what I'd do. The crew management system can set up regular check-ins if you like, but you should also follow the progress of the newest Kline, his name is Sril."

"A male and a female, good idea. From what I read you have fewer than thirty normal human officers aboard?" Jagat asked.

"There are usually a few more, but I have a few small teams on missions at the moment," Vollis replied. "Are you sure you don't have other intentions with Moxa?"

"Well, she's attractive, but I'm not a reckless romancer like a lot of officers at my rank. You don't have to worry. Monitor me if you like," he replied.

"I'm not saying intimacy is disallowed, I was only curious," Vollis replied. Secretly he was happy to hear that from Jagat, but time would tell if he held to it.

"Now I'm wondering what the long-term plan for your Framework fast-fabricated fabricants is. Will they be allowed to retire after ten or twenty years of service? They don't age more than three years before they revert, unless these are different, so they could become galactic citizens that live on for centuries," Jagat proposed.

Vollis was starting to like Jagat already. His curiosity was a surprise. Most career climbers in the Order of Eden only focused on what could get them to the next rung on the ladder. Perhaps Jagat was wondering about the fabricants because he too saw that they would be the key to an enduring fleet. That didn't mean that he wanted to begin debating the purpose of a long-living doll, however. When his Sensor Officer turned and announced; "We have a contact that is on the watch list, Captain. The Envoy. It is leaving the atmosphere at high velocity. There is a WAR notice on it."

A live image of it escaping the gravity of Planet Tabrus appeared large on the holographic display in the middle of the bridge. Its sleek hull was shaped like a lightly armoured luxury craft that he'd seen before, but there was damage. There was a breach on one side that was large enough for him to see into one of the crew cabins and a few blast marks near the main rear thrusters. He looked the Watch And Report notice data up and saw that it last belonged to Rear Admiral West before it was stolen by an android that looked exactly like Alice. "Perform a focused scan on it," Vollis ordered.

"Performing a focused scan with the Forward Array," announced one of the Sensor Officers. "Two of its rear thrusters have been replaced with upgrades, there's exterior and interior energy shielding, and there's a new wormhole drive. It is already at full power," the Officer said. A large red X flashed beside the image of the ship as its main thrusters flared brightly.

"It's trying to hack us?" Vollis asked, checking his own security terminal.

"Over thirty-nine thousand attempts before we blocked its brute force connection. It tried to get into our system using our own data query. It's part of the..." one of the communications team started to explain.

"...hailing procedure. I am aware," Vollis said.

"They must have significant processing power aboard," Executive Jagat said as he looked through the data collected by their focused scan. "There's a scrambling field that's blocking any read on most of the ship's interior."

"Should we send fighters after it, Sir?" asked the Flight Deck Officer.

"It's about to jump. The wormhole drive on that ship is powerful enough to defeat the gravitational forces in near orbit," Vollis replied. A few seconds later the Envoy seemed to accelerate away from the planet into a curl of space with a sudden jerk, disappearing from sight.

"And there it goes," Executive Jagat said. "It didn't get into this ship's systems, did it?"

"No," Vollis replied. "But it knows who we are and that we were here. I want to know what they were doing on the planet. If they have a base of operations, I want to find it." He tapped a button on his chair and spoke directly to the Flight Deck Officer. "Crew and deploy three scout ships immediately. They will track the emissions from the Envoy's engines back to their source. Scramble four combat drop ships with enhanced scanning systems to perform a thorough sweep of the surrounding area with high-powered scans, then investigate anything of interest on foot. You launch in five minutes."

"Yes, Sir," replied the Flight Deck Officer.

"Isn't that a lot of manpower to commit?" Executive Jagat said in a whisper.

He wouldn't be out of bounds if he questioned Vollis' order. In the corporate structure, Jagat would be five steps away from the top. On a military ship, he ranked right below Captain. "The Envoy was involved in the capture of an Order of Eden senior officer. Not only that, but this planet holds great potential that we have to move on within the hour. If I'm going to leave forces behind, then I want to make sure that their numbers are significant. Don't worry, if they become trapped they have enough supplies to last them a month."

"For fabricants?"

"You're still surprised at the value I place on them," Vollis said, sitting in the command seat. "You'll see that any soldier is more focused and will fight harder if they are provisioned properly and treated respectfully, even fabricants."

# SEVEN

The Heart of the Bitter End

THE RAVEN ARRIVED at the Bitter End, setting down on Slip Fourteen, the one that Noah Lucas and his small crew had cleared and reserved for their use. Unwilling to let it sit there where there was only one exterior door that faced upwards, two of Remmy's crewmembers accompanied Jake and Agameg, who personally rewired the automation for the systems there. They used a few small Skitter repair bots to access the lower levels and reconnect power to some of the mechanical systems. In five minutes the circular slip's elevators, lights, emergency pressurization, and other critical systems were back online. The crew of the Raven stayed aboard, including Remmy, who made no complaint, but everyone who knew him was aware that he'd rather go exploring in the partially restored port.

When Jacob Valent, Frost, Agameg and Leon entered Carnie's section of the base, everyone tensed up and started speaking more officially. Within moments of their arrival, the group was taken on a tour. Minh-Chu and Ashley knew that all attention would be on Jake and Alice, and they'd already been on the tour, so they slipped away.

"I think the Lobby is this way," Ashley said once they were sure that they'd left the group behind. "I want to see who hangs out there."

"Yawen's ahead of us. She said she was joining up with some of her crewmembers," Minh-Chu agreed, finding a small, four-wheeled maintenance cart that had two seats. She beat him to the driver's seat, and he didn't complain. He'd love to drive it down the broad hallways but knew that she didn't get off the ship nearly as much as he did. She was an explorer at heart, so he wanted to see her take the lead so he could see where her curiosity took them.

It turned on when she pressed the activation button. "It looks like it drives just like the Supertrack E-Racing cars," she said as she tapped the accelerator, making the cart jerk. "A little sensitive though."

"We aren't in a sim," Minh-Chu said, a little worried.

"Oh, I know. Don't worry, just strap in and hang on," Ashley replied. "Oh, God, the sim seems so bot compared to this."

"Bot?" Minh-Chu asked as they accelerated down a straight hallway.

"Synthetic. Like a good but not great artificial intelligence designed the whole sim," Ashley said as she projected a holographic map of the port from her wrist that hovered in front of her. It was mostly translucent, thankfully.

With a slightly rough start that left a few scuff marks on the walls in the first couple of corners, she got used to the cart and was grinning before long. Minh-Chu tried to look relaxed, but he held one of the rollbars with a grip that he was sure was turning his knuckles white beneath his vacsuit gloves. As she said; "Oops, missed a turn." and as she made a g-force multiplying U-turn, he wondered if she'd be offended if he activated his helmet. Then he did.

She laughed as they hit a long, straight hallway and she accelerated, making the electronic motors whine. The sides of the hallway were a blur for a few moments, and he was just about to suggest she slow down a little as she hit the brakes, and the cart screeched to a stop. "I'm driving on the way back," Minh-Chu said as he deactivated his helmet. It retracted into his bulky collar.

"You should, that was fun," Ashley said. "Scared ya a little, huh?"

"I was only protecting my face from wind burn. I need to preserve my looks for my young fiancé," he replied as they passed through the inner doors of the airlock that led further into the port.

"I hear she likes a few wrinkles," Ashley replied.

As the heavy outer airlock security doors parted the smell of hot food and chicken broth filled his nostrils. Yawen was waiting there, her curly hair loose, sidearm strapped to her thigh, and a layer of red-tinted transparesteel plate armour covering her upper torso. "Hey, Ronin, Swift. I saw you two coming this way on my tactical monitor. On your way to check the Lobby out?"

"Yeah, I have a feeling Carnie skipped over the most interesting thing about this place," Minh-Chu replied. He barely knew anything about Yawen. Her records didn't have anything more than the official story on her. She'd come to the Haven System with other Irish rebels like Ruby Sima, entered the Haven Fleet Apex Officer Training program, graduated somewhere in the middle of her class, and was killed shortly after. The person she was meeting had all of Yawen's memories and rights. She was a result of Haven Fleet's Resurrection Program, one of the fifteen percent of subjects that were classified as a full success. The records got foggy after that, since the Fleet had no involvement in her career path after she went to the Rose System with Alice. What Minh-Chu knew for sure was that Alice gave her command of a captured Order of Eden Advanced Destroyer called The Renegade and she'd been her captain for over three months. The vacsuit she wore was definitely a recent Haven Military design, but the new plate was unlike anything Fleet used.

"You're our guide?" Ashley asked.

"Yeah, I'll introduce you around. It's a good time. The Prowler just got here and they've got a hell of a haul," Yawen replied as she started to lead the way with Ashley on one side and Minh-Chu on the other.

"Wait, the Prowler, that rings a bell. Wasn't that the Justicar ship?" Ashley asked after pondering for a moment.

"Bingo. Oh, you probably haven't heard," Yawen replied. "When Alice left the Prowler was in Noah's hands. He got it back here with the help of a few Issyrians who knew something about flying a starship. I was pretty sure that he'd take it for himself, I think everyone was. Last Crisis made him an offer on it too, but it was way too low. Even when they told him that he'd become part of their leadership. Then we found out that he gave it to the Issyrians. It took them a month to get it into shape and another to really use the ship, but they've been keeping busy ever since. Captain Rikan and his crew have surprised everyone."

"So, it's an Order ship with a crew that's mostly Issyrian?" Minh-Chu asked, thrilled at the thought.

"They're all Issyrians. They even flooded a few decks so they can start building some kind of formal social group in an underwater habitat. There's a lot more to it, but that's the general idea," Yawen explained.

They passed through another set of airlock doors that were dark brown with silver gilding. This was the Lobby. There were several ways out through doors like the ones they'd come through, a transparent wall that showed a darkened transit car platform, and elevator banks. It took Minh-Chu seconds to find all the ways in and out of the place, but the rest was worth taking in slowly.

There was a space reserved on a wall for pieces of metal that had been cut away from ships, he assumed, since every one of them had the serial number of an Order of Eden or other corporate vessels. His computer scanned and looked each one up, tagging several that corresponded with reports on the Stellarnet of ships that had gone missing or were destroyed. He was drawn to it, and touched a thin slice of an Order of Eden destroyer's hull, the Regulator Nine. "Nice trophies," he cooed.

"Captain Marda and I took that one down. They had no idea what was happening for half the fight," Yawen said.

Across from that trophy wall was the bar. It was once the

check-in and customer services counter, but a variety of stools, vending machines, and a pair of Stick Men bartenders had been installed. There were more bottles and boxes with exotic lettering and designs on them than he could count at a glance. He could see something else past them.

The wall behind was transparent, tinted light red, and there were humanoid shapes in a room there. He couldn't make out the details, but he guessed they must be security droids, out of sight, but ready to come out from behind the bar if there was trouble. It was just starting to get busy. Several members of Yawen's crew, most of whom wore yellow or black suits with Renegade, the ship's name spelt across their backs in bold letters, were finding their places near and at the bar. Every one of them carried a sidearm that could pierce personal armour. A few of them already had their drinks and were at tables where they munched on something from baskets as they socialized with Issyrians for the most part. The name of their ship, Prowler, marked the grey-blue uniforms of the shapeshifters, who weren't in their native form, but had taken the look of humans, Nafalli, and other species that Minh-Chu didn't recognize. Mixed in were a few Kodden whose low, rumbling voices were unmistakable in the din. "That's a Kodden, I've never seen one in person," Ashley said.

"Me neither," Minh-Chu said as he watched one lower his muzzle into a basket of curled sweet potato fries. A pair of inner lips emerged from his hard mouth and they pulled a few inside, his dark eyes widening while he chewed. "Spicy," he rumbled.

The Kodden had a face with thick, hard lizard-like skin that ended past the top of his head, where hair that split at the base to naturally entangle and mat so that it made a kind of blanket coat from there down. He couldn't see past the collar of the man's hard suit, but he imagined that the thick coat gave him a thick-bodied appearance except for his hands, which were much like the creature's face - hard-skinned with tough claws for digging. Minh-Chu realized he was staring and nodded respectfully at the Kodden before looking at Yawen. "Not everyone here is involved with the Rebel Captains?"

"About two-thirds of them are today, but you're right, there are a lot of people who were pushed off their settlements by the Order. They find out about this spot on the Stellarnet. We're careful who we tell, but everyone knows that we'll be found eventually. That's why there's a hangar full of hardware that we've been cutting out of the bigger captures. We usually run out of time before we can get much, but there are shield generators and a few big cannons down there."

"Carnie didn't get around to telling us about that," Ashley said.

"I'm not surprised it wasn't on the tour. It's not his secret to tell. All the captains involved with this place and the Rebels have been contributing to the stockpile. Our problem is getting the workforce together to fix the power grid and other fortifications so we can install what we have and keep it going. Most people don't trust artificial intelligences, even the really narrowly programmed ones, so we want flesh and blood manpower to watch the scanners and fire the guns."

Minh-Chu considered what he'd seen already. Kilometres of corridors connecting hangars added up to hectares. A port with most of its slips and exterior spaces in the dark or even more heavily damaged. Crews that wanted a place to spend short shore leave where they knew Order Soldiers or Corporate

Forces wouldn't come after them, and broken down facilities that suggested that the port was many times larger than he could guess. Then an Issyrian that had styled herself darkly moved away from a pillar and he saw an interactive board that was showing a guide to the hotel and port facility. "I need to see that," he said, walking over to it.

"Oh my gosh, this place is huge," Ashley said as they looked at the complex, which featured the surface slip spaces with hangars beneath it that were typical of a major commercial port. Minh-Chu selected the Hotel Guide section and saw that there were in fact three hotels, each with several levels beneath the main hangars. There were other import-export facilities that didn't present much detail there, but it was enough to make his head spin. "No wonder Noah felt it was reasonable to take two or three hangars along with a surface landing spot," Minh-Chu breathed. "Even if three-quarters of this place has caved in, there's enough space for thousands of people to live and work."

"Yeah, that's the problem," Noah said from behind as they scrolled through some of the other details. He had a can of Aero Shine Light in each hand.

Minh-Chu took one as Ashley accepted the other. "Hey, long face, you look like someone stole your dog," she said sympathetically.

"Yeah, uh, can I talk to you two?" he asked.

"What? I'm not invited?" Yawen asked, feigning insult.

Noah turned and gave her a brief hug. "Hey, Corker, just didn't want to rain on you during shore leave."

"It's all right. I should buy a round anyway, you know, keep morale up. You guys enjoy your serious chat," she said, accepting a parting hug from Ashley. "Welcome to the Bitter End."

Minh-Chu's attention was drawn to one of the entrances as a crowd of people, many of whom had obvious cybernetics, came in. The Lobby was huge, and there was a lot of space, but it was getting full. The entry of a pair of thick-bodied, plate armoured beings that he recognized as Rapsu, seemed to bring the energy of the room down a little. Everyone got a bit quieter and all eyes turned. They were almost three metres tall, had three long opposing fingers on their hands and toes, and reptilian features that reminded him of the less popular synthetic komodo dragon pets some people used to keep, only their heads were thicker, taller. "Ah, shit, I should warn Iruuk," Noah said under his breath. "Come on, I'll send him a message while we take a booth."

They moved to one side of the room where a number of booths had been installed. They looked newer than everything else with black and dark blue colours that didn't match the rest of the lobby. "Why do you have to warn Iruuk?" Ashley asked.

"Rapsu and Nafalli are natural enemies. They've gone to war a few times in and around the Iron Head Nebula. It's always territorial and brutal," Noah replied in a whisper. "I'm not worried about Iruuk starting trouble, but Torssen will. He's got the biggest ego I've ever seen, and he'll have to show everyone who's boss if he sees a new Nafalli here. He's the captain of that Edxi ship and the Shrisso. Oh, and don't mention the Flutes around this guy. His people eat them. They are as chickens are to humans."

"What? Wow, that's nasty," Ashley said as she opened her can. "They grew them in captivity for food?"

"If you believe the stories, yeah," Noah replied. "The Rapsu aren't exactly the approachable type."

"I'll be right back," Minh-Chu said as he started for the bar across the lobby. He took a look around as he made his way between tables then across a large clear space, watching as everyone who wasn't a part of a crew gave the Rapsu a wide berth. He nearly tripped over a cleaning droid with a few dents in the top of its once-shiny dome.

As he made his final approach to the bar, he noticed that there was a kind of social order to where the people waited for their drinks or sat down to chat. The humans mixed with other species, especially the Issyrians, while a part of the bar and one of the Stick Men was left alone. That's where the Rapsu ordered their drinks and something called a Kifsal Sille. He considered taking the safe option so he could avoid the pair of reptilians, but walked right towards them instead. He leaned against the bar, looked over his shoulder where Ashley was smiling at him from the booth and Noah was regarding him as his jaw was lowering towards the floor. Minh-Chu waved at Ashley and then looked to the Rapsu on his right. "My fiancé, we're getting married in a month."

The Rapsu stared down at him, nictitating membranes closing and opening over its black and yellow eyes. "What does it say?"

Minh-Chu definitely felt the tension that must have come when someone stood next to a big predator for the first time. Rapsu jaws looked massive up close, and its teeth had definitely evolved to tear at flesh. It would be a mistake to show fear, and if anyone else asked, he'd admit that there was a little of that, but he pushed past it easily enough. "I'm Ronin."

"What is Samurai Squadron?" the other Rapsu asked, touching the emblem on the back of his jacket.

"That's my fighter squadron. We fly off the Triton, you'll notice it," Minh-Chu replied as the Stick Man regarded him with its simple, round face. "Just a clean glass, please."

"The Triton. What is the ship for?" asked the smaller Rapsu who was still over a head taller than Minh-Chu.

"We're here to join the Rebel Captains, but don't tell anyone, the ink isn't dry on that yet," he replied.

"Ink? Are you going to spray us? Are you afraid?" asked Torssen, the larger of the two.

"I wasn't planning on spraying anyone today. Not really, just thought I'd say hi," Minh-Chu said as he accepted a glass and started for the booth. "See you around."

"So, how'd it go?" Ashley asked as he handed her the glass. She started pouring the clear, bubbly contents of her can into it.

"Oh, you know, pretty good. I've never felt like a snack before. They're not really up to date on human lingo either. Oh, I wouldn't laugh for the next couple of minutes, by the way. They might think I'm making fun of them, and I don't really want to shoot someone. At least, not on my first visit," he replied.

"Good call. They don't really understand human culture," Noah said. "Or laughter."

"Do they really eat any kind of mammal they can get away with eating?" Ashley asked.

"Well, I haven't seen them eat a human, but that doesn't mean we're off the menu," Noah replied. "I asked Torssen if he was hungry once when we were in an elevator alone, you know, as a joke, and he just stared at me until I got out."

Minh-Chu snickered then stopped himself. "Talk about a tense moment." He tried the Aero Shine Light and found that it was just carbonated water sweetened with lychee flavouring. The can said there weren't any inebriants in it, and it was refreshing, so he said; "That's pretty good."

"I'm glad to hear you like it. We've got about fifty cases left," Noah replied. "We hit a freighter that was on its way to restock the Sweet Eats fast food places on Rodus. Half of what people here are eating and drinking here is from that run."

"You guys have been really busy. This place is amazing," Ashley said before sipping from her glass.

"We didn't do too much with the lobby," Noah replied, looking around. "After we set up the bar and put the security bots behind it, the rest of the Rebel Captains chipped in, especially Sel Marda. He loved the idea of having a good place for him and his crew to hang out. I thought it would be way too big when we got it started, but now I wonder if we won't have to open one of the halls up on some nights. Right now only Sel, Yawen and me have codes for them," Noah explained, his brow still creased.

"So, what's got you down? I mean, you're back home. That's something, right?" Minh-Chu asked.

"Yeah, that's sinking in, and it's not good," he replied, his worry worsening.

A few of Yawen and Sel's crews started dancing near the bar as an Electro Swing track started playing. It was in sharp contrast to the mood in their booth. "I guess the tour didn't go so well?" Ashley asked.

"It was great," Noah replied, settling into his seat, taking a tall, slender can of Armour Paint, a misnamed light inebriant beverage from the inside of his coat and opening it with a pop. "I showed them everything you guys saw and a little more. Jake - it still feels weird to call him that - listened, looked then told me he was surprised. I mean, he gave me the whole acknowledgement, congratulating the crew, me and going on for a minute about how we did a lot with so few people. Leon, the guy from Fleet who's taking over the whole Privateering thing, started up then. He was all about telling me that I was a shining example of an independent leader who took the resources I was given and made something amazing happen."

"Well, that's all true, right? I mean, you worked with other captains, sure, but that's how we're going to win," Ashley said encouragingly. "Through cooperation."

"Well, yeah, but while he was shining me up I kept thinking about all the parts of my little corner where the lights were out, or how we had a couple months but couldn't get real defences in place. I mean, the Control Centre is in good shape, but it isn't wired to much of anything and we have volunteers from the Renegade sharing shifts with a few kids who work up there. I mean, they do a good job, but there are child labour laws for a reason, right?"

"I'm guessing there aren't any schools around, and you make sure those kids are taken care of, right?" Ashley asked.

"Well, yeah. I did, sure, then Yawen's people took over and that's working out pretty well. It's a little tribe, though. You can't exactly send them to their rooms or set a bedtime. I get it, I was raised by carny's, so my idea of childhood is pretty close to what they're living. They'll be all right as long as people bring in food and protect them. But that's one of the things that has me feeling like I'm under a million tons of it right now. I'm the Rebel Captain who barely left this port after we got here."

"You feel stuck and overwhelmed," Minh-Chu said, watching the pair of Rapsu stare at the group of humans dancing at the other end of the bar. A Joy Metal classic was starting up, and a few of them stayed to spin and thrash.

"See? You get it. I think Jake thought I was leaning in the other direction. Maybe I was in pitch mode because he took one look at the fabrication setup we were trying to put together and told me; 'we'll help you get this going.' I mean, I know he can. If there's anyone who can get us a few tons of rare parts that are super expensive for even the Triton to make because they're all super-dense and made of rare materials, it's that guy, but..." he took a long swig of his Armour Paint then shook his head and went on. "Man, I saw the next year of my life right then. The manufacturing stuff would get going, and I'd become the leader of the port. I mean, when you're making everything from booths," he knocked on the table, "these were made on the Corsair, by the way." Then he went on, engaging in a rant that kept Minh-Chu and Ashley riveted. "Right, so we can make this stuff, hull plating, armour, food, and if we get the right materials, we could eventually expand the manufacturing stuff. That's great, but that would make me the richest guy here and I'd have so much control over what happens in the Bitter End that even if someone else was named leader, I'd still be deciding what goes on most of the time. What everyone gets, what parts of the port get rebuilt, and my reach would just keep going and going, especially as we build the defences and a huge shield."

"But you don't want that," Minh-Chu guessed.

He nodded as he took another swig and went on. "You

know what I was thinking when I was with Alice, hanging at her place? When I was sitting in that fighter on the way here? I was thinking; I miss this. Man, I miss being with my girl. I miss flying in formation with people I can trust. I'm gonna miss the Corsair, and being able to fly away from all this. I mean, if I were a visitor here, it would be amazing. I'd love this place. We even have fricken' lizard people. Sure, they're a bit intense, but they're interesting, right? There are people from all kinds of worlds here. Places the Order hasn't seen yet. I think there are even a couple guys from Grace who haven't left yet. That's who Yawen got that armour from, by the way. Not that they're competitors or anything. They gave that getup to her to thank her for helping one of their ships out."

"Oh, I was wondering," Ashley commented. "Do you think they've got some for sale?"

"I'm not sure. My point is that some of their people are coming here now. This is a so-called hidden base, but the word is creeping out over the Stellarnet," he spread his fingers out in the air in front of him, slowly moving them towards the air between them as he spoke. "It's just a matter of time before those few people who know where this drifting rock is tell a few more, and they tell a few more, and then some Order of Eden asshole makes his bonus by tricking someone into telling him where it is. I want this spot to be ready, but man, I mean," he shook his head, exasperated. "This place won't be set up to defend itself unless I beg and trade everything I've got with everyone who will listen and a few I'll have to blackmail to break their backs so this becomes a badass battle station. Then what? I rule like some kinda moon king? What's that look like?"

Minh-Chu opened his mouth to reply but was interrupted as the young man went on.

"I get to stay on this rock, making sure that this free port can stay open, supplied, the kids go to school or something, the Issyrians have access to all the water they want, and no one eats anyone else. Then you get the worst thing ever; big politics. Hell no. I mean, no way am I going to be on top if I have to deal with a bunch of political bullshit that's more complicated than one captain making a deal with another. That, I can handle, but when this place goes big, like with a hundred thousand people living here full time, the politics will get complicated. No way do I want to be here for that. I'd rather be in a starfighter, or on some ship like the Errand, within an hour or so of a nice visit with my girl." He chugged the rest of his Armour Paint then brought the can down on the table. "Sorry, that might have been boiling on the back burner for a while."

"Sounds like you made your decision though," Ashley said with an encouraging smile.

"You want to be a space pirate, or a starfighter pilot," Minh-Chu added. "I wonder how long that's been true."

"You know, I think I started daydreaming about those two ideas when I was a kid," Noah replied wistfully. "Man, I wish I could get the Corsair back."

"I can't do that, but I would welcome you back to Samurai Squadron in a half-second," Minh-Chu replied, hoping it wasn't too soon to ask.

"What about all this?" Noah asked, nodding towards the Lobby in general.

"Your allies are already here and they are already helping," Minh-Chu said, looking at a table next to the trophy wall where

Sel, Yawen and Rikan were sitting down. There were other Rebel Captains, but he suspected that those were the key to the whole organization. "They have come to meet with Alice and Jake so he can join them. I'm sure they'd give you a moment."

Noah's eyes snapped wide open. "What if they took over? I mean, what if the Rebel Captains just ran the place, especially after Jake and the Triton sign on?"

"I'm vying for a seat at that table too. There will be enough influence there to make sure what you built doesn't go to waste," Minh-Chu said quietly. "And you will have your own seat."

"I already do," Noah said, thinking for a moment. "That's good. I mean, I'd have to give up the gun operation, which would kinda suck since I've brought a lot of rebels into the fold, but, I mean..."

"Maybe not," Ashley said.

"Well, I guess I could keep the whole Stick Man processing thing going, but if I'm off doing things with the Triton, or the Samurai Squadron, then..."

"Talk to Alice and Jake," she said.

"What are you thinking?" Minh-Chu asked with narrowed eyes. He was aware that she'd known Jake for longer than most. He'd trained her as a pilot and treated her like a daughter.

"Well, there are a few manufacturing systems on the Triton. One really big one, a few smaller ones," Ashley replied before taking a drink. "I love lychee," she breathed as she finished.

"Oh, what?" Noah asked, surprised. "You think he'd give me time on those to make hardware and sell it?"

"Maybe, but that's not just up to him. Stephanie will have a say," Minh-Chu said. She was a practical Captain, and he wasn't sure if she'd go along with it. "One step at a time. First, you negotiate your freedom. Then you see where you go from there."

"Yeah, I'll take that deal all day. Thanks, guys," Noah said. "I'm switching to something that won't make me hyper." He tapped the empty can of Armour Paint and it spun in the middle of the table. "I shouldn't get too worked up before everyone gets here."

# EIGHT

## The Puzzle

IT WAS ALWAYS interesting to see how people reacted to a group entering the room. The Lobby's features told a story as well. The new booths were made by the Corsair's manufacturing systems before the Clever Class Corvette was given back to Haven Fleet. There was a crack running across the floor and ceiling that had been filled and repaired but not covered up. Supports overhead suggested that there was once a chandelier or some other fancy fixture up there. Everything was classically decorated, and Minh-Chu was fairly sure that the rest of the hotel was similarly set up in shades of brown, black and silver.

This space was never meant to be a bar, but it had become a massive one. He wondered if anyone who had never seen a traditional human hotel would guess at its former purpose. For the people who had seen old period entertainment featuring human culture, Minh-Chu was sure that the place had some effect on them. He watched as they took their time chatting, dancing, drinking or eating. Many stuck to their own corners, lingering with their own tribes. Ashley was beside him, doing the same as she checked the local Stellarnet, flipping past advertising, and checking in on local conversations and videos.

When Elyub, one of the more long-term Rebel Captains entered, he was greeted warmly by Captain Rikan and several of his Issyrian crew. Then there were other humans who wanted to say hello. "People watching?" asked Ashley as she followed his gaze.

"Just looking at all the pieces. Do you know if both of the Issyrian leaders have seats with the Rebel Captains?" Minh-Chu asked. Earlier in his life, he'd be mingling with as many people as he could, but he wanted more information before he started introducing himself this time.

"I don't know. Elyub does, that's in Alice's file about the Captains," Ashley replied. Normally she'd be out there socializing too, but she may have been staying in their booth because he wasn't amongst the crowd. "It's amazing, though. This is what the Order is probably afraid of. So many people from different worlds getting together. Being treated as equals."

Minh-Chu nodded as he watched most of the people at one end of the bar stop talking and look towards the entrance there. A man with skin that looked fake, waxen but dense entered. He'd seen pictures of people with that kind of skin replacement, most of them went bald even outside of an atmosphere, but this one wore a hood that was anchored to his forehead and cheekbones with metal clips. Elyub and a few others approached him and his entourage of well-armoured crewmembers respectfully, offering hand shakes. "That's Captain Ethan Asher, the leader of Last Crisis. People have been wondering if he'd show up to this meeting at all," Ashley said.

"Alice's last update said even she wasn't sure if he'd come. I'd think he owes her an appearance since she gave his group a captured Order Destroyer," Minh-Chu said, considering what a challenge it would be to have to attack one with a small group of fighters. It was an Advanced Destroyer with enhanced point defence systems made to repel missiles, torpedoes and small craft. He hoped it wasn't the direction most Order ships were headed in, design-wise.

"She gave him one of the three?" Ashley asked.

Minh-Chu nodded. "I thought you read the history she wrote up?"

"Well, not all of it. Okay, I started listening to it. I like the way she records reports, and I don't think she realizes this, but there's a little of her mother's accent in the way she talks," Ashley replied.

"I never noticed," Minh-Chu replied as they watched how Yawen and Sel's crewmembers reacted to Captian Ethan Asher. Sel and Yawen paid their respects, but their people didn't go any closer to anyone from Last Crisis than they had to. "I wonder what they mean by their name? Do they mean that this will be the last crisis? Or that they're still working on the most recent crisis? Or are they supposed to be the final crisis for their enemies?"

Ashley snickered and replied quietly; "Maybe you should ask them."

"Not yet. I want to see what the rest of the puzzle pieces do when our other friends arrive," Minh-Chu replied as he watched a group of people from Grace wearing vacsuits that were made of two overlapping pieces under mostly translucent armour approach Captain Asher. They were all smiles, offering their greetings as though they knew it was a pleasure to meet them. Captain Asher gave them a nod. Then he walked past them, leaving a subordinate with a bare metal cybernetic arm to shake hands with them. The rest of his entourage followed him through a set of doors that led to the nearest banquet room. "Ooh, chilly."

"Uh-huh. Asher either has a great big ego, or he's got bigger fish to fry," Ashley agreed. "You know, for some reason, I expected him to be more approachable. Alice said she got along with him well."

"Maybe he doesn't like being in a room with so many armed people," Minh-Chu guessed. "He has a few bounties on him."

"Do you think someone would try to hunt him here?" Ashley asked.

"For the kind of money the Order and everyone else is offering for him, I think the worst and best hunters would try all the time," Minh-Chu replied, knowing that she'd heard Jake say that a few times about other bounties he'd decided not to chase. It was wise of Jake to believe that he was usually a middling bounty hunter, even near the end of his career when he caught several high profile targets and brought them back alive.

"You know, I'd think that he'd want to try to hang out in this place. It's probably the only place where someone would help him out if a hunter did try something. He must have friends here," Ashley supposed.

"I don't know, he might have allies around, but I don't get

the impression that he has a great big group of friends," Minh-Chu said under his breath.

"You're probably right," Ashley replied.

The entrance closest to them opened, its doors parting to admit Alice, Iruuk, Jake, Leon, and Frost in that order. Iruuk retracted his helmet, leaving the rest of his fur looking like it was made of metal. The bar quieted, and all eyes turned towards them. A bawdy electro-swing tune came to its conclusion, completing the stillness with silence until someone dropped a glass. Yawen, Sel, and Elyub all started to cross the Lobby to greet Alice, and by the time the next song started playing through the emitters in the ceiling - a jumpy jive track that was hop-inducing - most of the people looking on sort of went back to their drinks and conversations.

That was except for a group who didn't seem to have an affiliation with the people Minh-Chu knew of, who slipped from their booth and left through the far exit. They didn't seem much rougher than the rest of the occupants, though their combat armour was more like adapted extreme environment equipment and their weapons didn't look as modern. He watched them leave and noticed that one of them took a long look over his shoulder as the doors sealed behind him.

As Minh-Chu and Ashley left their booth to join their friends, he noticed how everyone who could call Haven home still looked like they belonged to a military unit. The only difference worth noticing in their equipment was Alice's powder blue vacsuit, but it was covered in the same style of black military boots and long coat her father was wearing. Noah brightened the group more in dark purple and blue, but that wasn't enough to make them look less like part of a platoon. Their lack of rank insignia didn't help at all. "We all look wrong for this place," Minh-Chu said as he joined the group, looking Jake up and down specifically.

"You know I stick to black whenever I can. Maybe everyone else should get a little creative, just not too creative, and not yet." Jake replied. "We're here to make an impression."

"A good one, I hope. A lot of these people look like they're looking for a way to make life here easier, but I don't think they'd like people around who want to enforce rules," Minh-Chu whispered, watching as Alice stared at him with that look that suggested she might be reading him. "Yes, I'm feeling uneasy," he said to her with a little smirk.

"Sorry, I just caught it. You come through really clearly," Alice said.

"A clear mind is its own gift," Minh-Chu replied, really treading water. Expressions like that were easy to say and often gave him a moment to figure out what he would say next while people were thinking about it.

"We've been people-watching. It's a pretty interesting place," Ashley said, smiling at Noah in particular.

"So, what do you think of the crowd?" Jake asked Minh-Chu and Ashley.

Alice was exchanging hugs with Yawen, Sel and Elyub the Issyrian, who had transformed into a fairly average-looking human man. Minh-Chu identified him by the thick blue and green environment suit he wore. Introductions were next, and Minh-Chu knew that the moment to give his friend advice about the upcoming meeting would disappear soon, so he considered what that would be quickly. Jacob Valent was so much like the man Minh-Chu spent many years with before, the one who Jake grew out of, Jonas Valent, but there were several distinct differences. Jonas enjoyed good conversation with almost anyone. When it came right down to it, he was a social person. Jake was more selective, perhaps a better listener, but he definitely didn't have the patience. He'd also seen many more terrible people and places during his time as a bounty hunter. Jonas had a keen edge to him, but he had to be pushed. Jake wasn't a savage but was even more of a warrior, and that edge had been honed. That sometimes came through when he had to negotiate with people. "Have you met Elyub? Captain of the Opal?" Alice asked, introducing him to the smiling Issyrian.

Then the thing that would get his friend thinking in the right direction dropped into Minh-Chu's mind and he whispered to Jake; "What is something you can gain by giving?"

Ashley greeted Elyub with a hug and smiled brightly at him. "I was hoping I'd get a chance to meet you. Alice said a lot of nice things. I'm Ashley, the Master of the Helm aboard the Triton."

"Oh, it's good to meet you. That is a very large ship, you have an important job," Elyub said, his eyes widening a little more than a normal human's. "Alice speaks of me?"

"She dedicated a chapter of her report to you and your ship," Ashley replied. "I'll send you a copy later."

"Um, this is Wing Commander Minh-Chu," Alice interrupted, turning Elyub towards him.

"Wing Commander?" Elyub asked. "There is a fighter squadron in the area?"

"Samurai Squadron. We fly off the Triton," Minh-Chu replied, giving the Issyrian a brief hug. "It's good to meet you. How's the Opal?"

"A little damaged. The last raid had an escort. Some fighters would have been helpful, but we were victorious," Elyub replied, a little surprised at being asked about his ship.

"Your crew are all right?" Minh-Chu asked.

"Oh, yes. Only one breach, but our aquatic environment saved everyone in the compartment," the Issyrian Captain replied.

"Ethan signalling. He wants to get started," Alice said, glancing at her left command and control unit. She looked up at Minh-Chu. "Are you going to ask for a seat with the Rebel Captains?"

"Not yet. I want to see them at the table first," he replied. "I have a feeling that rushing won't help me or the Squadron here."

"Are you sure?" Jake asked as the group started moving across the Lounge towards the doors that Captain Asher used.

"I'm very unsure. That's why I'm not committing to a decision just yet," Minh-Chu replied. "Figure it out?"

"No. I don't have much bandwidth for riddles and I don't want to cheat," Jake replied, tapping his left bracer. "Better tell me the answer now or I'll be distracted during the meeting."

"Is it food?" Iruuk asked. "Something you can gain by giving? You feed something then eat it later?"

Minh-Chu laughed, joined by Frost, who was more amused by Leon who cringed and said; "Nasty. I'm a vegetarian when I have a choice."

"That's not bad, but it's not quite right," Minh-Chu said, turning back towards Jake. "It's grace."

He took that seriously, nodding as he muttered; "Clever. I get it. Walk lightly, listen carefully."

It was a privileged position, to be a close friend to someone like Jacob Valent. Minh-Chu knew that if that advice had come from most people, Jake may have seen it as condescending, but he had his ear and his trust. He was sure that it wouldn't be tested, but everything else was about to be.

# NINE

Rebel Captains and Old Business

THERE WAS a delay as the Rebel Captains sat down along one side of several tables that had been put together length-wise. Minh-Chu noticed that the table was the focus of the whole hall right away. The otherwise empty space decorated like some ancient twentieth-century Earth spot for modestly sized ball-room dances and fancy dinners. From everything he'd seen on the Remmybase, the massive collection of entertainment from across human history, it was a good match, right down to the giant chandelier hanging high above.

Before Yawen took her place at the table, she showed Minh-Chu, Ashley, Leon, Frost, Iruuk and Jake to a long row of chairs against the wall near the main entrance. Noah and Alice were still in the hallway. Minh-Chu overheard the beginning of the conversation that was causing the delay. Noah told Jake and

Alice that he wanted to hand control of the port, with the exception of a small section reserved for his own use, over to the Rebel Captains. He was also offering access to his private hangar and landing slip to Alice and Jake, and he was smart about it. His manner was similar to someone telling a guest that they could come back anytime.

Jake took it at face value, but Alice kept him behind in the hall to discuss it further. "I wonder if she's telling him to take his time with that decision?" Ashley asked, looking at the doors.

"Probably. It's a lot to give up," Jake replied. "They got a lot of work done in not much time. I might let it go if I were in his boots, but I know a lot of people who wouldn't."

Minh-Chu nodded, aware that Jake was probably thinking about Ayan and a few other people they were close to. When they were in rough shape on Tamber with too many people for the ships they had, she planted her feet and led the way in an effort to make a home. Ayan's tenacity and leadership saved lives and made her the new founder of the solar system. If that had led to peace, Minh-Chu was fairly certain that he'd still be in the Haven System, flying around with Ashley as they explored the centuries-old ruins of cities and the other sights that were abundant there. The new settlement that Ayan founded on Tamber became a threat and an enviable place instead. It was one worth fighting for, so peaceful exploration would have to wait.

The doors opened and everyone sitting nearby heard Alice as she was saying; "...as long as you're sure. There's no taking it back."

"I'm sure, it's like a weight is off my shoulders already,"

Noah looked at Jake then. "Can I talk to you out here for a second?"

Without a word, Jake got to his feet and followed the younger man outside. Minh-Chu would have wished he could overhear what they said if he wasn't fascinated by the Rebel Captains. Thick-bodied Sel, slender Yawen, waxen-faced Ethan, dishevelled Inod, wide-eyed Elyub and uncertain-looking Rikan sat along one side of the long table in that order. There were other seats there too, some of them were left empty beside the captains, spacing them out, but there seemed to be a pattern there. "Are all the captains here?"

"No, I overheard that there are a handful missing. Asher has two votes because his second is a full-fledged captain at the table too," Leon answered quietly. "Yawen said there are a bunch of them waiting to join up too."

"That must be encouraging to you," Minh-Chu said as he noticed that most of the captains watched Jacob Valent and Noah Lucas leave. They were curious about all of Alice and Noah's guests, but Jake was the one who drew the most eyes.

"You might get a lot of leads for the Privateering Program here," Ashley said to Leon.

He nodded. "I'm hoping to start with the Rebel Captains. I don't think they need more incentives to attack the Order, but it couldn't hurt. I can offer some support at least."

"Frost?" Jake beckoned as he opened a door.

The heavy-set man got to his feet. "Last minute plans," Minh-Chu muttered to himself. Sel noticed that he was watching the captains and nodded respectfully, Minh-Chu returned the gesture and watched as he leaned towards Yawen to ask her questions in a whisper. She put her arm across his shoulders and they took turns whispering into each other's ears. "Chummy," Minh-Chu said under his breath.

"Just a bit," Ashley said with a smile. "They've worked together before, right? That's what I heard?"

"I couldn't tell you for sure, but I'd guess," Leon replied.

Noah, Jake and Frost returned, the first walked directly to the table while the other two took their seats beside Minh-Chu. "We're going to use Hall Three next time," Noah said to the captains sitting at the table.

"The one with the gallery?" asked Sel.

"Yeah, we'll have security up there and at the exits. We have to be ready for meetings where there are ten times as many people here," Noah said. Alice was about to sit down and he took her chair, carried it to the head of the table, and put it down. "And there's another change happening right now."

Silence fell across the room as, after a moment's hesitation, Alice walked to the head of the table and sat down. "Do you know what's going on?" Minh-Chu asked Jake.

He shook his head. "No idea."

No one spoke a word as Inod took a chair and walked it to the other end of the table with Ethan on his heels. He put it down and Ethan was about to sit down when Elyub kicked it over. "No. He doesn't deserve to sit at the head of the table. She does." The Issyrian was deadly serious.

"No one sits at the head of the table. It's been that way since we formed the Rebel Captains."

"Pardon? Who called the first meeting? Who brought us together when we were still putting the Oasis base together?" Sel asked, booming across the table without getting to his feet.

"The first man standing doesn't matter as much as the last,"

Ethan replied. "I have…"

Alice silenced him as she got to her feet, drawing all eyes. "All right, you don't want someone at the head of the table. I hear it's been over six weeks since everyone here got together even though Sel called a meeting, Noah called a meeting, even Elyub called a meeting. No one from Last Crisis showed, Inod didn't show, and five other captains haven't bothered to turn up for this meeting. There are a lot of empty chairs here."

"I have Captain Mark Cavel's proxy. He couldn't get here in time," Yawen said.

"I have Dagnus' proxy," Ethan added.

"Why isn't he here? I saw his ship in orbit." Alice asked without looking up at him. When he hesitated to answer she asked; "Is he listening in?"

"There is an open channel," Ethan replied.

Alice reached into her jacket and flicked a device the length of her little finger onto the table. It blinked and spun until it came to rest in the middle. "It's a jamming device," Iruuk said in a hush. He was fascinated by the exchange.

Ethan and Sel cringed, and the latter tapped a control hidden behind his ear. "Right, I suppose keeping these meetings private is a good idea."

"No one transmits what goes on here," Alice said. "There won't be any more recordings, either."

"She comes back with her father backing her and she's making rules right away," Ethan said as he picked up his chair.

"She doesn't need anyone else backing her to sit at the head of the table," Elyub said.

"Thanks to her, you have a shipyard fresh advanced destroyer, Ethan. I would still barely be a concern to the Order if it weren't for her too," Captain Sel Marda said, pointing at him. "Oh, and she could have done it without your help, I am certain of that. You got what you wanted out of all that action and didn't give anyone else you owed a full share to their lot."

"That's true, I'm still waiting for the supplies and equipment you promised as our cut in exchange for your destroyer," Noah said.

"I didn't want to finish splitting that up until Alice came back," Ethan replied.

"Well, I'm here now, and I want my share. Where can I pick it up?" Alice asked. Then she cocked her head. "Wait, you don't have it, do you?"

"I gave two shipping containers to your boyfriend while you were away," Ethan replied.

"Filled with damaged guns and armour with a couple burned out portable shield generators," Noah said to everyone at the table in a loud, clear voice. "There wasn't a thing in there from the Order of Eden supply yard raid."

"Most of the supplies from that raid went into stocking and arming the destroyer she gave us," Ethan retorted.

"You don't think I had to do the same?" Sel Marda burst. "I had to scrape everything I had together and spend plenty of treasure to outfit that marvellous killing machine. It was worth it, but my crew went without pay for weeks so we could get it done. I'm just catching up with what I owe now, but it would have been easier if I had the three cargo containers of supplies and equipment you owed me for playing my part. Maybe I should tell my crew that your broken promise is why they had to wait for their platinum? I wonder how far their opinion of you and Last Crisis would fall?"

"Now, I'm sure we can do something here..." Ethan started as the rest of the captains, eager to hold him accountable, started shouting over each other.

Alice didn't let the disorder gain too much momentum. Instead, she shouted; "Shut it down! Back in your seats, now!"

"I wonder where she got that drill sergeant bellow?" Minh-Chu asked in a whisper, looking at Jake.

"The academy?" Jake whispered back, not taking his eyes off the table.

"Says the girl who has been given the head of the table by her boyfriend," Inod grumbled. Alice sat down and spoke with perfect confidence. "That's Captain Lucas. When we're at this table, there are no boyfriends, girlfriends, spouses or old relations, only brothers and sisters. He's told me all about how the Rebel Captians are drifting apart, and it was my idea to take control. When I left I was pretty sure that I gave the Prowler and the four Advanced Destroyers to the right people and that it would bring you together. Now I see Sel, Yawen and Rikan working together whenever they can, but you and Last Crisis are still on your own. Do you want out, Captain Asher? I'm going to bring this together whether you let the Triton join or not, do you want to be a part of that?"

To Minh-Chu's surprise, pride didn't seem to get in Captain Ethan Asher's way as he leaned forward and answered; "Yes. Since I have the proxy for all of Last Crisis, I speak for them as well."

"Good. I'm willing to forgive all your debts to me if everyone else is so we can move forward. Anyone else interested in wiping the record clean for Captain Asher and Last Crisis?" She looked to her left.

Noah nodded and said; "Aye."

Sel did the same, followed by Yawen. Inod chuckled; "He doesn't owe me a thing, but aye."

Then Elyub and Rikan did the same. Alice made it official. "So you're clear of every debt to the Rebel Captains. Screw us again and we'll decide how you'll be punished."

Ethan leaned back and replied; "Thank you," as he looked around the table.

"She's completely turned this around," Ashley whispered without moving her lips. "Asher has been put in his place."

"There will be bylaws. A set of rules that will keep things fair for all of us, you'll get them once the meeting is over. I'll take suggestions for the next few days then we'll vote on them when we meet next week. The Rebel Captains is going to be a real democracy starting today," Alice said. "I need a majority at this table to keep sitting here. We're voting for my leadership right now."

"This table is weighted in your favour," Inod said, pointing down its length at Alice. "I barely know you at all, why should I stick with the Rebels when it looks like all you'll bring are laws and restrictions?"

"Haven't you been listening? Do you have eyes in your head, boy?" Sel asked. "Her little crew got us the four biggest fighting ships we have and she just forgave debt worth a quarter million plat so we could get on with our business."

"What business is that?" Rikan asked. When the Issyrian saw that his question wasn't going over well with most of the table he added; "Asking for a friend."

"That's a good question. What we do won't change. We're here to ruin the Order of Eden's work and to make things better for ourselves. I want us to cooperate more, but we'll still work on our own goals. Come with us for a while, let me show you," Alice replied.

"All right, but I think Captain Asher should take the first turn at the head of the table, so I'll put him up," Inod replied.

"Any other nominations?" Yawen asked.

They waited for a moment, and then Sel said; "We go around the table."

Noah nodded and said; "Alice."

Yawen, Sel, Elyub and Rikan did the same, leaving Inod to vote for Ethan, who surprised his only supporter when he said; "Captain Alice Valent."

"Thank you, I won't let you down," Alice said. "Noah Lucas, Captain of the Errand has something to bring to the table."

"What happened to the Corsair?" asked Elyub, his eyes widening.

"It got repossessed by the military," Noah replied as he stood. "I'm hanging on to the Errand, maybe upgrading it a little, but don't be surprised if I leave it here in my hangar. Speaking of which, I want to give most of the Bitter End to the Rebels. I'm keeping a section for myself, but I'm appointing a temporary mayor while we finish getting the first manufacturing plant together. Shamus?"

"Aye, God help me," Frost said under his breath. "Aye, just call me Frost, only my lady calls me Shamus. I'll be taking a crew down here to secure Noah's part of the port, which doesn't amount to much compared to the rest, then I'll be setting up a lot of bots to take care of whatever's unearthed and working already. By the time that's done, you lot should be able to find a mayor to replace me and I'll hand things off."

"He comes with the deal," Noah said, turning towards Rikan, who was getting to his feet. "What's up?"

"I want that job," Rikan said. "I came here to announce that I'll be giving Elyub the Prowler. I'm not a good captain. The ship can barely fight, and we've had to close whole sections off. I would like to say it's been nothing but cash and prizes since the crew put me in charge, but I picked the cart and donkey."

"He lost me," Minh-Chu snickered. "I think I get what he's saying, but the reference just went over my head."

"He's talking about an old game show in the Remmybase called Let's Make A Deal, it's so strange and hilarious," Iruuk explained.

"Oh, we'll check it out," he replied as Ashley agreed.

"And you want to be a mayor?" asked Sel. "Are you sure?"

"Absolutely," Rikan replied. "I have education and experience with civics and was in charge of trade for a whole space station before this. I know I'd do well."

"Okay, then follow Frost around after you finish handing Elyub command of the Prowler over. You okay with having a shadow, Frost?" Noah asked.

"If it means I finish up down here faster so I can get back to the Triton, aye," Frost replied.

"Anyone against the Rebel Captains taking control of the Bitter End when it's ready in a couple weeks?" Alice asked, sending the vote around the table.

No one was against it, so she was about to move on when Sel said; "Thank you, Captain Lucas. That's quite a thing. You sure you want to give over what you built up?"

"Most of it, yeah, but I'm taking a cut of everything that comes out of the manufacturing setup I'm building," Noah replied.

"There it is," Yawen laughed, and there were a lot of snickers around the table.

"Hey, I'm no saint," Noah said with a shrug and a smirk. "By the way, does anyone know where I can salvage some heavy manufacturing parts?"

"I know a place, I've even got a crew going back and forth with full loads," Sel said, looking around the table. After considering it for a moment, he went on. "There's a world the mad bots made dead, almost no one on it, and there's tech just laying around with no law watching."

"Keeping that to yourself, huh?" Yawen asked.

"He hasn't told you about it?" Noah asked.

"This is the first I hear of it," she replied.

"Hey, everyone's got two hands and a right to hide one behind their back," Sel said.

"Well, out with it. You can't tell everyone you've got a secret looting spot then not share, not at this table, at least," Yawen pressed.

"Right, you're right. I get a discount on that manufacturing rig when you're done building it," he said to Noah. "And I want twenty-five percent of whatever you sell from that spot."

Some of the captains laughed, others shook their heads in objection, and Yawen punched him in the side just hard enough to make him wince.

"All right, all right," Sel said, holding his hands up. "You'd think you were all thieves and hardened criminals or somethin'.

Fine, there's a lot there, just remember that I shared next time you find something juicy."

"Deal," Noah replied. "And I'll give any captain who sits at this table a discount on my manufacturing. We should all be sharing what we can. Where is this spot?"

"Well, you'll want to send your ships to Tabrus. I'll show you the way. I'm telling you this place was a bloody wonder, but the bots scraped every breather off the planet before the antivirus came along and shut it all down. Bring big ships with lots of empty space and plenty of people to load them up with. It won't be too long before the word gets out," Sel said.

"Tabrus? That's a shame. I visited with my family when I was a boy," Ethan said. "Well, I'll send two freighters."

"I appreciate it. The Errand is going, of course. I have an old Postal Ship that's ready too," Noah looked in Jake's direction. "Can I count on the Triton?"

"You can," Jake replied. "Regardless of how things turn out here."

"I was going to ask," Elyub said, looking towards the seating by the door. "Why are we letting outsiders listen in?"

"They're petitioners, and what they're bringing to the table is so big that I'm sure you'll give them at least one seat," Alice said. "Besides, we have the votes."

Minh-Chu's jaw nearly dropped as he realized that the whole situation was tilted in the Triton's favour. Alice made herself the facilitator of the meeting. There were Captains missing and the ones who showed up would back the Triton and the ship's owner. All he had to do was sit back and see how it would all come together. It took a great deal of effort for Minh-Chu to hold a chuckle in check.

# TEN

Coveted Advantages

"NOW I'D LIKE to present a new Captain for membership," Alice looked towards Jake. He got to his feet and strode to the empty side of the table. The similarity between her confident gait earlier and that of her father was impossible for Minh-Chu to miss. To him, he looked like he already belonged there, but Jake was doing something that made him less domineering than he had in previous similar moments. Perhaps it was a change in his expression, or maybe his posture was a little less rigid.

"Good, he doesn't look like he's about to take over," Minh-Chu said for Ashley's benefit.

"I was afraid of that too," she replied in a similarly hushed tone.

"I didn't think I'd ever see this," Sel said as he stared at Jake with a look of disbelief. "Sorry to hear about your troubles at home, but if it's brought you to our table with something to offer, then I hope ye don't hold it against me if I thank my lucky stars."

Minh-Chu wondered if being reminded that he'd just been kicked out of Haven Fleet bothered his old friend. If it did, Jake didn't show it as he replied; "You have no idea how lucky you are. For anyone who doesn't already know, I own the Triton and share rights to some of the most powerful technology in the galaxy."

"The Quad Drive," Captain Inod said, leaning forward. "The fastest interstellar travel system out there. I wouldn't believe it if I hadn't seen the Renegade use one while I was scanning her."

That's something Minh-Chu saw coming. The Quad Drive system was a simple idea. The smallest ones were one square metre in size. Inside that space was a micro-fusion reactor, a pre-programmed secure navigational computer, a communications system and a dimension drive that would send your ship skipping through a specific energetic space as you were protected by a wormhole. It didn't allow you to explore, but it got you to your destination in the safest, fastest way possible. It was safe, tamper proof and if you got stuck in the energetic space outside of your home dimension, it would spit you out so you emerged somewhere inside your local galaxy. There was something in how the whole thing worked that ensured that result every time the Quad Drive system failed or was deactivated early.

Only Haven Fleet had them, and they protected the technology jealously. Word was obviously getting out though, there was no stopping information from spreading once it hit the Stellarnet. Minh-Chu braced himself for Jake's response. "I won't be handing out Quad Drives. What I'm here to offer are Haven Nodes," he projected an image of a contained cylinder with ports at the top and bottom. It was about a metre tall. "This is a full-sized image of one. Hook it up to your ship and you will have a near-zero latency connection to every other Haven Node along with access to the Stellarnet. Right now the only reason why the Stellarnet is getting constant updates is because the Renegade and other ships that are tapped into Nodes are in the area, By installing one of these you can throw away every part of your communications system except the interface. I'm giving you one for free, the backup will come cheap," Jake explained.

"Those are built into Quad Drives. They use them to update navigation," Sel said. "You know I've gotta ask; why does Captain Blake over there get a Quad for the Renegade while we get passed over?" He leaned forward and added; "I'll give you whatever kind of treasure you ask for if I can get one of those drives. Name your price."

"She was a part of Haven Military forces and has been in constant communication with them as she makes the transition from officer to free actor. Technically, I've hired her, so I own the Quad Drives on her ship. They're on loan."

"So, how much of this table is under your influence? Are you going to be pulling the strings through her?" Inod asked as Ethan crossed his arms and leaned back in his seat.

"I'm a free agent," Alice said. "I may be his daughter, but I'm not in the Fleet anymore. The Clever Dream is an independent ship as well. I get to keep the technology inside because I earned their trust. Oh, and I traded everything I own outside her hull and still owe an eye-watering sum that I may be paying off for another ten or twenty years."

"That still sounds like the military to me," Ethan said. "Independent or not."

"How'd you earn enough trust with Haven Fleet to get you a pretty ship like that?" Inod asked.

"I led a small half-squad of soldiers into an Order Base Ship and assassinated Admiral Tafford before blowing it up from the inside with an antimatter bomb, among other things. There's verified footage, here," she swept her finger across her left command and control bracer, sending a copy of the interactive holograms and all the other data to everyone at the table.

"Some of that's still classified," Jake muttered.

"Oops," Alice said with a shrug.

He laughed for a moment then said; "I can't get every Captain a Quad Drive, but how does a free Haven Node sound? How about being able to transfer data to each other at near-instant speed anywhere in our galaxy? That's the bribe I'm offering today. Oh, and you can encrypt your transfers however you want. Aside from that, I'm willing to give you access to the Triton's navigational database and I'm bringing in the master of the ship, Captain Stephanie Vega. She'll want to work with you on raids."

That gave everyone at the table pause until Inod said; "Sorry, still not impressed. I hear that ship is fifty years old or something."

"Have you tried to scan her?" Sel asked, offended. "Signals slide right over that ship's hull. My crew have been making curiosity sweeps since she arrived in orbit, there are no cracks. Even if that ship's upgrades stop there, look at the size of her! The internal space is so big that it would take three and a half of our destroyers to come close to the volume."

"So it's big," Inod said with a shrug, his face turning red at the irritation of being confronted.

"Captain Marda's right and he's also missing the point," Elyub said. "Everyone who is interested in technology or ship construction is eager to see what Lorander is going to start producing in the Haven System. The rumour is that they have the most advanced technology and the highest standards. When Captain Lucas joined us, he was able to make upgrades for our ships and equipment for our people that was as good as the best we could buy anywhere else. There were also things that we'd never seen that were better. Now a legend is politely asking to join us with an offering that is beyond that. Jacob Valent owns a large stake in the Haven System and will have access to whatever is made there. Access that he may share with us. I don't have to ask him any more questions. I vote we welcome him, the Triton and everyone he employs. Before you ask, I have no involvement with him or the fleet that he was ejected from. Maybe I'll be lucky enough to in the future."

"If you don't like the fact that I'm technically one of his employees, then I'll abstain and I won't use Mark's proxy vote to get Jake in," Yawen said. "But hear him out."

"Full disclosure; my brother's still in Samurai Squadron, the flight that man over there leads," Sel said, pointing at Minh-Chu, who waved and smiled at the captains. "My Da is still in Haven Fleet too, but I won't be pulling my vote off the table. I want to see what the Triton can do up close, and I hear Captain Valent was a hell of a bounty hunter before he was an Admiral."

"It's just Jake now," he said with a little humble bow.

"He looks too much like the law for me," Inod said, shaking his head. "I'm sure the Triton runs by military order, regardless of whether or not it's independent. When the Aucharian military collapsed I was happy to get away from all that, so I have to vote against him and Vega, especially since they're holding the most important tech he's got back."

"I agree with you on that, Captain Inod," Ethan said. "Is there any way one of us could earn a Quad Drive? If not from you, then from Haven Fleet or some manufacturing company?"

"Yes," Jake replied as a smile played at the corner of his lips. "But not through me. Right now I can give you this and the Triton's support as long as Captain Vega agrees and we're not busy with something else already."

"How?" Sel asked.

"That's not a question I can answer. I brought someone who can, and he has a proposal for all of you that'll have to wait until I'm finished," Jake replied.

"We determine the order of things at this table," Inod grumbled, looking past Jake.

"No, I do," Alice said. "There's a vote running right now. We haven't heard from Rikan or Noah and Ethan hasn't made his choice yet. Do either of you have more questions before you decide?"

"Yes," Ethan said. "You own the Triton, but you said she has another master. Will we be dealing with you or Captain Vega?"

"She ultimately decides where the Triton goes. I put her in charge of the safety and direction the ship takes. I'm speaking for all my concerns at this meeting, but you're right, there's a good chance you'll be speaking to her in the future when the Triton is involved."

"Then this is a vote for a shared seat," Ethan thought for a long moment. By the time he spoke again, everyone was looking at him. "You have a fighter squadron and other ships aboard that you use, with more resources than even Captain Lucas, right?"

"Yes, and I'll probably be flying missions off the Triton, not actually operating aboard," Jake replied. Minh-Chu could see that his friend was trying to answer the question at hand and the next one at the same time.

"Then you and your people will be pursuing more than one mission at a time," Ethan concluded aloud. He paused once more before saying; "The Triton should have two seats. Her Captain and the owner, especially if the Haven Nodes that he's offering to every person here are real. I don't think everyone understands the incredible advantage they could provide."

"If we start using those Haven Fleet could listen in on everything," Rikan countered.

"Who cares? Just use quantum encryption," Captain Sel Marda said with a shrug. "We should be using that for every signal anyway."

"That's true," Rikan said. "I vote that Captain Vega and Jake Valent should have seats."

"So they can overwhelm this table?" Inod asked, outraged.

"The only reason why Alice, her relations and her friends have so much power here today is that the other captains didn't show. There are five of them. Some haven't come to a meeting in over two months," Eluyb said. "I expect that one of the rules in the proposed bylaws Alice is sending us is some kind of mandatory attendance."

"Once a month, minimum," Alice said.

"That is reasonable, especially if we can use something like the Nodes. Perhaps we can encrypt holographic transmissions as well, increasing attendance," Elyub said.

"There's a provision for that," Alice nodded. "You'll see it in the bylaws."

"Then the Valents and their friends will not have an automatic majority," he said, half standing so he could make eye contact with Inod. "Besides, you already voted against him. Shut up."

"Watch your mouth, squidie," Inod said through clenched teeth.

"Careful, we're all armed here, lad, and the only one who's a faster draw than him is Rikan," Sel said.

"It's all right, I won't shoot him for that, but if we have a problem, then I'll resolve it after this," Elyub said calmly, staring at Inod. "Unless you were only carried away by the moment."

"Yeah, sorry, I just see this whole Rebel Captains thing turning into something else and I thought we were getting along fine," Inod replied.

"That'll come to an end if we don't grow," Noah said. Even Minh-Chu noticed that he'd sort of faded into the background until then. The young entrepreneur and captain stood up. His gaze moved across the Captains as he spoke. "I've got one big cannon ready to mount on the surface to protect the Bitter End. We've got a few bases out there that are armed, but there's nowhere near enough firepower to fend off raiders, let alone an Order of Eden force. They're coming. Word about this place is making its way from ship to ship and across the Stellarnet. It'll happen faster when we've all got Nodes in our ships so our crews can talk to whoever they want. We need to grow so we have allies like Jake who can help us set up defences, and so we can get organised behind real leadership. I mean, Alice may be my girl when we're not at the table, but this is a woman with officer training and experience. That is a leader, and her connection to powerful people will only help us out. We need her, and we need Jake. Change and growth are the only ways that we'll be able to keep what we have. I mean, the other option is to pick up and go on the move, to shrink as people get knocked off or drift away as we go along. How does that sound?"

"Yes, that," Inod said. "We can pick people up as we go, but it'll be safer if we keep moving and hiding."

"No," Ethan stated darkly. "Last Crisis has invested a lot of time and resources in our base."

"Where the hell are we going to store and trade our hauls when every corporation and friend to the Order starts shutting down free markets out there?" Sel asked no one in particular. "We need a free port. Even places like the Doxan System will eventually organize, and that means a lot of them will shut down black markets and freeports. The Bitter End can be ours, and if word is spreading, a whole bunch of buyers will come to our dark little market. If we have to pick up and go, then we will, but I'd rather have this."

"The only way we'll be able to plant our feet and have our own port of call is if we bring in allies who can help us arm it, even run it," Noah said in agreement. "Everyone here knows which way I'm voting, but I thought you had to know why. Come on in, Jake. You and Captain Vega each deserve spots at this table just for what you're bringing to us."

"I re-state my position," Rikan said at last. "I vote that Jake and Captain Vega both have seats."

"I vote that they get two seats as well, but Jake needs to bring his own ship. We're all Captains here," Sel said.

"I can do that," Jake replied.

"Good, then there's only one vote we haven't taken," Sel said, looking down the table at Alice.

She was leaning back in her seat, quietly considering something. When she looked at her father it was with a serious gaze. "Think you could sweeten the bribe a little?"

Minh-Chu's jaw dropped, as did Iruuk's, and he heard Ashley gasp quietly and ask; "What is she doing?" in a whisper that only he was meant to hear.

"How?" Jake asked. He didn't seem irritated. As his daughter answered, it became clear that the opposite was true.

"It would take the Triton about three days to manufacture a shield system that would protect the entire port. What if you come to Tabrus with us, gather all the rare materials you'll need there, manufacture the shield system, have the techs from the Triton install it in the Bitter End and train a few people to use it. Oh, and I'm hoping that we'll find a few planetary defence cannons on the trip, so maybe you could spare a couple hangars so we could get them back here."

"Done, but I can only guarantee one trip," Jake replied.

"Then I vote for the Triton to have two seats at the Rebel Captain's table. It passes," she replied.

"All right, now it's Leon's turn," Jake said as he gestured for him to come forward.

He was polished and poised as he took Jake's place. "I'm a consultant with Haven Fleet, and I'm here to offer you official Privateering Licenses that will make your pursuit, capture, and destruction of any ship allied with the Order of Eden or military assets from that organization legal. Here is a list of companies and allies that are enemies of Haven Fleet and their allies." He projected a long list of names and logos onto the table.

"Oh, we took a Peregrin Company Freighter last week," Sel said, pointing at one of the names.

"Get me the proof, and I'll pay you a fair bounty. You get to keep everything you took during your raid too. We'll even give you documents legitimizing your capture if you came away with vehicles or high-priced items," Leon said. "I'm willing to certify captures and pay bounties for any capture or kill going back one month from today if you join up."

"So, what are the terms? There are drawbacks, yes?" Elyub asked.

"You must give any beings a reasonable opportunity to leave their ships using escape craft and emergency equipment when you make a capture or are about to destroy one of their ships. You must send an emergency signal as you leave the area on their behalf so they have a chance at rescue. Any prisoners you take must be delivered to a Haven ship or outpost and you will be punished for cruel treatment. I know that may sound restrictive, but you'll be surprised how loose the regulations are for prisoners of war. You'll get a chance to read through it all, you don't have to accept or decline right here," Leon explained.

"Nothing else? There are no other catches?" Sel asked with an upraised eyebrow.

"Only one. I have to approve your ship and my small staff has to interview each captain. Haven Fleet wants to know who we're dealing with and that your ship is ready for a fight. I doubt I'll turn anyone here away. If you could use a few repairs or upgrades, you can visit the Haven System, where you'll have access to military facilities. You'll find the cost will come below market price, you can trade goods that you acquire to offset that burden, and you will eventually get access to proprietary Haven technology."

"Quad Drives?" asked Ethan. "I'd rather pay a mountain of plat for one of your drives instead of the alternative."

"Yes, eventually. We want to reward the most trustworthy, hard-working captains and crews for helping us fight the order. If you follow the rules and make things very uncomfortable for the Order, then you deserve access to the best we can offer you," Leon said, relaxing a little. "You are not alone. The British Alliance, Lorander, Mergillian Fleet and other smaller concerns will be on your side and they are all adding to the bounty list."

"Didn't Lorander just buy the Spacerwares chain?" Rikan asked, his eyes widening.

"They did," Leon said with a grin as he projected a new menu above the table and scrolled until he found a bounty. "Lorander is actually paying anyone who raids then destroys Spacerware locations that are being run by the Order of Eden. There is a list of locations here. Make sure you hit the right ones and not an actual Lorander controlled store though. Oh, and they don't want any harm to come to civilian employees. That's their condition."

"There must be hundreds of locations," Sel said. "Wait, is that a list of warehouses? Spacerwares warehouses?"

"It is. Destroy the stock or steal it, Lorander doesn't care. They just want these off-license locations shut down. Haven and the British Alliance feel the same way because most of these warehouses and the larger stores double as Order of Eden resupply sites," Leon said. "You smash, grab and burn them down behind you. Everyone wins except for them."

"I like it," Ethan said, his waxy guise grinning for the first time. "We can keep this list?"

"I'm going to give you encryption keys so you can see the bounty board and get access to the intelligence database that you can use to find targets. You'll need one of those Nodes to get access. Oh, and something Jake forgot to tell you is that the nodes are untraceable. That is, with any technology we've been able to find," Leon replied. "Anyway, I'll send you all the information you need to decide whether or not you want a privateering license. The interview and ship inspection take about two hours, and I'll be available to answer any questions while the Triton is in the area. Oh, and if you can put some good defences up, we'd like to rent some space for an office somewhere in the Bitter End."

"Rent?" Elyub asked, surprised. "You're not asking for a seat at the table?"

"No, Haven Fleet will be happy to pay our way to be a part of this. Captain Lucas was just saying that it would only be a matter of time before everyone knew about this place, so why not bring a little more legitimacy to it by having a small Haven Nation presence? We want to have offices wherever independent captains who want to stand up to the Order drop in for supplies or repairs. Why not start here?"

"We'll talk after the meeting," Rikan said, his Issyrian mouth spreading into a tight-lipped smile that was almost frog-like.

"It'll come to a vote before that," Alice said.

"If it's about this privateering enterprise, then I'm pretty sure it'll pass," Sel said as he continued to look through the slowly scrolling list of bounties hovering above the table. "I've got to get another look at the terms and conditions, but I think I'll be the first to sign up."

"No one reads that crap, I'm in. Sign me up. I'll even give you a list of the places I've hit over the last month in case anything qualifies for one of your bounties," Inod said.

"You know about this privateering effort, right, Alice?" Ethan asked.

Minh-Chu was sure that she'd read everything about it and watched all the introductory videos along with the interactives. "I know it backwards and forwards. I just wanted Leon to have his pitch. We'll get rich and dangerous if we stay busy. I didn't know about this list, though. Some of these warehouses are on Rodus. They could have military defences."

"Well, putting that aside a minute, do you think we should get legitimate?" Sel asked.

"Yes, but I think every Rebel Captain should take the five minutes they need to look over the terms and decide for themselves. Anyone who doesn't take the deal is crazy. Inviting them to have an office here is another vote for another day though," she replied.

"So, the terms are fair, there are no surprises in there?" Ethan asked without looking away from the digital bounty board.

"No. It's all reasonable. No killing civilians, no ransoming in Haven Fleet's name, fair treatment of prisoners with stasis being preferable, and there are a few common spacer laws that we should be following anyway. You know, like making sure that we don't interfere with escape pods unless they start shooting us."

"And then?" Inod asked. "You know, if they escape and come back with guns blazing in their little life boats?"

"Oh, it's not an escape pod if it's firing its guns at you, it's a combat craft. Slag it," Alice said, finishing with a shrug.

"Sounds fair to me," Sel said with a chuckle.

"Thanks for the presentation, Leon," Alice said. "I'm pretty sure most of us will sign up."

"Well, I've got more. The whole thing is about an hour and a half long," Leon said uncertainly.

"Take the sale, man," Noah laughed.

"We'll take a few pamphlets and leave them in the head, but he's right, we'll be signing up," Sel added.

"So I'll leave you with the data package then," Leon said a little awkwardly.

Alice looked in Minh-Chu's direction. "Are you up next?"

"Not yet," Minh-Chu said, noting the disappointment on Sel Marda's face. "I'll see if I can get an invitation to the next meeting." He wanted to see more, but another thing was just as important. He wanted to show them what Samurai Squadron could do.

"Well, I think we've all got enough to process out of this meeting. I'll tell the rest of the Captains that they missed out. We'll meet back here in a week and anyone who doesn't show will have to have a good reason or they're out," Alice said with finality. "Let's take some time to relax and reconnect in the Lobby before we start planning our trip to Tabrus. First round's on me, but nothing expensive, right? I still have a ship to pay off."

# ELEVEN

The Whistle Blower

THE COMBAT INFORMATION CENTRE aboard the Rixe was half-manned. The crewmembers who were supposed to fill the rest of the posts wouldn't be finished for weeks, thanks to interference from the program Scanlon launched when her death was confirmed.

Captain Vollis Mikan tried to let his frustration go as he looked at a display at one end of the large compartment. His ship was staffed and functional, but every department could use more intelligent leadership and crewmembers. There were a hundred-nine tubes with fully grown fabricants that were ready to have the final, refined memory engrams implanted. Those would have been the training packages that would make them ready to become highly trained crewmembers. The pods hung from the sorting and storage areas in the centre of the ship like grapes on vines. There were other sections, other vines with hundreds of pods with growing bodies in them that were staggered in age so they would be ready several weeks apart. As for the ones that were fully grown, they had been placed in stasis. The final training engram data they needed to finish them was deleted by Scanlon's program. Another kind of revenge she took posthumously.

The virus responsible was gone. He and every department involved were certain. It was time to check on the damage and recovery. "How is the restoration for Engram Sets Eighty-Four through Ninety-Eight progressing?"

The pair of technicians in the central chamber of the ship where all the experimental fast maturation systems were kept turned from their stations. They were fabricants as well, some of his oldest, a male and a female named Uddo and Ussa. Uddo shook his head; "You were right to suspect that restoration would barely give us a starting point. Less than three percent of the data was recovered. There's only one shortcut to recreating the engram sets. We'll have to bring as many living and active crewmembers who were imprinted with those in as we can."

Ussa picked up where he left off. "If we can deep scan them and sequence their memories right, we will be able to create new engram training sets, so your next generation of officers will not only wake up with the memories they need to serve, but they'll have at least another year's worth of experiences to draw on." Her excitement at the prospect of more advanced engram sets was showing.

"I want more good officers, expedition leaders, and investigators as soon as possible. Is there any chance to adapt the little engram training data we have so it'll work in the framework quick regeneration systems?" Vollis asked. It wasn't the first time.

"I wish that were possible. There is a root incompatibility that we're still adapting to. You'd think a brain is a brain, but there's a subtle difference in how the common framework systems fabricate biomatter compared to the art of how they're grown here. Bridging that gap should be easy, especially since early-generation experimental frameworks were able to use Vindyne's memory engram sequencers to set up entire personalities, but we haven't been able to replicate their process."

That was an irritating fact. Vindyne, a corporation that was wholly owned by Regent Galactic and the Order of Eden, created software that could imprint an entire lifetime of memories on a framework capable of regenerating its whole body in minutes, sometimes even faster. It was used on prototype framework models, like the ones that at least one Valent had, but that technology was lost as far as he knew. It meant that a being made with a framework couldn't have more elaborate sets of memories. Every one came with limited training and engram implantation took a long time, over a hundred one-hour sessions for a year of memories.

When engram implantation was finished in a properly grown fabricant, they awoke with perfect, elaborate memories of a life during which they learned what they had to. There were even variations in their memories so no two were alike. He missed the emergence events, where he would have the pleasure of meeting a few of them at a time. "How long will it take to scan and build engram sets?"

"My conservative estimate is that it'll take two weeks for the first three sets to be rebuilt and refined. Priority?" asked Uddo.

"Intelligence analyst officers, programmers and expedition leaders. We need intelligent leaders who can expand the presence of this ship and its mission. We are joining the effort to quell resistance on and take Planet Rodus for the Order," Vollis said, watching the pair of fabricants as their interest was piqued. "When we finish that, I promise you will both have a nice vacation there."

"It's a nice world?" asked Uddo.

"From the reports I can tell you that there is everything you could want ranging from forest retreats to modern cities with major entertainment centres," Vollis said. "I'll make sure you can go wherever you like with your team for an entire week." They didn't need incentives, they enjoyed their work, but they'd enjoyed a few leisure excursions in the past and always came back to their duties with fresh ideas. It was another one of the differences between grown fabricants and the framework-generated type.

"The team would appreciate that. Now, about the scanning schedule," Ussa started.

One of the officers behind him interrupted her. "Captain, we have an emergency message from a ship called the Lendi."

Vollis regarded the pair of Developers in the Genesis Chamber. "I'm sorry, I'm being called away. I trust that you'll be able to responsibly schedule scans of the crew."

"Sir, I hesitate to ask, but..." Uddo started to say, cringing with uncertainty.

"He wants to ask if we're really at war. If our stealth mission is at an end," Ussa said more boldly, but still hesitant.

They rarely asked about the greater mission, and neither of them was prone to distraction. "We are following through with our merge with the Order, so, yes, we are going to provide support for the Messenger, their Base Ship. Don't worry, I'll make sure you and your people are well-insulated. The Order will not be allowed to interfere with your work."

"That's good to know, thank you, Captain. We'll start scanning officers within an hour. Will you be volunteering?" Uddo asked, more confident as he was once again speaking about something relating to his profession.

"Not this time," Vollis replied.

"Well, we'll contact you with regular progress reports," Ussa said, adding; "Work, work, work. We've gotta get the next generation out of the tubes."

Executive Jagat entered the Combat Information Centre, letting light spill through the metre-thick security doors before they slid closed behind him. "I got a notification that there was an emergency message, Captain?"

"I was just about to look at it," Vollis said as he turned towards the main holoprojector at the centre of the semi-circular room. "It's from the Lendi. Are there any important situation tags in the metadata?" he asked the Communications Officers.

"The only tag of concern is; piracy. Other than that, I can tell you that the message is thirty-eight hours and five minutes old. It was recorded by Alibell Okuda, the First Officer of record. They were transporting high-end medical supplies, thirty thousand tons of diridion, several commercial shipping containers containing packages from Amio, and fifty containers of agricultural supplies. It was an expensive high-speed shipment."

"Worth tens of millions at least," Jagat said appreciatively. "What kind of agricultural supplies?"

"Nutrients and seeds in stasis," the Communications Officer replied.

"With that many containers, someone could restock several grow towers. Enough to feed a small country."

"Not exactly something that would be easy to sell on the black market," Vollis said. "We'll have to start scanning the Stellarnet for information on this cargo. That is unless it was destroyed. Do we know?"

"There is no official final report," came the reply.

"Play the emergency message," Vollis said.

The head and shoulders of the First Officer, Alibell Okuda appeared life-size with the bulkhead of an escape pod behind her. The walls were padded and the restraints held her fast as the ship rumbled. It was probably accelerating, judging from the whining sound in the background. She was in one of the more recent styles of space traveller suits from the Order Civilized worlds that had more durable materials in areas that were more susceptible to wear and tear. There was piping down its length in an unflattering pattern that contained all the critical systems for short term survival in space. "I'm looping this through the transmitter aboard the Lendi so I can use its emergency alert beacon to get more attention. Then I'll be posting this recording on the Stellarnet before I move on. I'll probably be fired once the company sees this, which is fine. They lied to us. When we took this haul they said the Rose System was safe, so they don't deserve me. Screw all of you at corporate headquarters."

"So, we're dealing with the honourable sort," Jagat muttered.

Alibell went on with a frustrated scowl. "Long story short: I was First Officer aboard The Lendi, Slyden Enterprises medium-sized Commercial Hauler. We just finished a run from Amio to the Rose System when we were jumped only an hour after finishing our final deceleration thrust. It was a Regent Galactic military ship, a destroyer, I think. My personal recorder got some video. It's for sale to the right news outlet. Sorry, I don't have scans, we were jammed the instant they were on top of us. They pretended to be Order of Eden at first, and told us that they had to board and inspect our ship. Sabine," Alibell hesitated for a moment. Saying that name brought grief, they could see it on her face.

"This is the aftermath of a tragedy," Vollis mused aloud.

Alibell pressed through it and continued. "Sabine, the communications and protocol officer aboard, spotted anomalies in the ship's transponder code. She said it didn't look right, and Captain Hecham questioned the representative from the Order ship. That's when they fired on us. I was ordered to lead the defence gunners and I got into Turret One. That may have been an Order ship, but it wasn't being run by an Order crew, obviously. Some band of assholes had captured one of their major military craft and was trying to take our shipment. The Lendi was armed, but not as well as a military destroyer. When Captain Hecham refused to stop resisting for the second time they took out the bridge. They could have done a lot of other things, like break our connection to the cargo train, or hit our power vault, but whoever was on the stolen Order ship killed the bridge crew instead. We're just jobbers, working towards that Level One Life, you know? Half of us were going to settle on Rodus, it was going to be our last run, our cash-out payday, but now I'm going to be hiding my savings and finding some other way to get that L-O-L because I'll be fired for this. I might even get charged for the value of the shipment, and I'll have to join the Order to get protection from that debt. No way."

She took a deep breath and continued. "Yeah, I said; 'long story short,' but I got rambling, so I'll get to the point. When we left Amio three weeks ago, we were told that the rumours of piracy and crime in this area were overblown. Now I know better first-hand. The rumours don't go far enough to explain how bad it is here. For anyone who doesn't get it yet: we were just taken out by a real, full-sized, fully armed military destroyer that someone was able to steal from the Order of Eden. Not only are there pirates, but at least one group of them have a ship that is so powerful that only a military transport with an escort could even stand a chance. Don't let the propaganda fool you, there's trouble out here, and it ruined me. For all we know, there are Edxi roaming around too. Stay away from the Edwin Cluster, and if you see this while you're already on your way, get ready for a fight, just in case."

"Trace?" asked Jagat.

"I've been trying, but I can only trace this back to the Lendi's beacon. I can't find further data on Alibell Okuda either," replied one of the Communications Officers. She checked one last time and shook her head. "We'll have access to more information when we arrive in the Rose System. I'm sorry, Sir."

"It's all right, I'm not surprised. She's right, she'll probably be fired," Executive Ozof said.

"So, one of the destroyers stolen from a Rodus Orbital Shipyard is crewed and operating," Vollis said, looking at the Executive.

Jagat sighed and dropped into a well-padded seat. "It looks like the secret's about to get out. Over the last three months, the incidents of piracy against the Order and several companies associated with us have been rising steadily. Commanders have been doing their best to compartmentalize the information, to take care of the problem in their own territories, but it's not working. The more they patrol, the thinner they are spread. The thinner they spread out, the more vulnerable their ships are."

"Why slow the reporting down?" Vollis asked. It was alarming that the problem was so well spread.

"No Order commanders wanted to be punished out here, especially by Scanlon. She believed in demotions and fines. Letting a couple of customs corvettes and shipments get taken in your region could cost you millions and get you demoted to Private. The flow of information in her direction was kept slow, especially when it involved piracy. Now that she's gone, I guess that'll change. Eve doesn't punish people the same way. Her default is to reinforce her people and get revenge against troublemakers. If there's one thing I like about her, that's it. To be clear, there are a lot of things I like about our leader."

"It's always good to be clear," Vollis said as he looked at the frozen image of Alibell. She had high-arched eyebrows and was full-faced with nice skin. "She has done harm to the Order's image out here. People will see this on the Stellarnet and wonder if the Order can protect them. Alibell has done me a favour, though. I don't know how long it would take me to discover how common piracy is. Now I know enough to tell you to get me access to every report, every scrap of data that you can and to request more once we're in the Rose system."

"It's a lot of reading material, but you'll have it right away, Sir. What do you plan to do?"

"I need more information before I make a plan, but I'll include you in the work when it's time to put one together. Now, start at the beginning. I want to see the oldest report on piracy in the Edwin Cluster that you have."

Executive Jagat Ozov brought an interactive holographic interface up and unlocked a classified section of the Order of Eden database that Vollis had never seen. "Here we go. This is going to take a while."

# TWELVE

A Night At The Shattered End

ALICE and her crew tried to relay what was going on with the Rebel Captains without going into details that would betray them, but seeing them first-hand was a completely different experience. Minh-Chu and Ashley had an insatiable appetite for stories about that group before they arrived in the Bitter End. Being there when Alice took the head seat was something that they would talk about for hours later.

Minh-Chu called most of the pilots who were babysitting the fighters to the Lobby to relax for a while. They found one of the small, four-wheeled utility carts and arrived together with Cooper at the wheel and the rest piled on the small flatbed behind him.

By then the music in the Lobby was turned up, people got to their feet and while many mingled, the rest danced. Alice, Jake,

Leon and most of the other captains weren't jovial, but still focused on business as they gathered around a large round table. It would be no surprise if Jacob and a few of the other people at that table who seemed to take themselves too seriously would never make it onto the dance floor. That didn't stop Minh-Chu. As soon as he finished working with Slick to finish scheduling patrols and checking the status of every member of the Fighter Wing he signed off. After sympathising with poor Slick, who was stuck on the Flight Deck of the Triton, he looked back towards the centre of the festivities.

It only took a couple of seconds for his eyes to find Ashley, who had reshaped her vacsuit into a short red dress that looked like it was made of liquid metal. It was a contagious style that spread to other dancers who could alter their clothes. Dame was a gorgeous angel compared to most, and she'd borrowed the pattern from Ashley and made it so long that it ran down to her ankles. Cooper's outfit was just as stretchy and metallic but it was an open shirt with tails that came to points behind his knees. That was something Minh-Chu didn't expect. He would have bet that the new pilot wouldn't bother with the dance floor, but he'd lose, because Cooper was having plenty of fun between Dame, whose real name was Edda, and Knud, who wasn't wearing much but was either painted metallic blue or had tattooed his entire body so he could change its colour whenever he wanted. It was difficult to tell. There were over two dozen people there, most of them from other crews, and seeing them cut loose had Minh-Chu grinning before he knew it. The most flashy dancers were the Issyrians, who were still human-shaped, but had large fins or thin tendrils that stood up from their heads and shoulders. They looked more like strange exotic birds as their skin changed colour with the style and movement of the music.

Most of Minh-Chu's attention was on Ashley, who was lost in the mood and pulse of the music, her dress shimmering as it highlighted her curves. Her jet-black hair was loose, sweeping and twitching across the metallic material, finally falling in her face as the intensity of the music started rising to what promised to be a powerful peak. Seeing her have so much fun made his spirits rise so high that it felt wrong to stay in his seat.

The song slowed down for a moment, rising to a howl of notes before setting off into a blast beat, and in that instant, Ashley flicked her hair back and stared at him with her dark eyes. That got him on his feet, and he changed his vacsuit into a proper tuxedo with a shiny jacket that had the same texture as her dress. It was a preset from the night he proposed. That was the first and last time he saw Jake on a dance floor. He'd proposed to Ayan that night as well, and the party that followed got out of hand. It was also the first time the mobile military station, the War Forge, registered a noise complaint from any of its rooms.

The only captain to join some of his crewmembers on the dance floor was Sel Marda, who had as much fun as anyone. Probably the wildest one there, it was comical when the young man and Edda started dancing together and didn't part ways for several songs. They were still at it when the crowd thinned as people decided to take a break and the music moved onto less danceable genres. Many members of Sel's crew and others watched as he escorted her to the bar and he bought her a drink. This was an interesting pairing that Minh-Chu guessed was born of pure chemistry that he wouldn't have expected. No one was saying a word about it, but they were well observed. "I need to go on more missions," Ashley said as they broke the seals on condenser bottles and then took long pulls on straws.

"There's barely ever dancing," Minh-Chu said with a wink.

"Maybe the fates smile on us because you're both here," Cooper said as he accepted a drink from Yawen. He regarded her with surprise. "Thank you."

"I saw you out there and thought; Now, Yawen, he's going to be thirsty when he's finished flashing all the dancers his tails," she said in her trademark Irish accent. "So I thought you should try this. It's Melema, juice from Doxan Three. It tastes like mint and sugar."

"How am I going to feel after I finish the glass?" he asked as he looked at the cold, cloudy white drink.

"Like you've got a little more energy, maybe a little less inhibited, that's all," she raised her frosted glass to him then took a sip.

"That's good," Cooper said as he did the same.

"Would you two like to try?" Yawen asked, looking past Cooper. This was either an honest offer or she was trying to point out that Minh-Chu and Ashley were watching and she wished they weren't.

"Oh, no, I'm flying back in a couple hours, thank you," Ashley said first. "And the Wing Commander has to stay dry from now on."

"Aw, but I want to try everything the cool kids are drinking," Minh-Chu pouted as they started walking away from the bar. They were headed roughly in the direction of the captain's table.

Ashley laughed and played along, saying; "You'd be amazed

at the trouble he'd get into if I weren't here to watch him," over her shoulder at Yawen, Cooper and everyone else within earshot at the bar.

They settled in at the booth just past the table where Alice was holding court. Jake, Noah, and Leon were just as busy talking to people who seemed very interested in the new state of affairs. Someone was projecting a map of a massive industrial city onto the table, Minh-Chu guessed it was a part of Tabrus. It was the kind of serious business that Minh-Chu wasn't in the mood to get into just yet, especially when Iruuk and Theodore were in a booth next to that table, inviting him and Ashley to join them. "Do you know why most of the people here are treating me like I'm about to try to eat them?" the young Nafalli asked.

"Maybe they haven't seen many Nafalli here?" Ashley offered.

"That was my theory," Theodore said. "I think you're the first one to visit the Lobby since I've been here."

"Maybe the Tree Tribe people are misunderstood," Minh-Chu offered.

"Oh, I wonder why? My sisters called me a woora until I was nearly full-grown because I always looked harmless. My growl didn't lower until I was over two metres tall," Iruuk replied, a little distress in his eyes.

"Woora?" Ashley asked.

"It roughly translates as; 'puppy,'" Iruuk replied in a tone almost too low to hear.

"Well, I don't think anyone would call you that now," Minh-Chu said, making a point in looking up at the tall, broad-shouldered Nafalli.

"What do I do? I might have to come here often," Iruuk asked.

"Aw, does the woora wanna dance?" Ashley asked playfully.

Minh-Chu wondered if the young Nafalli would have taken offence if anyone else asked him that way as he watched him roll his eyes. He finally nodded, his tongue almost lolling out of the side of his mouth. "Okay, yeah. I saw you guys having so much fun out there."

"Follow me and Minh when things start up again. We'll show 'em you're just here to have a good time like everyone else," Ashley said with one of her trademark smiles. She had a talent for making people feel better.

"That's an excellent idea," Theodore said, nodding. It was easy to forget he was an android under his perfect synthetic skin. "The only way to break whatever stereotype is through demonstration. If they see that you're like everyone else in a sense, then their comfort level will rise."

Minh-Chu was starting to wonder if there was another reason why people kept their distance, and he looked for what he guessed the cause. The space that the Rapsu occupied at the bar before the meeting had been overwhelmed by humans and Issyrians. There was no sign of them anywhere. "The Rapsu have a reputation here that keeps people clear of them, so maybe your people inherited a bit of it since you're natural enemies?" Minh-Chu asked.

Iruuk instantly changed the mood at the table with a low rumbling growl and a sneer that bared most of his teeth. "They're back?"

"No, I don't see them," Minh-Chu said reassuringly. "I was just..."

A flash of light and the sound of a round breaking the sound barrier inside the Lobby stopped everything in the place. Minh-Chu's sidearm was already in his hand as he looked towards the table to his left, where Alice, Noah, Leon and everyone else wearing military-class gear were getting to their feet as plates emerged from their jackets and boots to seal over their entire bodies in complete suits of power armour. The rest of the captains there were scrambling for cover, most of them activating personal shields as they drew weapons.

The scorch mark running across the surface of the round table pointed at one of the hallway entrances, where a group of five humans in old heavy, thick plated combat suits stood. Three of them carried automatic rifles with barrels so large that they required a carrying harness for support. "I'm here for Valance!" shouted one through a crackling voice amplifier. "Jake Valance! If you survived that, then come with me and no one else needs to die!"

Then Minh-Chu realized that Jake was the only one he hadn't seen and followed the scorch on the table in the other direction, away from the gunmen. That first shot hadn't missed. Jake had been thrown back into a booth behind the table and was extracting himself from the ruins of the table. The scorch mark on his vacsuit told the rest of the story. Even still, Minh-Chu checked his friend's status on his command and control unit. He was relieved to find that he was saved by his personal shield and his heavy vacsuit, which was repairing itself already. There were two broken ribs which were being moved back into place and re-fused by nanobots and recovery medication. His concern eased as he became increasingly sure that the five armoured gunmen who had come for Jake had made a huge mistake. They had the element of surprise, but gave it away the moment their leader decided to make a statement instead of making sure Jake was dead then running away as fast as they could.

The expression on his old friend's face was more worrying than the gunmen for Minh-Chu. He had a deep scowl and a steady stare. Jake wasn't activating his heavy armour either. Instead, he flung the remains of the booth's table aside and got to his feet. "They call me Valent now," he announced as he flicked his long coat so it trailed behind him and it was clear of his sidearm.

Minh-Chu looked for the shimmer of a personal shield or some other defensive device, but didn't see any. Alice and Noah started to move into position in front of him, the latter saying; "You crashed the wrong party."

Jake walked slowly, confidently, and stepped between the pair. "This is old business, don't worry," he said to them.

"You killed my cousin, you son of a bitch!" shouted the gunman in the lead.

"I did a lot of work under that name, you'll have to refresh my memory," Jake said, his hand coming to rest on his sidearm. It was a special model, the last version of the Violator Handgun. A low mechanical sound it made for a second that only those nearest to him could hear was a sign that Jake activated its highest setting. He would only get seven shots before its battery and ammo cartridges were expended but the damage it could do would be horrific.

The security bots that hid behind the bar rushed out. There were seven of them, and each carried a very serious-looking type of pulse rifle that Minh-Chu hadn't seen before.

Noah put his hand up and they stopped, half of them already beyond the bar after leaping over it with ease. The five gunmen couldn't see them from where they were standing, but it seemed to Minh-Chu that this was a fight they'd definitely lose.

Most of the other patrons were armed as well, and there were enough guns out of holsters to stock a respectable sized shop. Captain Sel Marda left his weapon in the holster strapped to his middle as he approached the armoured men from their left. "Hey, Captain Raines, what's the issue here?"

"Stay out of this, Sel!" came the distorted response from the gunman in the lead.

"No, really, I've got to know what got you so crazy that you'd try this shite," Sel said, actually stepping so close to the gunman that he was between most of the bar and him, even blocking Jake's shot.

"You want to know? You really want to know?" Captain Raines asked, his voice amplifier distorting as he shouted. "That man stunned my cousin to death, stole my ship and left me lying beside his corpse on a landing platform with nothing but debt and a funeral to pay for!"

"Well, I'm sure there's a reasonable explanation," Sel said, looking over his shoulder at Jake.

"Sure. Captain Raines here was a deadbeat. He stopped making payments on his ship and I was hired to take it back, so I did. As for stunning someone to death, I admit I didn't stop to check on everyone's health on my way out, but it was a mistake. You know what? You took a shot at me and hit your mark. Showed all these people that I can be caught off guard. I say we call it even."

"You think a scorch mark on your armour is going to satisfy me after what you did?" Raines shouted.

"It better, because I'll put you down if you don't put your weapons down and..."

Jake was interrupted as Raines snatched Sel Marda by the belt and put his arm around his neck. Before anyone could do anything, he was holding the well-liked captain in front of him like a human shield with the muzzle of a gun against his temple. "Listen to me, you scumbag bounty hunter! Corporate puppet!" Raines raged.

"We're listening, don't do anything we'll both regret," Sel interjected.

"Shut up! You're barely old enough to drink, and that blonde peach fuzz on your face isn't fooling anyone!" Raines shouted, the pistol shaking.

"No reason to get nasty," Sel muttered.

Raines, the lead gunman, looked back to Jake over Sel's shoulder. "I ended up in prison! Wired up to a goddamned neural rig so a company could use my grey matter for data processing until a crew came and let me out! That favour came with a price, and it would have taken ten years to work it off if I didn't lead a goddamned mutiny! When I went back to get the rest of my people, I found out the Order beat me to it and I nearly got took for my trouble!"

"A touching story, too bad about how it's going to end," Frost said to a reception of snickers and some outright laughter.

Raines wasn't laughing. "You surrender now or I'll shoot his goddamned head off!"

In the blink of an eye, Jake's sidearm was in his hand and

pointed at Raines. "Do it and you're gone. Is that the exchange you want here?"

"Don't do anything rash," Sel said. Who he was talking to wasn't clear.

"That's it!" Alice said as she stepped in between them. "You so much as twitch the wrong way and you're dead, Raines. There's only one solution here. Put your guns down, let the Irishman go and I'll let you get on your ship and fly away."

"Why the hell would I listen to you?" Raines asked. For a second it looked like he was about to point his sidearm at her, and Minh-Chu cringed.

He was pretty sure that if that happened, it would be anyone's guess at how many people would take the chance to shoot at him from any angle they thought they might miss Sel. Some of them might not even consider the fate of young Captain Marda.

"They just voted her to the head of the table," Yawen replied as she dropped her gun back into its holster. "You know, made her a Major, a Commodore, or an Admiral, depending on whatever order of rank you're used to."

"You put that girl in charge? This place is going to shit!" one of Raine's men exclaimed.

So many guns shifted their aim to him that you could hear it in the rustling of clothing, grips and rifle straps. "You guys are getting less popular by the second," Minh-Chu said, earning a nudge from Ashley.

Alice sighed and leisurely stepped out of Jake's line of fire as she said; "You have five seconds to let Sel go, drop your guns and power your armour down. I don't think you'll like what happens when I stop counting."

"And I almost didn't come tonight," Captain Inod said with a chuckle. "This is gonna be good."

"Don't just take the leader down, I want all five of these assholes slagged," Alice shouted before she started counting down from; "Five!"

"If I'm going out, I'm taking..." that's when Raines made a critical mistake. The muzzle of his gun left Sel Marda's temple and started to turn towards Alice.

Alice's armour would have protected her from several if Raines bulls-eyed her with his sidearm, even without using an energy shield, but that wasn't a consideration for whoever made the shot that took the weapon out of his hand. At a glance, Minh-Chu saw that it was Noah, who had moved out of Raine's sight one booth up.

When Minh-Chu looked up, Sel was ducking and running. Raines was reaching for the heavy rifle hanging off his side, and the shooting started. Between the sounds of energy pulse weapons, old-fashioned slug throwers that were usually used ornamentally, and new kinetic-energy hybrid blasters everyone could hear Captain Marda as he shouted; "I just got this armour, for mercy's sake! Watch your damn aim! Shoot around the Irishman!" He made it to the bar and dove for cover, even though he was well out of danger at that point.

Raines didn't get a shot off, and his companions only got a few rounds out before the mob's attack broke through their armour. After what must have been at least ten seconds Alice shouted; "Whoa! Cease fire! Cease fire!"

When they finally listened, she walked over to the pile that was once five intruders and looked down. The only sound in the place was a lingering sizzle that brought with it a sickly sweet meaty scent loaded with ozone. Everyone watched her as her armour retreated back into her boots and long coat. As she surveyed the damage with her back to the bar. Then she shrugged. "I didn't finish counting down to five." Then, looking over her shoulder, she added; "What a bunch of savages."

Yawen burst out laughing with a shriek and she was joined by most of the other people there. "Is anyone injured?" Theodore asked.

"Those five guys over there, I think," Sel said as he stood up and got ready to pour drinks. "Damn good shots, the lot of you. I came away without so much as a graze. Next round's on me." His hands shook as he picked up a glass and checked if it was clean.

Minh-Chu was surprised to see Ashley laugh along with everyone else, even though he did see the humour in the situation. He'd forgotten that she'd seen her share of dark things, having been with Jacob Valent's crew for years. It was also a reminder that she didn't talk about it much.

Before long, droids were cleaning up the mess and the environmental systems had cleaned the smell out of the air. People had drinks in their hands and were socializing again only minutes after the incident. "You know, I remember the job where Jake repossessed Raine's ship," Ashley said, piquing the interest of Theodore and Iruuk. "I wasn't there when it happened, but I remember it didn't take them long and they came back with oranges."

"I saw the whole thing, played my part too," Frost said as he slipped onto the seat beside her. "That place was a real nice place for sun lovers. A vacation spot. That was right before everything changed for the Samson and crew."

"You don't talk about that much," Minh-Chu said to Ashley.

She shrugged. "They kept me away from most of the action. Probably a good thing because I was a recovering teenager, barely in my twenties, still more interested in learning to be a good pilot and the ship scuttlebutt."

"Then I'll get the whole story if you tell it while you're sitting beside each other," Minh-Chu said, regarding Frost and Ashley. "So, tell me about Captain Raines and the repossession. Start at the beginning and don't leave a thing out. I've only heard a few stories from the Samson days and it'll be a way of sending the guy who just got cooked off to the next thing."

"Well, it's been a bit," Frost said, starting to slip out of the booth.

Ashley pulled him back as she put his arm around his shoulders. "Okay, so we landed at St Kitts and I was excited because it was a good time of day for tanning. I made sure I was wearing my bikini under my vacsuit and Captain - that's what I called Jake back then - left me in charge of most of the crew while they used hand scanners to check the outer hull. The deal was; we finish that then we get to lay out and relax, but I didn't want to rush it because I wanted to show him that he could trust me with more responsibility."

That opening brought Frost's interest back, and he leaned forward as he picked up where she left off. "She was making a few of the lazier crewmen a little worried for their jobs. She was eager and pretty good at most things he trusted her with."

"Thank you," Ashley said.

"Well deserved, it was true," Frost said before continuing. "Well, Jake took me and young Finn, who had never been on a job with us before, into the port. The heaviest weapons we could carry were stunners, so our teeth were pulled for this one."

Iruuk cringed at that and Theodore said; "He's not speaking literally, I assume."

"Aye, just an expression. We weren't as well armed as we would have liked," Frost explained. "But the port allowed small ships with antimatter to land. I never understood that. Anyway, we set off into the port..."

They looked up as Jake approached the table. "We're setting out for Tabrus first shift. Stephanie's calling the crew back to the ship and I'm taking the Raven back in an hour."

With a disappointed sigh, Minh-Chu said; "I'll tell my pilots to get back to their ships in time to escort you. Frost and Ash are telling us the story behind all the commotion, care to join?"

Jake looked like he'd been put on the spot as he silently looked at each person - Theodore, Iruuk, Ashley, Frost and then Minh-Chu - before shaking his head. "I'm still processing the ending." He took his leave, returning to the scorched table where Alice, Noah, the Captains and several other people had resumed their gathering.

"So, do go on," Minh-Chu said to Frost before taking a long pull from his water. "I want to hear the whole story before we have to go."

# THIRTEEN

Overnight Turbulence

Returning to the Triton and then retreating to bed was disappointing to everyone who got to spend time in the Lobby, even Minh-Chu, who would have liked to extend their stay. "Pilots need their beauty sleep," he told them as everyone was rounded up to be wheeled back to the fighters.

The rough outline of a salvage mission was sent to him while they were flying back, so Minh-Chu took a little time to do some planning. Ashley was a lot of help, asking about different points of interest and doing most of the preliminary math. She also included herself in the mission as one of the pilots, subtly marking one of the Archangel fighters with her callsign, Swift. "Pixie was going to take that spot," Minh-Chu said.

"Maybe I could fly the Raven instead? You haven't assigned anyone yet," Ashley countered. "I'm trained on it and have a mission in a Clever Class Corvette under my belt."

"I know. Okay, that saves me a lot of trouble. Everyone's training on Archangels, no one's interested in doing extra work to get a name for flying bigger ships right now," Minh-Chu replied.

As soon as the rough version of the mission was finished, Minh-Chu turned the holographic display in the living room of their quarters aboard the Triton off and he followed her to the bedroom. Despite the adventure they had that night, sleep came easily. Being back aboard the Triton in what he saw as lavish quarters, with Ashley wasn't as strange as he expected it to be. It was easy to get used to a new bed when it made a point of adjusting to you, after all.

A sympathetic thought was spared as he half-dozed on his way to sleep for the poor team that was transferring to the Bitter End from the Triton. They would be sleeping in more basic bunks that lacked the perfect comfort of self-adjusting membrane beds and self-cleaning linens that conducted more or less body heat depending on how warm or cool you were. They would be on firm mattresses instead. In the morning they'd get to work on enhancing the security and fixing up a massive list of broken-down features in the section of the Bitter End that Noah was keeping. Then they'd work their way outward, repairing every part of the port that could be pressurized with the help of a small army of robots. He wondered what it would be like to be under the command of Shamus Frost, who had a reputation for big reactions and a very direct style.

There were two squads of soldiers down there, which would leave the Triton a little short. They'd be back in a week, maybe two if there was more work than they expected. The plan was to leave a few volunteers to work in the docking and manufacturing facilities. They'd get paid well while they trained crewmembers from the other Rebel Captain's ships and managed the hangars that Noah would hold ownership of. It was a relief that the pilot was stepping away so he could rejoin Samurai Squadron at least temporarily. Minh-Chu needed pilots.

With Ashley in his arms, and the bed adjusted to Minh-Chu so well that he felt like he was resting in a warm cloud, he drifted off to a sound sleep. There was no telling how long it was before he felt like the world around him was spinning.

Minh-Chu clung to a railing with his arms and legs as the massive, multi-tiered garden module ripped away from the station along with another large section that depressurized suddenly. The large garden had its own inertial dampeners, but they struggled, failed, and reset over and over as they were strained past their capacity. Artificial gravity was tricked into pulling him and everything else - plants, mostly - in odd directions.

The leaves, branches and vines seemed twisted, wrong somehow, and the view through the transparasteel window beyond the railing he clung to was worse. Chunks of the station were tumbling, spinning into unyielding asteroids. He could see a group of people in one, looking at him, some of them pounding on the glass instants before the sealed corridor smashed against a tumbling mass of stone. The lights went out. The reinforced metal corridor was crushed and twisted to pieces, sending the atmosphere and some of the people inside into space in a rush.

An abrupt shudder that threatened to fling him from his railing struck, then another, more violent shake followed along with the sure knowledge that the garden pod - once the housing for a massive reactor - had shattered against a great mass of an iron-rich asteroid. He woke up looking at Ashley's peaceful face in the nearly complete darkness. She was still sound asleep. That wasn't a memory, but the exaggeration of one.

The botanical gallery that he found in the Blue Belt years ago saved his life. True, it was torn from the station along with several adjacent compartments, and that was the most violent thing he'd ever experienced, but he survived. Minh-Chu concentrated on the present, one of the tricks that started working for him after therapy sessions and over a year of medication that helped him put the memories of his near-death experiences in their place. He didn't tell anyone that he started talking to Quan when he grew tired of what he called 'a faded spirit.' The medication made him feel like he was sometimes not fully present, and when he met Quan, a telepath, he asked him how his people dealt with the kind of echoing horror that he had running through his life.

That was when Quan started guiding him and Ashley, who refused to be anything but a partner in the journey, and they discovered that she had some lingering echoes along the way. Memories of being in harm's way and of incredible fear when she discovered Zoe, a young Nafalli. If it wasn't for Quan's guidance, Minh-Chu doubted either of them would be able to join the crew aboard the Triton.

As Minh-Chu followed Quan's advice by taking deep breaths and observing his surroundings, which were comfortable and warm, Ashley's eyes opened to slits. "Dreaming, huh?" Ashley asked.

Guilt at waking her threatened to undo any effort he made at calming down. "I'm sorry, it's all right."

"You're here with me now, it's okay," she whispered, stroking his arm.

There was a time when he might shrink away from that so he could protect her from what was going on in his head. He'd come to know better. Ashley would listen. "It was a classic. The one I can't shake." He smiled at that unintentional pun. It took a lot of work to get to the point where that was possible, where that dream wouldn't screw up the day to follow. "The station breaking up."

"Wow, that came back when we transferred to the Merciless," she said. "That's the oldest one, huh?"

Minh-Chu nodded. "I used to have that one almost every night after I got things set up out there when I was adrift." Sleep was the enemy then and after. "I'm just glad the decompression dream hasn't come back for a while."

"Hey, you're back here with me, 'kay? There's a lot of ship between us and the cold," Ashley said reassuringly.

"I know," Minh-Chu said, aware that there was an unhealthy instinct at work trying to pull him back into a pattern of dark reminiscence that would have him reviewing every regret and nightmare that had left its mark on him over the years. Some time ago it would have been impossible to resist, but he tried to reach past it.

Then Ashley said something that she picked up from their sessions with Quan. "You have a new day ahead."

"Thank you," Minh-Chu said. "It's just an aftershock." He knew why the dream came back, too. Things had changed once again. It didn't matter that he liked it, or that he thought it was for the best where his friends and Ashley were concerned. Change made things uncertain and his mind would always react in its own way. This time it seemed to want to remind him that change could be violent, destructive, scary. The impact of the dream was fading though, and he was starting to move onto other things.

"I wish I could make the aftershocks stop," Ashley said.

"I know. I love you," he said, aware that she was waking up more and more. He wanted to get up and get his day started, and he glanced at the communication band on his wrist. It lit up just enough for him to see that there were less than two hours left before their alarm would go off.

"I love you too," she said, a smile playing on her lips. "Feeling better?"

"Yeah, no shakes or sweats this time. Hasn't been that way for a long time now. I think I want some time alone though. You hang out here and get a few more winks."

"You sure?" Ashley asked, so clearly ready to join him.

"Yeah," he replied, remembering the lesson that a little time on his own was a good thing sometimes as long as he had something constructive to do. "There's a lot of last-minute stuff left over, and I want to talk to the Maintenance Chief. You can sleep through all that stuff."

"Okay, love you. Call me if you want company, 'kay?" Ashley said. "I'll track you down if I can't get back to sleep."

"You can try," he teased, kissing her briefly and slipping out of bed.

Being wide awake before his alarm went off was nothing new, but it didn't happen nearly as often. It took a long time for Ashley to accept that she didn't have to get up with him, no matter the time, and it was a relief that she finally had. He'd know if she was able to get back to sleep in the next fifteen minutes. She'd either join him or be completely out. He hoped for the latter but suspected that he wouldn't be alone for long. There was too much to be excited about, and her nightmares were more sparse and random.

In the main bathroom off the sitting room in the middle of their quarters, he stepped into the double-sized hygiene closet and turned it on. Having a water shower was a luxury in space, he usually used a vibrating mist with a little rinse. This time he wanted to get drenched. He turned it on and found it already set to Ashley's preferences - extremely hot with several jets of water from all directions that were set so high that it felt like they could strip paint. He danced out of the shower, laughing at himself, turned it off, made a preset that suited him with less pressure and the same temperature, and took a relaxing shower.

As he stood in the jets of water, letting the nozzles move around the stall walls so they hit every angle of him, he considered the nightmare. It wasn't like most of its kind. A normal nightmare faded, but he could still see it in his head as clearly as most memories. The exaggerated, fear-soaked feeling of it had faded almost entirely, however. The work he put in towards recovery had given him the ability to look at it as one of the most important lessons in his life.

When he thought all was lost, that he'd be killed in the seat of his starfighter, he found that hardened section of the Blue Belt Station and was able to shelter in the old reactor, which had been turned into a massive garden. Minh-Chu found good fortune just as his death seemed certain. Even though that led to an experience that would haunt him for the rest of his life, he was sure, it was also his salvation. "What's the lesson?" Minh-Chu said amidst the water jets.

Several passed through his mind. Disaster and opportunity can come at the same time. Blink and you could miss something important. Don't question good luck. Then he focused on the lesson that he wanted to believe in most and said it aloud; "I'm lucky to be here."

# FOURTEEN

Fifty-Five Minutes

THE FIRST PART of the briefing was like any other where half of the people attending were new. It started with Minh-Chu reiterating standards for everyone so they knew when and where to show up for every part of their job, what gear they should bring, and what they should check on or refresh their memories on before they got there. Put simply, the meeting and calendar functions were handled by their command and control systems. The locations they needed to turn up at were usually presented with the reminders they would get with those too. As for what they needed with them, well, Minh-Chu had changed the standard so they had to be fully equipped at all times with their vacsuits, armour - which was hidden in their jackets and boots except for their new helmets - along with their flight and ground kits. The only time a combat pilot could go without all their gear was when they were in their bunk or quarters. That got some groans from the group of pilots who sat in chairs that were exact copies of the cockpit seats in the Archangels.

It was a full house, with fighter and corvette pilots in the front rows. To the left and right sat holograms of Captain Marda and Captain Blake. The rest of the rows were filled with officers from the Sciences, Bridge, Communications and crews who would be piloting shuttles on the next mission. All of them had been through the Haven Fleet Clearance Program, there was no doubt that they could be trusted. Everyone there would have some part in the mission, and Minh-Chu knew that even more people were listening in, like Captain Vega, who was sitting on the bridge. Well, not all of them were listening to the details of the new standards for his pilots, at least he hoped they weren't. Unless you were a pilot, they were pretty boring, despite his efforts to keep things moving along.

The last point he highlighted during the first fifteen minutes of the briefing - the Standards Review - was that every pilot had to be completely up to date and tested on the features, capabilities, and operational characteristics of their fighter. They also had to be aware of the same for every ship involved in the mission whenever possible. All the pilots in the room were up to date on the ships they would be flying except for four of his squadron members.

It wasn't one of those that asked the question when he came to the end of the Standards section of his briefing and gave everyone a few minutes for queries, however. It was Pixie. She had set her seat to the largest size and was sitting with crossed legs in the middle of the expanded seat cushion. He was happy that wasn't her habit when she was in a cockpit. "So, why do we have to know what every ship on our mission list can do, even if it isn't going to become directly involved with the action?"

Minh-Chu glanced at Ashley, who was suppressing a little smile from where she sat beside Dame. They both knew what was going on. Pixie had studied everything, Minh-Chu and all the other officers in the Wing had seen that in her file, but she wanted to give him an opportunity to indirectly tell everyone who wasn't as well studied the answer. She didn't have to. He would be telling them to get to work individually later.

Regardless of that, he answered. "You need to know what to expect when you're flying near any of these ships, or what to consider if and when a fact in the mission changes. Let's take Captain Marda's ship for example," Minh-Chu said, bringing up a holographic image of the long, heavily armoured destroyer.

"Oh, let's," the live hologram of Captain Marda said as he stood up from the virtual captain's chair to the far left of the front of the Ready Room.

"If you know the combat and flight characteristics of this model of the Regent Galactic Corporation's Advanced Destroyer, and you should, then you'd be expecting the launchers along the upper port and starboard sections to be filled with missiles. Its turn rate, acceleration and time to jump along with a lot of other factors are all well recorded and you wouldn't expect them to be altered. You would be wrong. You might even know which ones were built in a Regent Galactic dry dock and which were outsourced. That can matter too, unless you consider the Hammer. Captain Marda's crew has spent two months installing turrets where several of these large missile pods were. The launch doors have been enlarged so the firing arc of each turret is broader. There are also flak guns in place of four of the original missile launchers. The thruster configuration of the ship hasn't changed, but the mass is different. That tells us how fast the ship can turn and accelerate. The ship is also carrying borrowed tech at the moment, so the amount of time it takes to take off into a wormhole is shorter than it was when it left the dock."

"So, you know all that about my ship?" Captain Marda asked Minh-Chu.

"That and more," he replied. Minh-Chu looked back towards the rows of seats, specifically running his gaze over the pilots who were going to be staying close to the Triton under Slick's leadership in Blue Group: Rip, Sass, Gren, Garma. "How about an example of why we need to know what the Hammer can do?"

"Oh, this ought to be good," Captain Marda muttered.

"Please save comments until he asks for questions," Dame whispered over her shoulder.

"Oh, sorry," the Captain replied, his hologram glitching for a second.

Minh-Chu went on with his example, the shortest one he could think of. "Let's say that a pair of Order of Eden Corvettes have turned towards the Hammer and they're armed with Electromagnetic Countermeasures, short-range Faster Than Light Interdiction Systems and Directed Electromagnetic Pulse beams. You know; ECM, FTLIS or Fitliss as you kids pronounce it, and DEMPs, the trifecta nightmare for any ship trying to get away."

"Throw the whole fleet at us, why dontcha," Captain Marda said to the amusement of several people in the room. Dame shot him a dirty look and he put his hands up.

Minh-Chu wasn't irritated at Sel Marda's antics in the least. It was helping him keep the pilots who knew exactly where he was going with the example awake. With a nod to him, he pressed on. "So, you need to know if the Hammer has anything to counter any of what's coming, how fast it can accelerate away, if it's carrying weaponry that can stop those Corvettes before they get all their weaponry in range, and if it can jump into a wormhole before the interdiction waves reach it. There's also a chance that the Hammer has a Quad Drive aboard, which will overcome the kind of FTLIS that a ship the size of those corvettes could carry. It helps if you know the energy signature of that type of FTLIS, so you can identify it and estimate its effective range."

"Sorry, Wing Commander, but I've got software here on the bridge that does all that," Captain Marda said, earnestly curious. "Wouldn't your fighters have something like that too?"

"We do, but we train for software crashes and manual flight," Minh-Chu replied. "We've got backups but you would be surprised at what can go wrong when you're getting shot at."

"Aye, makes sense, sorry for interrupting," Captain Marda said.

"No problem, Captain," Minh-Chu replied. "Any more questions about Standards and Practices?" He gave the room a moment then nodded. "Well, congratulations to everyone for staying awake for the whole thing. Now for our next challenge: Groups and the mission."

Carnie, who was sitting between Alice and Pixie, shifted to the edge of his seat. He already knew that he had been assigned to Green Group, but no one had been told what that would mean. "Maid, Shep, Scythe, and Crashrabbit are in Grey

Group. Your Flight Leader is Maid. You will be providing support for the Hammer, commanded by Captain Sel Marda and the Renegade under Captain Yawen Blake. Each of their ships will be launching two cargo craft. How you split up to cover them will be up to Maid. She'll brief you when I'm finished."

"I was wondering why she was sitting over there," Pixie muttered as she looked to her left, where a perfect hologram of Yawen was sitting beside her.

"Under Slick in Blue Group, we have Rip, Sass, Gren and Garma, the four pilots who didn't do all their homework. Since you don't know what our friends' ships can do, you'll be staying close to the Triton. Your job is simple: extend the immediate scanner reach and intercept trouble as ordered by your Flight Leader. I hope all get thoroughly bored by the end, because nothing interesting should happen in your area." He gave the other pilots a moment to chuckle then, after looking at Carnie, Pixie and Breaker, who were starting to look a little excited, he gave them the good news. "Easy, Breaker, Pixie and Carnie; you're with me in Green Group and we have the pleasure of escorting the Clever Dream on a special mission. Dame, you're flying the Clever Dream, which is under Alice Valent's command." He looked towards his fiancé then. "Swift, you're flying the Raven which is under Jacob Valent's command."

"Damn, I've gotta do my homework next time," Rip said, rolling her eyes. "You get to see the sights while I stay home."

"Covering the Triton is an honour. You're lucky to be flying at all," Slick said loudly enough so everyone could hear. "We'll be talking about this later. Seal up and listen for now."

"Yes, Sir," Rip replied.

"Boring is good for you on this operation, you should definitely hope to be bored but be ready for something exciting, not the other way around," Minh-Chu said, looking at each member of Blue Group as Slick nodded. "All right, time for you to follow Slick to the briefing room across the hall so he can fill you in on the plan and fill a few knowledge gaps."

They stared at him for a moment and he asked; "Questions?"

"I thought we'd get all the details on this operation. Wouldn't it help if we knew what the rest of the squadron is doing?" Sass asked, shifting uneasily in his seat.

"Right, I thought the secrecy stuff was going away after we left the Fleet," Rip added.

Alice started to laugh then stifled it. Minh-Chu regarded her and invited her to join him at the front of the Squad Room. Seriousness returned to her expression as she did. The back door opened and Jake quietly took a seat at the back while she turned to address the pilots and commanders. "Secrecy is even more important now," Alice said, and not just to Blue Group. "We already have people involved in what we do who were never, and will never be properly screened. With the Privateering Program underway, there are going to be whole crews signing up and we'll have to coordinate with a few of them. A few Order spies will definitely come into contact with people from the Triton. We expect a whole undercover Order crew to eventually sign up as Privateers. We're already watching but we're preparing for some of those spies to get through our net. So we'll be compartmentalizing information whenever we can, whenever it makes sense to. This mission, even though we're not raiding something critical to the Order, still has to be treated like it's sensitive. Part of your pay bump is there as an incentive to study the information we give you and to keep quiet about what you know with anyone who doesn't have your clearance level. We don't have to tell you about what comes next in the briefing for you to do your job, so we won't be sharing."

Gren spoke up tentatively. "With respect, I wonder if we would have stayed if we were able to study the materials on the other ships?"

Alice looked to Minh-Chu, who replied; "Not this time out. There was no way you and Garma could have caught up on all the reading because you were recovering. Come to me if you want help catching up after the mission."

"Yes, Wing Commander," the pair of Mergillians said together.

"All right, I'll be filling you in on what you need to know," Slick said as he stood up. "Rip, Sass, Gren, Garma, follow me. We'll be back when it's time to go over contingencies."

When they were gone, Minh-Chu brought a holographic tactical map of a solar system with a pair of stars at its centre. "Solar System Thirty-Three in The Cluster. It is a system with two stars that are only nine million kilometres apart in a stable gravitational lock with each other. There are only four planets in orbit and, from the scans Captain Marda gave us, the Sciences department has determined that they are in regular orbits with no predicted deviations. There are five major asteroid belts and our group will be passing this one, the third from the sun. Since we'll be over seventy million kilometres away, we don't expect any trouble, but there is every chance that our scanners will pick up something the Hammer's didn't when they came this way. That's why all three flight groups will be out and ready along with the Raven and the Clever Dream, just in case someone tries to jump the Triton, the Hammer or the Renegade. It will be their funeral. If something fires at us, any one of the Group Leaders, Triton Command, or commanders from the Raven, Clever Dream, Renegade or Hammer can give the order to open fire on it. That's going to be the same for every part of this mission. If they start something, we end it in a hurry. Questions?"

"Nope, that's pretty clear," Carnie replied. "Where's the Errand in all this?"

"It's shadowing the Raven. Remmy Sands is taking command personally. I told you I'd get someone who knew what they were doing. He's listening in from the Errand's bridge," Minh-Chu replied, happy to see that Carnie was satisfied with the answer. "All right, this is what we're doing today," Minh-Chu said as he started an animation cycle that showed the Triton, Hammer and Renegade arrive in Solar System Thirty-Three and start moving towards the blue-green planet of Tabrus. "We'll pass the asteroid belt with the fighters ahead in three groups so we can increase everyone's sensor range. All our fighters have the smallest version of the Haven Nodes installed, so it'll be zero latency all the way. Don't try to call home or use it for browsing the Stellarnet, I'll know. Once we get into a high orbit around Tabrus, the Clever Dream and Green Group will do a sensor sweep of the southern continent, here," he pointed to a land mass on Tabrus that roughly looked like a human footprint missing two toes. "Grey Group will stay close to the Renegade and Hammer's salvage ships as they wait for the Raven and four of our armoured shuttles. Say hello to their pilots and copilots, who have been quietly sitting at the back." Minh-Chu waved at them and got the laughs he wanted out of the group, who were completely new to the Squadron. "These guys are from all parts of the Triton's crew and they've each got over five hundred non-simulated hours in combat shuttles or similar craft. They know what they're doing. They're carrying workers, loader droids and some of our armed guys who will provide cover when they descend on what I call; The Toy Store." Minh-Chu pointed at a massive factory complex on the coast of the southern continent.

"Niiiiice," Captain Marda said. "I was hoping we'd be hitting that."

"I know, it was top on your list," Alice said, smiling back at his hologram.

"Jake?" Minh-Chu said, tilting his head to look at him at the back of the room. "Fill us in?"

"Right," he said, standing and rushing to the front. "I looked at the list of places that Captain Marda gave us along with the scans, and this one looked pretty much untouched. The parking garage for employees has been mostly raided for vehicles and parts, and someone took half the security fencing, and it looks like someone made off with whatever wasn't bolted down to the loading docks, but the rest seems mostly untouched. Sursytos was a leisure product manufacturing company that went bankrupt right before The Fall. It looks like the tech inside hadn't been sold off yet, so there are whole multi-purpose manufacturing lines that are intact and ready. I saw a rough scan of a section that was still locked up with palettes of spare parts that'll finish the fabrication system in the Shattered End, so if our time there is cut short, we can just load those boxes and run. If we have more time, we'll still take all that, but our plan is to disassemble three of the smaller manufacturing lines apart, load them into shuttles and get them off world, back to the Triton, Renegade and Hammer. When Sel told me that Tabrus was a picking paradise, I had no idea how right he was."

After a nod in his direction, Jake went on. "If that site is contested or defended, we'll move on to the other site, which I've called The Duty-Free Shop, a smaller fabrication plant that will have all the parts we need, but we'll have to take a lot of the systems in there apart to get them. Ideally, I'd like eight hours to work down there, but I estimate that we can get everything we absolutely need from the Toy Store in fifteen minutes if those spare parts are still in storage. If not, then we'll need forty-five at either site so we can take the parts we need to finish the project at the Bitter End."

"Thank you, Jake," Minh-Chu said as he watched his friend take a seat beside Ashley. "Grey Group will go ahead of the shuttles headed for the Toy Store, watching for any defences. Captain Marda tells us that the ground-to-air emplacements are dormant, but here they are. You studied them, you dreaded them, they're the H-3-B, pronounced Heb, particle cannons that can reach right into orbit or cut one of us in half. Set your ECM packages to start up the instant they detect that you're being tracked by any of those or another type of ground-to-air defence. As for the unknown element - other salvagers - Captain Marda tells us that they give each other a lot of space. There's some trading, but no interference. He who gets to something shiny first, keeps the shiny thing."

"It's been good on all three trips," Captain Marda added.

"Oh, and we'd like to take a few of those H3B's with us if there's time," Jake said, half-standing.

"If we have time we'll unbolt and make off with all the toys we can," Minh-Chu said. "Once Grey Group has determined that there are no active defences, Maid will call the shuttles and the Raven in. If there are defences, Jake will determine whether or not you'll be going forward based on the fresh scans you give him. When the defences are neutralized, you'll stay overhead, watching for signs of trouble and addressing anyone who heads in our ground team's direction. Maid is great with people, so she'll be saying hello to anyone who gets too close to our operation, and she'll warn them to stay clear until we're finished. If they go aggressive, then we end the encounter with prejudice."

"With prejudice?" Captain Marda asked.

"We slag 'em from above," Pixie replied.

"Oh, right," he said solemnly.

Minh-Chu enjoyed watching their exchange and momentarily thought that Sel Marda and Pixie might get along well. He had a great sense of humour while she was known for her spunk and high energy. He shook the observation off and pressed on. "You're going to see a lot of abandoned buildings, a few scavengers here and there, and there is a chance that someone from the ground will contact you. Forward every signal to the Triton. They have a whole department that handles non-vital communication for us. If someone wants a ride and you have to say anything to them, the only answer you can give them is 'no.' We are not space taxis. When the last loads get off the ground, you'll escort them back to their ships. After that, you'll make sure the Triton, Renegade, Errand and Hammer get far enough away from the planet to safely jump then we start recovery operations. If we encounter anything that wants to stop us, Blue and Grey fighter groups will be assigned interception targets. Once our targets are defeated or the order to retreat is given and the Triton, Renegade, Errand and Hammer are clear to jump, we will latch onto the hull of the nearest ship or recover in a quick and orderly fashion then head for a long debrief, where I'll see all your smiling faces again."

"There are a few more details to work out for Grey Group, so we'll talk after this," Maid said, running her hand over her bald head, something she probably didn't realize she was doing.

"All right, as for Green Group, you're stuck with me," Minh-Chu said with a grin. "We're going to the same continent, so our scan data will be shared with everyone else. The Clever Dream has a special mission on the surface." He looked at Alice, who was leaning against the window overlooking the fighter hangar. Most of the fighters were on racks along the walls, and one was slowly moving as the ships were being loaded into the launchers, called punters, beneath. Several fighters were being maintained on the deck between the racks, but anyone who wanted to see that would have to stand near the front of the squad room and look down a little.

Alice took Minh-Chu's place and her officer training kicked in. She was calm and clear as she brought up an image of a woman who looked just like her. "I've led everyone to believe that going to Tabrus was Captain Marda's idea. The truth is that I asked the captains I trusted if they knew about the place before the meeting with the Rebels because I received a message from Rogue, a prototype android that was made during a previous mission. I realize there's a resemblance, that was the point. She also thinks like I do. I'm guessing she's the one who stole a hyper-transmitter system from the Doxan System and turned it on in orbit around Tabrus. I'd do the same thing if I wanted to contact the Haven System in days rather than years. A lot of looters are using it too, and it's clear that she is using their activity to cover her activity. I'm not going to fill you in on what Rogue had to say, but she's called me to Tabrus to get an encryption key that's loaded onto a drive hidden on the same continent as the Toy Store. That's why we looked in that area specifically for what we'd need for the Bitter End facility."

"I'm just wondering, how long before the meeting of the Rebel Captains did you get this message?" Captain Marda asked, earning another glare from Dame. He spoke to her more quietly; "I know, no interruptions, but I forgot to ask this twice now, so I thought I'd just get it out. I'll button it up from here on out."

Alice smiled for a moment then replied; "An hour or so before. I was already wondering if there was a place we could get all the parts we'd need for the Bitter End other than the Triton's fabrication system when it was forwarded from the Haven System. It looks like luck would have us going there either way. So, what Green Group will be doing is giving us cover while we go to the coordinates that Rogue sent me, retrieve the drive and whatever else she left for us, and move on to the second part of my mission. We'll be connecting to the largest local Stellarnet we can find so my team can determine what exactly shut every computer on Tabrus down. What we know about the situation there doesn't completely line up with what we know happens to artificial intelligence-heavy worlds that are infected and then cured of the Holocaust Virus. I'd like to find out what's going on if we can. The retrieval mission should take no more than half an hour, but I'm allotting more time for complications. Up to eight hours. I have to make sure I get whatever Rogue might have left for me and the encryption key. If there's resistance, I'll have to either retrieve that or make sure every copy of the encryption data is destroyed along with everyone who saw it. My understanding is that this is sensitive, and I can't let it fall into the wrong hands. My crew's second objective, determining what happened on Tabrus, doesn't have its own mission time. It'll be over whenever our salvage teams are ready to leave or when we get our answer."

"We'll be providing an eye in the sky for them," Minh-Chu said, picking up where she left off. "The Clever Dream will drop Alice and her squad off on the planet then rejoin us with Dame in command of the ship. If there is resistance we can call on the Raven. It's set up for it and there are some soldiers in there who want to go flying around in their armour if they have to. I salute your bravery."

"I know you think it's like flying naked, Ronin," Jake said, taking to his feet. "But I believe we can capture an enemy ship or two if we run into one. I want their data and their hardware."

"I wasn't criticizing, just highlighting a symptom of your madness," Minh-Chu replied. "Green Group's mission is to provide whatever cover Alice needs to get there in the Clever Dream, while she's down on the planet, and when she decides to leave. Questions?"

"Oh, so many, but I don't think you have answers right now," Breaker said with a chuckle as he looked at the holographic overhead map of Tabrus.

"You're right, there are more unknowns than I could list on this mission, but let me try," Minh-Chu replied. "We don't know if someone's turned the defences on, or if a few scrappers got it in their heads to shoot something down so they could raid its hold. There are thousands of satellites in orbit that are dormant, but who knows if any of them will be turned on, and there are ships coming and going from that world. Who knows if we'll be competing with someone for parts, or how long exactly Alice will need on the ground? For all we know, she could pop down, find the drive, then connect with the local 'net, get her answer and decide to join Raven Team so her people can help them load up? Maybe we'll find a long-lost pop star who Jake wants to rescue, and we could become her backup singers after freeing her from a bunch of overzealous fans. Who knows? I could go on, that was all just off the top of my head."

"They don't let you make toasts at parties much, do they?" Captain Marda asked with a raised eyebrow.

"Not since that one time a long time ago," Minh-Chu replied with a snicker. "So I make the most of these opportunities. Speaking of which, it's time to go through a few real contingencies I put together. Using these we should be able to pivot and address just about anything with a few minor modifications," Minh-Chu brought up the next mission slide, one where an Order of Eden fleet tries to trap the Triton, Renegade and Hammer in orbit, up at the front of the room.

"Do you still need me?" Alice asked in a whisper.

"Not up here, you can sit down," Minh-Chu said. "But you're staying for the last fifteen minutes of the briefing. Three of the contingencies include you and the Clever Dream."

"Oh, okay," she said, taking a seat beside Dame.

Minh-Chu signalled Slick and he came back, leading his group into the room and asking; "Contingency time?"

"Contingency time," Minh-Chu replied. Even though he made sure he got through the plans as fast as he could while making sure everyone understood them, it felt good to have the core of a good squadron there. He'd missed flying with Carnie, liked Breaker, was glad to see Slick flying again and was relieved to have the other pilots he'd seen improve since they found the Haven System, like Maid. It was also good to see how excited Ashley was about flying a mission off the ship. It seemed that she especially liked being Jake's pilot, something that Minh-Chu was seeing for the first time. She'd worked as part of his team for a long time, and as he presented several contingency plans, he started to get the feeling that the whole squadron was starting to fit together like a puzzle. Even the pilots who hadn't earned a callsign but would be flying the Triton's cargo shuttles. They had all passed the highest security checks in Haven Fleet before they left on good terms to serve aboard the Triton, and he wondered how many of them he could entice to become fighter pilots full-time.

More than all that, Minh-Chu found his heart lifted by something he saw in abundance: potential.

# FIFTEEN

Approaching Tabrus

THE COURSE that took the battlegroup past the dense asteroid field, which they called Ring Three, was more exciting than Minh-Chu predicted. He knew that every ship with a high-quality scanner package was constantly sweeping the stony features of the belt as the group decelerated towards Planet Tabrus.

The view was incredible. Tabrus was a little dot in the distance, growing nearer at a steady, slow pace. The ring of asteroids was so thick that they could still see it like a road suspended against a starfield that stretched into the distance. Green Group was at the head of their ships with Clever Dream. The light their Archangel fighters' ion-Xetima thrusters burning reflected off of its glossy black hull. This was the suspension of time, when seconds moved slowly before the first real information about their surroundings came in.

"I've detected wreckage, we're focusing our scans now," Iruuk said from the small bridge of the Clever Dream.

"This is Triton Sciences. We see it. Send us your detailed data while we continue omnidirectional scanning."

The communication channels for Samurai Squadron and most of the Battle Group were silent for several minutes afterwards, and then the Science Officer aboard the Clever Dream, Iruuk, cleared his throat and announced; "Lewis and I have identified the wreckage. There are the remains of three Io Yards defence craft spread around the empty hull of an Eden Fleet Mothership."

"Can I get a clarification on that, Iruuk? You said an Eden Fleet Mothership, not an Order of Eden ship?" Minh-Chu asked as he watched an image of the round, silver-hulled automated vessel appear on his tertiary display. He turned it off, fully aware of the ship's capabilities.

"Hell no," Easy said.

"Anyone else get shivers? I've got shivers," Pixie added.

"You are correct, Ronin," Iruuk broke in. "The hull is definitely from an Eden Fleet Mothership, but we are only detecting wreckage from the outer structure and permanent inner components. It looks like the intelligent computer core and most of the other components were ejected. There's no sign of them."

"How long ago? Was the hull destroyed after the end of the Fourth Fall?" Jake asked from the Raven.

"There's no way to know, exactly. The wreckage is over a year old, but for all we know, the Antivirus that defeated the

Holocaust Virus only reached this system eight months ago, or a year ago, or… we need more information," Iruuk replied. "There are a few destroyed drones in there too, and they were most likely destroyed at the same time. The damage I'm seeing matches the type of weaponry the Io Yards Defence Craft used. Maybe they defeated the Eden invaders before they reached the planet?"

"Well, if it factored into how this place went quiet, you'll find out," Jake replied.

"But no pressure," Minh-Chu said to the young Science Officer. "You just have to find what you're after and hook into something that recorded and remembers how things went dark here, that's all."

"I'll do my best," Iruuk replied uncertainly. "The team aboard the Triton are performing a more in-depth analysis of our scans. Hopefully, they can tell you more about this Eden Fleet Mothership. There was a lot of activity in the asteroid field too. In most of the dormant artificial craft and structures, there is evidence that there was a lot of mining going on here. I see a few active rigs that are harvesting. No life signs. Their cargo compartments have been emptied sometime in the last few days, so someone's operating here."

"Nothing special then, we'll leave that alone," Captain Vega said from the bridge of the Triton.

The main focus of their scans moved to the outer space around Tabrus. There were several freighters and a few cargo trains flying in a lazy course. Minh-Chu watched as a battered orbital lifter brought three heavy cargo containers to its hauler, where thin arms accepted a box and put it in place along the metal train frame trailing behind the large craft. He zoomed into the handler cab at the rear and saw a teenage boy chewing gum as he controlled the manipulators with gloves, his arms raised as the mechanism outside reached for a cargo box. He was bobbing his head to the beat of something Minh-Chu couldn't hear. Then the youth's eyes went wide and he looked up. Minh-Chu knew that there was no way the kid could see any of the ships in the Triton's battlegroup from where he was. The scanner data that made the young worker visible was reaching him from over a hundred million kilometres away.

Then, the explanation for the young man's shock came through as Alice announced; "We're getting a lot of acknowledgements from ships in orbit. Most, like the hauler we're coming up on, are announcing that they don't want any trouble. The rest of the ships in the area are sending friend or foe pings and standard hails. Passing them on to you, Triton. You were right, Captain Marda, there's almost no activity. Fewer than twenty ships so far. Wait, there's a challenge, putting it through to the Command Channel now."

"This is the Siren Development Ship Fine Day. Fine Day to the battlegroup on approach: We are engaged in revitalization operations on the surface of Tabrus, specifically in the equator city of New Zero. I'm sending you the coordinates now. Requesting that you stay clear of that area." It wasn't a challenge, but a request, and whoever was issuing it was speaking clearly but he didn't sound threatening.

"Fine Day, I'm Captain Vega of the Free Ship Triton. We're here on a salvage operation. Is there an authority enforcing salvage registration?" replied Captain Stephanie Vega.

"Say again, Captain Vega? I- the most recent record we have

of your ship is as a Haven Fleet Heavy Close Combat Carrier." said the voice on the other end.

"Things have changed, Fine Day. We're a free ship along with the rest of the battle group you see with us. We're after a bit of salvage today on the southern continent. Nowhere near the coordinates you've marked."

"Oh, I guess I have some news to catch up on. Have at it, Captain Vega and company. There are no governments on that continent at the moment, so there's no one to stop you from taking whatever you want, especially with all the friends you brought along. Just wondering, what are you after?"

"I'd rather keep that to myself, but we'll be gone before you know it," Captain Vega replied.

"Understood. I'm only asking because we're re-establishing a settlement in New Zero. You're welcome to stop in once we're ready. Guest areas should be open in five days if your people want a little R and R," the Captain of the Fine Day offered. "Oh, and spread the word. New Zero's open for business."

"Will do, but we won't be staying long enough to visit," Captain Vega replied, adding; "Best of luck in New Zero."

"So, who are these Siren guys to us?" Breaker asked on the Green Group's channel.

"Oh, they're the good guys," Carnie replied. "Corporate competition to Regent Galactic, and they make some nice gear. Don't tell them that I've been borrowing a few of their weapon and survival gear patterns for a few months."

"Do you know anything about New Zero, Captain Marda?" asked Alice over the Battlegroup's Common Chatter channel.

"Can't say I do. The Fine Day's new to these parts. There

are a lot of places on this planet that I don't know much of anything about, to be honest," he replied.

"From the scans of the planet surface that are coming in now, I can see that New Zero was a large city centre capable of housing nearly three million people," Theodore said from the Clever Dream. "The only life signs we can see from here are within a fifteen by fifteen block area that has a heavy Siren Corporation presence. It's the most population-dense section of the planet from what I see so far. Mostly humans, with a notable Nafalli presence."

"We'll have to take a closer look later," Jake replied from the Raven. "We stay on mission for now."

"I agree. If we start exploring, we'll be here for a month," Captain Vega replied from the bridge of the Triton.

The temptation to take a look at the scans of New Zero was very real to Minh-Chu, especially when he got a message from Ashley that read; 'Ooh, it looks really nice. They're reviving agricultural towers and planting things along all the pathways. We'll have to visit sometime.'

He was about to remind her not to text while flying, but saw that the message was made using a link between a transmitter sitting on the back of her head. She'd mastered the Brain Bud most pilots were starting to use to connect to their ships. He shook his head, then concentrated on replying through the mental interface of his fighter. 'We'll definitely drop in when we come back. I'm going to activate my tactical map now.'

'Okay, Bud you later!' came her friendly response. That was her slang, using 'Bud' as a verb. He didn't really think it would catch on, but that wasn't at the fore of his thoughts. He was sure that she was already seeing the growing tactical map in her mind and was having little trouble sending messages at the same time. Sure, they came through as text since she, like practically everyone else, couldn't actually do better while multitasking, but she was much better at connecting to telepathic systems than he was. Whenever he tried to record a message with his mind, like a simple thought-to-text message, everything else he was getting from the connection became blurry, like his tactical map and system status updates.

Thankfully, she knew and understood. It was something they'd discovered in simulations and he was grateful that she didn't tease him about it. Most people could only let a tactical map in through the telepathic link. Archangel pilots were required to be able to use the link at least for that. Everyone in Green and Grey Groups could receive and comprehend a tactical map and their ship's basic instruments. Minh-Chu activated the tactical map, targetting systems, ship instruments and status and watched them all come into focus in his mind's eye. It was like having a mental picture of the head-up display that didn't interfere with his vision.

It was better than the simulations, even though the awareness of his ship's condition slipped away almost completely. He set it to alert him if there were problems instead of maintaining a constant data stream and focused on what he could hold on to. He had a clear sense of where the planet was, feel where the nearest ships were and know their trajectories, speeds, and even the weather in high orbit became an image in his mind. "There are a lot of particles out there, high solar activity," he announced. "The atmosphere is really thick below that. We'll have to make a slow entry," he said on the Green Group channel. Carnie, Pixie, Breaker, Easy and Dame signalled that they heard him.

Triton Flight was late with their acknowledgement, responding; "Sorry we didn't give you a weather report before we emerged from FTL."

"Don't worry, Flight. We've got thi..." Minh-Chu stopped as a small ship appeared on their scanners. It was leaving orbit above the southern continent. "I've got something here, recognized as a Citadel Wormhole Jumper Drone."

"Good catch," Flight replied. "I can't believe the new scanning protocol we grabbed off the Stellarnet actually detected Cloaked Citadel ships!"

"So happy the stuff you found on the 'net works," Minh-Chu replied. "What do we do here, Flight?"

"We've signalled the drone with a request to divert and submit to inspection. Surprise surprise, it's running," Captain Vega replied. "Start scrambling and intercept it before it can get far enough from the planet's gravity to jump."

"On it. Green Group, on me," Minh-Chu said as he turned his fighter and led his group of five fighters in that direction. They accelerated, joined by the Clever Dream. Its turrets began to turn towards the drone as its rear thrusters opened up, giving it an aggressive flame trail.

"Four more moving to intercept. Three drones, one scout craft," announced Dame from the Clever Dream. "I'm marking the Defence Drones as Targets Two, Three and Four."

"Gunners, open fire," Alice said from the Clever Dream. A second later, every turret on the corvette was firing small, high-speed rounds using its new railguns.

The Citadel combat drones scattered, and Minh-Chu

locked three missiles onto the one in the lead. It wouldn't be able to jump into a wormhole for several more seconds, but there was a power buildup inside it that made it clear that it was getting ready. "Firing three M-Nines at the Jumper Drone," he announced as he flipped the trigger cover up and pulled it as many times. His missiles sped after the drone, turning in an arc after it as the small ship started to evade.

"Firing two M-Nines at the Jumper Drone," Carnie said. It wasn't unusual for another pilot to ensure that a mission-critical target was taken out by adding to its trouble with a few missiles of their own.

"Breaking, going after Drone Two," Pixie said as her fighter jerked out of the drone's line of fire then spun and started firing at it. She was chasing after it next.

"Drone Four is down," Alice said. "That scout ship is trying to get away. We're giving chase."

"Not much of a match for you," Breaker said. "Firing three M-Nines at Drone Three, then pursuing."

"Backing you with two M-Nines on Drone Three," Easy said as a pair of missiles shot from the launchers built into his fighter.

The Jumper Drone fired a countermeasure laser at two of Minh-Chu's missiles and was struck by the third. It spun out of control for a second, but as it righted itself so it could continue accelerating away from the planet, he put the crosshairs of his guns on the centre of its fuselage and opened fire. He performed a focused scan at the same time, turning the gain on his secondary scanner array all the way up. One of Carnie's missiles struck the Jumper Drone and its shields failed.

A flood of data streamed into the computers in Minh-Chu's

fighter as his sensors saw through a crack in its relatively thin armour. He didn't pay attention to anything that didn't appear in his tactical system, which told him that only the ship's armour had been damaged so far, that it was a Sol Defence design, and that it was approximately six months old. There were serial numbers and other data, like fuel load and a systems list, but it didn't matter as Minh-Chu opened up with his guns for another burst. His four anti-capitol ship railgun cannons all hit, drilling a hole through the Jumper Drone's middle. Its thrusters went out and it drifted along its last trajectory. "I read no power, it's toast. Good shooting, Ronin," came the congratulations from Carnie.

"My Drone's about to bite it," Pixie said as all four of her guns fired and pieces of her quarry's hull broke apart as it turned to fire back at her. Its particle beam touched her shields for half a second before it flew apart. "Down. That's Drone Two, wishing it never met me."

Easy and Breaker were in pursuit of Drone Three, which had managed to evade all their missiles so far. Two were still giving chase as the drone evaded, its rear pulse emitter spending more of its time slicing at Breaker's Archangel. His shields were deflecting most of the damage as he lined his shot up and opened up with his guns, hammering the drone's shields. The energy barrier failed, Breaker broke off and Easy took over, finishing the kill with a burst of his own. "Drone Three is inoperable," he announced.

"Nice teamwork, Easy. Just like the sims," Breaker added.

"Need help, Clever Dream?" asked Minh-Chu as he started manoeuvring back into formation behind the corvette.

"No, but you can watch," Dame said as a warning flashed in

front of the ship and five missiles were sent from its forward launcher. The projectiles accelerated at a shocking rate and impacted less than a second later, shattering the oval scout ship. Two humanoid-sized pods flew from the explosion towards the planet so quickly that Minh-Chu wouldn't have seen them if they didn't appear on his tactical map. "Escape pods. See them?" he asked as he marked them as EP 1 and 2.

"I've got them. Pursue?" Alice asked.

"No. We'll stick to the plan," Jake replied. "They know we're coming. Hopefully, that was the only scout ship. If not, rushing in after those pods will just make us more vulnerable."

The final drone failed to evade the Clever Dream's rear gunners as they blasted it to pieces and Green Group formed up behind the ship. Minh-Chu decided it was time to activate one of his contingencies. "Hammer, Renegade, how would you like to take a nice trip around the planet, just to see if there are more Order or Citadel friends around?"

"Aye, changing course," Captain Marda said.

"On it, we'll meet you back here in nineteen minutes," Captain Blake replied from the bridge of the Renegade.

"The Clever Dream is going counter-spin," Alice announced.

"We'll go the other way," Jake said from the Raven.

"All right, come back to the Triton if you run into anything too dangerous," Minh-Chu said as Green Group fell back into formation behind the Clever Dream. "I knew this would be exciting."

# SIXTEEN

Towers

THE NEWS WASN'T what anyone wanted to hear as Captain Marda announced; "We spotted a Citadel Scoutship right as it jumped out of the system. The Hammer is coming about and on its way back to the Triton right now. Scanning the surface as we go, but we're not getting good clarity because the outer atmosphere is so bloody thick and charged."

"Link up with our Sciences Officer, Kadri. She'll help you clear some of that up," Captain Vega replied.

Minh-Chu could see that the Hammer was accelerating aggressively in high orbit so it could return to the protective area the Triton offered. Meanwhile, the scans coming back from the Clever Dream weren't showing any threatening craft. Most of the ships they did see were on their way off world, and they engaged their faster-than-light drives as soon as they could. "Is this normal, Captain Marda? More ships leaving than arriving?" he asked.

"No, can't say I've ever seen that before," he replied. "My Sensor lads are shaking their heads at me too. Ships land and stick around to load up until they're at max weight. Stays last days."

"Maybe someone should try to get in touch with someone on the Fine Day, ask them if there's something scaring those ships away?" Minh-Chu asked.

"I'm seeing it too," Captain Blake said as Navnet data was sent directly to Minh-Chu's ship. "It's like watching fleas jump off a dog in a bath. Five ascensions and jumps in the last three minutes. That's escape speed."

"Maybe it's us? Maybe people see a real battlegroup and are assuming that the party's over?" Pixie asked from the cockpit of her fighter.

"I doubt it," Captain Vega replied. "We sent a message with our intentions out over the common channels. Most of the ships that are getting out of the solar system aren't fleeing from the same continent we marked. No, they're seeing something we haven't yet."

"All right, Green Group is going down to check. Shields to maximum, adjust barrier geometry for atmospheric entry and set the gain of your sensors to auto-level. If there's a chance we can see through the friction burn while we're on our way down, we should take it," Minh-Chu said as he set his fighter up properly.

"Right, better to see the anti-air guns fire at us the instant before they knock down our shields than take us out," Easy said with a chuckle.

"You know, sometimes I really don't understand your sense of humour," Dame said without a hint of levity. "The Clever Dream can lead the way, just in case he's right and there are live defences below."

"Ladies first, especially if they're flying more heavily shielded warships. Go ahead," Minh-Chu said as he led his formation of five fighters into place a fair distance behind the Clever Dream. "We're set for entry, out of range of your turbulence."

"Going in now," Dame said as the Clever Dream turned and shared its course with everyone in its group.

"We're doing the same about fifteen hundred kilometres away," Maid announced. "No reason why the Clever Dream and the Greens should have all the fun."

"That's why I like you, Maid, you're so practical. We will come down above the continent on a section where there are likely no surface-to-space weapons, while you and the Raven come in a few hundred kilometres off the coast, where we saw none," Minh-Chu told her cheerily.

"Well, there's a chance that they'll just have a clearer shot at us because there's nothing but the sky above and ocean below, you know," Maid replied. "But we're hoping things haven't changed much down there, right, Ronin?"

"Right," Minh-Chu said as his ship started to heat up. Their approach was relatively slow for atmospheric entry, but the thick atmosphere resisted them. His shields were reducing friction and deflecting most of the heat. Every ship in his group was faring just as well, with the Clever Dream generating the most friction because of its size. It was also providing the biggest target.

As expected, their scanners were almost completely over-whelmed by the interference created by the high temperature of the burn and electromagnetic energy of the highly charged atmosphere. As soon as it began to clear, an alarm sounded in Minh-Chu's cockpit and the Clever Dream, which was just reappearing on his tactical map, flashed red. "A targeting system is on us," Dame announced. "Going evasive."

"It's gone," Breaker announced an instant after the tracking signal from the ground disappeared as though someone turned it off with the flick of a switch.

"It came from that Navnet uplink dish, strange," Iruuk said from the bridge of the Clever Dream.

Minh-Chu didn't have to ask why he thought it was odd. The dish he highlighted on the ground was made to link to satel-lites in orbit, not to gather data. Someone had adapted it to that purpose, and it wouldn't be accurate over a wide area, so it wasn't a good candidate for that kind of job. There wasn't more than a second to ponder that, as he ordered; "Spread out, send extra energy to your shields, and be ready to go evasive."

Green Group did exactly as ordered. He wanted to extend the thin, fold-out wings of his craft so he could glide more than propel his way across the sky, but it made sense to keep the silhouette of his fighter small while there could be trouble below.

"That dish is completely dead, there's no power coming from anything affixed to it, but I see..." Iruuk was saying over the Green Group's Tactical Channel before trailing off.

"If you suspect trouble, tell us about it, Fur-Face," Alice was overheard saying in the background.

"It's just... I saw a shape down there, I'm doing another

scanner pass," he replied, highlighting a section of the landscape below and behind them.

Minh-Chu looked at it. The continent they were flying over was infiltrated by plant life, with few roads, buildings, or lots free of the grip of new growth. The forested areas seemed rudely healthy with green and orange trees thickly filling huge sections of the landscape. To Minh-Chu, it was a beautiful sight. He focused on what Iruuk highlighted. It was a cross street with several tall buildings on each corner and several landing pads, two of which were recently cleared of vines, suspended between them. What he spotted was highlighted red: what looked like a craft that was taking cover beneath the landing pads. "Good eye, that's definitely a Sol Defence drop ship," Minh-Chu said, the memory of its shape springing to mind thanks to the countless times he went through the database of known vessels. He hadn't done it in a while and took that as a reminder to re-invest time in the habit.

"Why didn't you see that, Lewis?" Iruuk asked the artificial intelligence aboard the Clever Dream.

"Of course I saw it, but there's only a forty-one point one percent probability that Ronin's assumption is true," Lewis replied haughtily.

"Ground chatter," Alice announced from the Clever Dream. "Encrypted."

"I caught that too. It was a short message," Carnie said from the cockpit of his fighter.

"It's Order of Eden encryption," Lewis announced.

Three missiles fired from the ground ahead of them and the Clever Dream was struck on the underside by one. "SAM's, evading!" Dame announced.

"The launcher is marked, we've got it!" Minh-Chu said, highlighting it on the tactical map with a thought. "They're warming a surface-to-space particle beam up."

"The missile that hit us was a Burster with an EMP pre-detonator and an explosive warhead made to take out shields then break through a ship's hull," Iruuk explained. "We haven't taken damage, but they're trying to get a lock on us again. Dame is taking us... low."

The Clever Dream was flying towards the ground in an erratic path as Minh-Chu and Breaker flew past it. Behind them were Pixie, Easy, and Carnie. Breaker was the first to fire, announcing the launch of three M-9 seeker missiles from a distance. To everyone's surprise, they all made it to the target.

The surging dome of an energy shield appeared clearly as they exploded. It neatly surrounded the top of a building clad in armour that gleamed silver-red in the yellow sunlight. Minh-Chu fired three missiles of his own as soon as he heard the tone that told him he had a lock. Then he lowered the nose of his craft a little and fired his four guns. The shield stopped the missiles from doing any damage, and the dozens of rounds he flung at it were halted as well. That was until they struck the thirty-fifth floor. Six more missiles from his fighter group hammered the shield, and the readings his craft took on it told him no one wanted to hear. "That shield may be connected to a power grid that's not sending power anywhere else right now. We may never get through, that is unless we topple the tree."

"Topple the tree?" Dame asked. A glance at where the Clever Dream was showed that she was busy weaving the ship between the buildings in the large city centre, slowing down.

"The shield doesn't extend past the top six floors. I'm

marking a spot beneath that," Minh-Chu said as he took his fighter down so he could manoeuvre behind cover.

"They're trying to target me now," Pixie said, audibly straining. "I'm ducking behind buildings, putting as much between me and that site as I can."

The anti-air turret fired five missiles and they crossed the distance between the launchers and Pixie's fighter in less than three seconds, screaming across the sky. A building she barely had time to get behind was the unintended victim as two impacted the roof and three more destroyed the top two floors from the inside. Her fighter's shields were down nearly fifty percent from indirect damage. "Get down lower and behind something bigger!" Easy told her.

"Bigger than a building?" she asked in an objecting squeak. "How about this: I distract them while you make a run on what's holding them up."

"What?" Carnie asked. "No way."

"Do it," Minh-Chu said. "Making my run now." With that, he flew down between the buildings, just above the street, then turned between a pair of them, then again and started firing his guns the instant he could see a sliver of the building ahead. Normally he could feel the rumble of his four railguns, and hear the whine of his shots accelerating out of his craft. That was outside of an atmosphere. The turbulence of those bolts as they left his barrels and fought the air made his ship shudder. The whining sound was buried under the rapid thunder as hundreds of rounds broke the sound barrier per second. His weapons were set to fire as fast as they could, the flight software built into his ship did its best to counter the force of his weapons using thrusters and dampeners as he flew towards the side of the building in the shadows cast by the others around it.

The armour cladding chipped and cracked as he did his best to keep all his bullet hits within a small ten-by-ten-metre area. If he had time to smile, he would, because he saw a large chunk of metal and concrete fall away. He launched three missiles then another volley right behind it, and then swerved away from the building where he used a row of skyscrapers as cover, just in case there were countermeasures below the turret.

"I see where you made a nice hole, Ronin, almost there," Breaker said. "Got a pair of Javelins loaded."

"That's going to cause collateral damage," Carnie said before Minh-Chu could.

It was too late for Breaker to change his mind. The torpedoes were away, accelerating at incredible speed, lighting the street and rows of buildings up around it with its white-hot thrusters. They both made it through the hole Minh-Chu's missiles had broken into the side of the building. For half a second there was no explosion, then an eruption that Minh-Chu felt even over ten blocks away changed their target and every building in its immediate area. The skyscrapers waved like wind-swept grass. They recovered, returning to their original positions, but they were severely damaged. The streets and walkways below were showered with glass, metal panelling, and concrete.

Breaker's fighter was sent sideways through the windows of a nearby building where it tumbled through walls until it rolled to a stop. Pixie was no longer being painted by the anti-air missile launcher, and the shield surrounding it collapsed. Minh-Chu took his fighter up and started flying towards it; "Breaker!

Are you all right? I'm not getting anything from the sensors in his ship."

"Did he just get caught by his own blast wave?" Easy asked.

"Yeah, oh, hell yeah," Carnie sounded astonished. "I wasn't too far behind. I got some of it too. Man, I can't get anything from him either."

"Breaker!" Minh-Chu shouted, seeing two Citadel drop-ships on the roof of the same building with the surface-to-air missile launcher system built into the top. The shield was hiding them before.

Then, to everyone's relief, the sound of Breaker laughing came over their channel. "I've never launched torpedoes in an atmosphere before, not even in simulation. Whoo!" he cheered. "That was a hell of a rush."

"Oh man, don't do that!" Carnie said. "I was watching you launch those bad boys one second, then they went off and you just disappeared!"

"I don't know what you did to earn your callsign before, but you just re-earned it now," Pixie laughed.

"Oh, did he ever," Minh-Chu said as he watched a dozen soldiers in Order of Eden uniforms run from the control room of the missile launcher system as the top of the building began to sway and collapse, becoming more lop-sided every second. They scrambled for their drop ships. One of the turrets on the dorsal side of the vessel started to rotate. "Everyone see my target?"

"I see it," Pixie was the first to announce.

Minh-Chu switched his comm system so he was speaking over every available channel. "This is Ronin, leader of the fighter group who just wrecked your little building. Stand down and you will be treated with..." a streak of turret fire crossed the sky near him and he shook his head. "Well, you just screwed up your chances of getting off that building before the top falls off," he finished before switching to Green Group's encrypted tactical system. "Take those drop ships out."

"My turn," Pixie growled as she opened up with her guns, raking the rooftop before ripping into the dropship and flying past.

"I have a lock on Dropship Two," Carnie announced. "Firing three. M-9's, not torpedoes."

"Firing two on your target, Carnie," Easy said and seconds later that side of the rooftop exploded along with the dropship, which was just starting to hover up.

The other Dropship, which was marked as the third, was struggling after being peppered with rounds from Pixie's guns. Minh-Chu saw her come around and didn't bother getting involved as she announced; "Launching three M-Nines. This is for trying to knock me out of the sky."

Her Archangel was within five hundred metres when she launched her missiles. As they left her launchers she banked, turned and was flying away, backwards so she could see the dropship explode. She was treated to an even more thrilling sight as the top six floors of the building tilted and dropped straight down onto the structure below. Somehow the main support in the centre of it didn't fail completely but held the remains of the upper section of the skyscraper in place. "Oh, damn, it's like a cock-eyed torch," Carnie laughed.

"We will be easy to remember here," Minh-Chu said with a snicker. "They'll just have to look up and, well, there it'll be. The bent building. Now, how are you really doing, Breaker?"

"Oh, this ship will fly, but I'm not airtight anymore," he replied. "I'll be out of the wreckage, but I'll have to hitch a ride."

"All right, land next to the Clever Dream later so we can take your ship aboard. We're moving on to check out the other dropship Iruuk Spotted."

"We're covering you," Minh-Chu said as he sent a silent order for the remaining fighters in his group to loosely form up around the Clever Dream.

# SEVENTEEN

Hollow People

BECOMING an empath taught Alice more than any other transformation or rebirth that had come before it. There was a culture that Quan could barely begin to tell her about because it was so large with so many variations. The kind of heightened empathic ability that she had would have made her sought after where he came from because people who had it could train as therapeutic, research, and tactical empaths among other types. The idea that she could specialize was a realization that made her shrink back from the idea because Alice wanted to know something about each branch of the empath training tree.

It took months for her to trust Quan, but once she did there were more questions on her lips than he had time to answer. There was also too much to each speciality than she had time to explore, so he gave her the exercises she needed to generally control her ability and that's what she focused on for the most part. The rest of the time she worked on her ability, she used the tactical empath training that he offered. Quan was not himself an expert in that kind of use but had the materials and sensitivity to begin teaching it to her. While she was playing royal guardian in the Cefa System, Alice honed her sense to detect deception, intentions, and to quickly locate people who were nearby. Alice's reach grew, her ability to separate her emotions from those emanating from the people around her, and she was ready to trust her own judgement before she was finished with palaces and royalty.

As she waited in the debarkation cabin at the rear of the Clever Dream with her small team, she took a quick read of everyone aboard. Dame was at the controls and calm. The feeling of someone who was taking in new information constantly and keeping it all organized in her head was firmly asserted in her. This was how the pilot was during missions, but Alice liked it when she relaxed more when she spent a lot of time just waiting to be included in whatever conversation was underway. She was happy to announce; "The Surface to Air and Space emplacement that the Order took control of has been destroyed. The others have been scanned and are not active."

"Yeah, well done, Samurai Squadron," Iruuk said.

The tower was over two hundred kilometres away, but it could make trouble for anything flying over the continent. "That is a relief," Alice heard Theodore in the background of the announcement before Dame turned the ship intercom off. He was working with Lewis to take over the sciences, copilot and communications stations. It wasn't much of a stretch for either of them, so Dame could concentrate on flying while the rest of the duties were well taken care of.

Tammy, a new crewmember on loan from the Raven, was taking care of tactical and leading the gunners aboard the Clever Dream. She was an impressive tactical officer and the twin sister to Ashley. Both of them were grown in a factory and programmed to become daughters to their new owners.

The other gunners from the Triton marines were glad to be on a mission, and in a state of eager readiness. They wanted to impress everyone on the Clever Dream, which probably meant Alice more than anyone and through that, her father. She made a mental note to talk to each of them individually after the mission, no matter how poorly or well things went. She didn't know if or when she'd be getting her Nafalli crewmembers back.

The people standing around her, waiting for the Clever Dream to touch down so they could disembark, were a mix of new and old crew. As usual, Iruuk was excited and alert - eager to explore and ready to protect his crewmates. Roscoe was on loan from the Raven, and was in a state of calm that reminded Alice of many seasoned soldiers. It was a little strange for someone his age, in his early twenties.

Mayu, who was the same height as Alice, a little over one point fifty-two metres, was delighted to stand beside her temporary commander. The fact that they were equally short set her off in a bright mood, and Alice wondered if there was a serious core to the young woman's personality at all for a few moments. Then the bald young woman looked at her command and control unit, did a very quick and thorough equipment check using the personal inventory system, made sure that all her weapons and armour systems could complete a quick power test, and then regarded Alice with a sweet smile. "Thank you for picking us for this mission. I was afraid they'd send me into the small spaces so I could unscrew things in that manufacturing plant. I'm sure that's happened to you. Well, maybe not, because you're, you know, a Captain, then a member of Special Operations, and well, you're Alice, after all. Um, well, thanks."

"She talks enough for the whole Raven crew. It would be a problem if she wasn't usually saying what we're thinking better than we can," Nigel said with a grin that reminded Alice of his uncle, Shamus Frost.

Mayu rolled her eyes at him, but Alice knew that the young marine enjoyed his sentiment.

Nigel was nervous and he was covering with humour. Perhaps he thought he had a lot to prove, being Frost's nephew. That wasn't so for Alice. He'd already completed more training than his uncle did, and scored high in his specialities.

Jake's voice came over the general mission channel then. "We're inside the Toy Factory. Someone left a few minor traps here, probably as a way of reserving this find, but we got past them without a problem and they're disarmed now. No one here. Most of the new parts are still where we thought they'd be so we're loading up. Finn is leading the rest of the team in disassembly on one of the fabrication lines."

"Thanks for the update. The Clever Dream just touched down. We're about to check out Beta Site," Alice replied as the large rear ramp at the rear of the Clever Dream opened and she led the team off the ship. They were in full armour, carrying heavy rifles made to kill Order Knights and small vehicles. They could be automatically re-tuned for precision on the fly as well, and that was how Alice's was set up at the moment. Iruuk, being almost as tall as his father, was carrying a beam weapon that required a generator backpack and a harness. He'd made some improvements including a high-powered scanner so he could concentrate on his science officer duties while staying very well-armed.

The street was divided in half down the middle. One side was definitely reserved for pedestrians judging by the planters and storefronts along the left, while the other was for some kind of slender vehicles. "What are those?" Iruuk asked, pointing down towards the corner. "Bicycles," Nigel said, nearly in awe. "I haven't seen one since I left the Core Worlds."

Alice spotted them, a neat stack of the two-wheeled pedalled things that had been bound together by vines. They also reached up the sides of the buildings around them, spreading green everywhere. Mosses and rough, bright grasses were growing across the street, but everything seemed fresh, not like the area had been overgrown over years. "Why would anyone use those?" Iruuk asked.

"It doesn't use power cells, just your own legs, so getting around is free," Roscoe replied as the group moved off the street into an alleyway. "That's what the pedals are for. My neighbours back home loved those things. Think they're dead now. Guess the bikes weren't fast enough to get away when the 'bots went wacky."

"You have an interesting point of view," Iruuk said, returning his full attention back to his scan data. "I see two soldiers coming this way. Nine hundred metres. The Clever Dream's cloaking system must have worked."

"Otherwise they'd bring a lot more or be running away,"

Alice said, reaching out with her mind. There they were. Two soldiers to the north. They were emotional twins, with the exact same dutiful dedication running through their minds like a looped recording. That was impossible. Each person, even when they were genetic twins like Tammy and Ashley, was a universe unto themselves with different perceptions and reactions adjusted by experience. She took a moment, turning and leaning against the wall of a building. "This isn't right."

"What is it?" Iruuk asked quietly.

Then a thought struck Alice and she opened her eyes. "Those soldiers are fresh frameworks. They can't be more than a day old."

"Switch to Munition Twenty-Eight," Iruuk said and every member of the team made the adjustment so their rifles would fire rounds specifically designed to defeat framework soldiers.

Alice pushed her perception and felt the presence of an entire squad. "There are three people with unique personalities, the rest - nine of them - are new frameworks. Soldiers. They're not specialists. They're running." She didn't take time to warn the rest of her team before Alice rushed from the alleyway and levelled her rifle at the nearest soldier. Her aim assist system steadied her arms, adjusted for her gait, and simply put the reticle she could see in her head up display onto the nearest soldier. It followed her target as she sent a burst of rounds its way, the cracking of each of them merging together in a sound that echoed so loudly that she was sure that if there were spirits in the ghost city, they would awaken. Her first shot missed narrowly, not a surprise from that distance. "Send a high-powered scan their way and update tactical."

Iruuk did so from behind her as her team caught up to her

and a second later the tactical map in her helmet was updated with the locations of the entire squad of Order of Eden soldiers. "Most of them are moving computer storage equipment to their drop ship from that building," Iruuk said, highlighting several of them who were carrying heavy cases. The rest were grabbing rifles and rushing towards the street. "Prioritize the nearest armed soldiers," Alice ordered. "No prisoners."

"I'll go high," Iruuk said, leaping up the side of a building and running along as though gravity had tilted ninety degrees just for him. There were still moments when Alice envied his mobility, especially with the help of his suit which could grip just about any solid surface.

"They're not in practical range," Roscoe said as he let loose with a reckless rattle of rounds.

Rain started to spatter the street as they closed on the nearest soldiers. The creak of the synthetic muscle layer of Alice's new black combat vacsuit as it helped her run faster nearly drowned him out. "I know, we need to scare them back while Green Group does the rest."

"I heard that. Ronin here, what do you need?" he replied from above.

"Keep that drop ship from launching, but don't destroy it. They're in the middle of a smash-and-grab," Alice replied.

"And you need what they're grabbing. I got it," Ronin replied from somewhere well above.

The rain came then. It was as though a bucket had been tipped over their heads and the visibility was reduced to a metre or less. "Switching to SEV," announced Mayu.

Sensor-enhanced viewing was an overlay that played inside their helmet that used data their suits collected to create a clear substitute for normal eyesight. In less than a second, Alice activated it and was seeing the street as though it was a clear day. The pair of soldiers that were nearest to them were two-hundred eighty metres away, give or take a centimetre, and she tried taking another shot. They reacted exactly as she wanted and rushed for the entrance of a burned-out store.

They forgot to look up. Iruuk reached down from above and snatched one by the shoulder then tossed him across the street, where he awkwardly collided with a window sill before dropping to the ground four stories below. He fired his beam weapon at the other, who was dropping to one knee, aiming his rifle up at the Nafalli. His arm was cut away by Iruuk's blinding beam before he could pull the trigger. The framework soldier started to clutch the stump but was interrupted by convulsions.

"Holy hell, there's a reaction starting in that one! He's turning into a living bomb," Nigel said as Iruuk leapt from the side of the building.

The Nafalli was struck in the back several times by armour-piercing rounds as he ran on all fours, putting two dozen metres between the fallen soldier and himself. Alice and Mayu were the first to score hits on the soldiers who broke cover to fire at the departing Nafalli. They were fearless in a way that was eerily identical. One mind stood out. There was a cool hatred at its core, the kind that someone who was trying to stomp the life out of some kind of vermin intruder would feel and Alice shut most of her empathic sense down.

The ground shook as both of the soldiers Iruuk disabled exploded. The young Nafalli made it, and other than some damage to his flexible metal hybrid armour, he was fine. The shots he'd taken from behind were only enough to take out his personal shield, which was regenerating.

The howl of something approaching from above was enough to send every soldier inside the drop ship running, and Alice dropped to one knee. Her team followed her example and when she opened fire at the nearest armed Order of Eden framework grunt, she wasn't the only one shooting. "Like level four target practice," Roscoe said as the nearest soldier was picked apart by a barrage of rounds from his rifle.

Alice did something she loathed the thought of in that instant and she didn't know why at first. She reached out to the mind of the soldier as he fell. To her surprise, there was no despair, shock, or regret at dying. There wasn't even enough pain to make her wince, which was saying something because it didn't take much for her to react sympathetically. Her own pain was easy to take, but the anguish of others as she felt it through empathy always seemed personal, even haunting. When the framework soldier died, there was almost nothing. It was biologically human, but that seemed to be the extent of it. She wondered if it even had the potential to become more than it was. "These are flesh and blood droids," she said.

That confused her team a little. Then she realized that she'd stopped shooting. As she took aim at the officer with a more unique mind she saw the soldier heft some kind of launcher. "Cover!" Alice ordered, highlighting the alley to their left as she got to her feet.

A warning tone sounded in her helmet and before she could reach the alleyway her personal shield came under fire. It seemed that every soldier on the ground took aim at Alice and fired at Alice, battering her defences. As her shield's energy meter shrank to a sliver, Alice felt a thud against her ribs and she was flung sideways. A pod the size of her forearm had affixed itself to her right side and her tactical system warned that it was a high explosive. She'd never seen a match for it but knew that she had to get it off. The rest of her team surged back out of the alleyway, rifles firing at the soldiers who were looking for cover away from the drop ship.

The howling from above was almost deafening the instant before the sound of anti-ship rounds ripping into the engine pylons of the dropship filled the street and three Archangels flew on. "They are not getting off the ground without their main thrusters," Carnie said with the kind of joviality she'd come to love.

Nigel and Iruuk started rushing towards Alice and she put a hand up. "Don't come any closer! She'll blow this as soon as you're in the blast radius."

"But I'm sure I can get that off you without..." Nigel countered, holding back.

Alice's training was already taking over. Approaching the situation as though she was standing on a crude land mine, she shifted the density of her armour to block as much of the blast as it could, sealing the metal slats on that side and sending material to reinforce the layers beneath the bomb. Then she did the grim work of setting instructions for her helmet up. If the bomb went off, it would seal at her neck, protecting her head, but decapitating her cleanly as she was put into emergency stasis. She pushed through the shudder that came with the mental image of it. "You ever see this before?" she asked Nigel as he and Iruuk backed up.

"No, it's not in our database, but..."

"Then shut up and let me take care of it while you kill everyone down range, soldier!" Alice ordered.

Iruuk turned, leapt out from cover and began firing his particle weapon at the enemy, starting with the officer who fired the special launcher earlier. She dove under cover, so he moved on to the framework soldier to her right, cutting a line from where she once stood across the trooper's hip. These frameworks weren't armoured like knights. Instead, they wore uniforms that didn't resist his particle beam nearly as well. He fell over, missing one leg, reaching for something to brace himself with for an instant before Iruuk caught him full in the face.

The rest of her team was doing an incredible job at taking out framework soldiers as the officers tried to get away. Alice concentrated on getting away from the bomb. She scanned it and found a receiver, a timer, and a membrane that surrounded both of them that served as a chemical trigger. If she pierced it or used an electromagnetic pulse, it would set the bomb off, which was large enough to take out anything within nearly five metres in every direction. Panic was the enemy, and she focused, aware that there were only two options left: She could take a chance and order her people to retrieve the detonator from the officer who launched the rocket propelled grenade. The other option was simpler. She could try and step out of her armour, which could open on the side opposite the grenade, then put a shield between it and herself.

"Everything okay down there?" came the question from Carnie, who was flying nearby.

He'd overheard her giving orders to her team, or he saw that they were fighting about fifteen metres down the street, forming a protective line between them and the enemy. Either way, she wanted to hear his voice but didn't want to tell him what was going on. She sent everything her sensors could see, hear, smell and otherwise detect to her father and their chief engineer, Finn. If anyone had ideas, it would be them. Even still, she couldn't imagine what fix they could come up with that she didn't already think of. Meanwhile, she had to keep working. Alice made sure that most of her suit moved to her right side to protect her from the bomb, then started slowly opening the other side. That was the moment she chose to tell Carnie, her Noah; "You know I'm crazy for you, flyboy."

"Oh, man, what's going on?" came his question.

"I'm just in a little trouble and I don't know how it'll turn out," Alice said as she felt the cool air and rain against her left shoulder. The suit started automatically opening on that side and she was surprised the bomb didn't go off.

"Alice, get out of that armour but try not to move until the last second. Keep your helmet on," came the response from her father.

"It's the only way," Finn replied grimly. "If you can palm a portable shield puck and drop it between you and the armour once you're out, then do it, but don't take extra time."

Alice saw an Archangel fighter lower to the street and slow. The officer who pinned a bomb to her struck the fighter with another rocket. It went off against the fighter's shields as it hovered, took aim at the officers trying to flee from the far end of the drop ship and tore them apart with a barrage of gunfire that rattled the air. Then the fighter turned towards her and the cockpit canopy opened to reveal Noah. "What's going on?" he asked over their private channel.

"Holy shit, he just played mayhem marksman from his fighter?" Roscoe laughed in disbelief.

"Stay back!" Alice said, getting ready to order her armour to open on one side. Then she felt the Order of Eden officer who hit her with the grenade die and the bomb affixed to her armour went off.

# EIGHTEEN

A Coordinated Aftermath

EVEN AFTER MILITARY TRAINING, experience in and out of the cockpit, and more than one time when he watched the worst thing that could happen take place before his eyes, Minh-Chu wasn't ready for what happened to Alice. The bomb went off. Her suit countered and absorbed most of the blast. Her body was sent through an opening on the opposite side while her helmet detached from the rest of the vacsuit so it could continue to protect her head.

Other than the helmet, Alice was left in her thin blue undersuit as she was sent over twenty metres down the street from the blast. Everyone and everything seemed to stop and Minh-Chu directed his scanners towards the body and saw that she was alive. Bleeding critically with a list of broken bones and other major injuries, but she was alive, and her medical system was putting her into emergency stasis while nanobots rushed to the stump where her left arm once was and the open wound on her side to stop the bleeding.

There was an ache in Minh-Chu's legs and shins as he remembered the instant flash of destruction when he once stepped in front of a grenade. The memory was vividly in his mind before he forced himself to focus. He took another look at the status screen and nodded to himself, saying; "She's going to survive. There's minimal head trauma. It could have been worse."

"Thank God," Pixie breathed.

"Alice!" Noah finally screamed as he ran to her, leaving his fighter hovering behind him. He was out-paced by Iruuk, who was a blur of silver and black, running on all fours down the street, leaping over the crater left by the blast. "She will survive. Let us do our job, Carnie," he said as he reached Alice well before anyone else and put a protective stasis bag around her.

He knew he was witnessing a show of magnificent professionalism on Iruuk's part, and the rest of their small squad was following his lead.

Carnie was the only one who was out of place. He stopped and watched Iruuk make sure that Alice was in stable stasis, no longer bleeding and made sure that she was ready for transport. "I'm on my way to you," Dame said from the Clever Dream.

"Alice would want you to do your job, Carnie," Iruuk said with surprising sensitivity even though he sounded absolutely certain. "Guard her ship."

The young pilot nodded then ran back to his fighter so he could get back into position. Minh-Chu was ready to give him permission to stay down there, but the stress levels he was seeing in Carnie showed that he was handling the fate of Alice better than anyone could expect. It looked like he was able to focus. "Carnie, are you all right?" he asked anyway.

"They've got her. She's going to be okay, so I'll be fine," Carnie replied as his fighter ascended back into position. "The best thing I can do is make sure nothing goes near the Clever Dream now."

That ship, Alice's ship, was swooping down to the street, expertly piloted down onto its landing gear with the rear hatch facing Roscoe. Theodore ran down the ramp at an inhuman speed and, with Roscoe's help, put the containment bag holding Alice onto a gurney. She was taken into the Clever Dream, the hatch closed, and the ship started its ascent immediately. "Go with them, Carnie, Easy. Give them cover. We'll watch Iruuk and his team."

"Aye, on it, covering the Clever Dream," Easy replied.

"Aye," Carnie acknowledged.

The fighters were in formation to the port and starboard sides of the ship in seconds.

Iruuk was taking over as the mission commander, his cannon in hand, pointed at the dropship down the street. "Mayu, Nigel, you're with me. We'll get every data drive in that drop ship and check the place they were raiding. Watch for traps, watch for enemy survivors. I'll perform the hard scans and plug a tuneler into the drop ship's computer. Raven, I'm requesting a pickup in fifteen minutes." There was a kind of confidence that Minh-Chu had never heard from the young Nafalli before.

"Yes, Sir," Mayu and Nigel said together as they got into place and ran alongside him.

"I'm coming," Jake replied. "Errand, you're going to have to pick up what the Raven is leaving behind at the Toy Store."

"Acknowledged, we'll move some furniture around," Remmy replied.

Minh-Chu started a private call with Jake. "She's going to be all right."

"I know," Jake replied sternly. "Her helmet and hard armour saved her. The Triton's med bay will do the rest. I just want to finish this up so we can get the hell out of here."

The words were right, but his tone told a different story. Jake wanted more than a pound of flesh for what happened to his daughter and the officer who fired the rocket-propelled grenade at her was already dead. "I wonder what they'll find when they check the transponder of that drop ship?" Minh-Chu asked, knowing that it would move his old friend's focus to something that might be actionable. Something he could fight.

"Start cutting whole sections off that fabrication line! We're past the point of careful disassembly!" Jake shouted at the salvage crew as the sound of engines starting up threatened to drown him out. Then he spoke into his communicator. "I hope they didn't wipe or destroy the ship's ID."

"Have faith," Minh-Chu said, meaning to add something clever, but then a blip appeared on his tactical map then vanished a second later. It was moving away from Iruuk's team. "Got something here, maybe. Scanning using the new parameters." He turned his scanners up as high as he could inside the atmosphere and sent a hard pulse out. The detail of the city below, the profile of every kind of energy emanating and reflecting off the surfaces and the air between increased exponentially. His hard scan revealed a moving craft below that was flying slowly down the streets using every cloaking system it had. "Marking a Class B Citadel Drop Ship," he announced.

"Take out its engines," Jake instructed.

"I'll try to make sure there's something left, but no promises. This thing's got enough firepower to wipe out five city blocks at a time," Minh-Chu replied, switching to the regional Navnet channel. "Citadel Ship: Power down and land near your current location or we will shoot you down."

The drop ship, marked as DS-4, accelerated so abruptly that it nearly collided with a building before it could turn and pull up. "Oh, they're running," Breaker said with a chuckle.

"Breaker, cover Iruuk and his team. Pixie, you're with me. We're knocking DS-4 down. Aim for weapons and engines."

All his pilots acknowledged their instructions. A tone, then a flashing circle overtop the icon showing the position of DS-4 indicated that he had a missile lock. "Firing three M-Nines," he announced as Pixie did the same. "Firing three more M-Nines," he said as he watched his first trio of high-speed tracking missiles disappear into the heavy rain. The next trio followed a second later. He could see the missiles going straight towards the drop ship as it climbed almost straight up. The enemy ship's missile compartment opened and a full volley of ten missiles was launched. They were larger, slower munitions. There was no warning tone or blinking indicator warning that the missiles were after him. Even still, he and Pixie strafed and jerked evasively to make sure they avoided the dangerous volley then launched countermeasure discs into their flight path. His counter-guidance electronic countermeasures started jamming them then, and all but three of the missiles either spun out,

losing their target lock or were torn to shreds by their countermeasure pellets.

It only took a moment for him to realize where the
remaining warheads were headed. "Iruuk, get out of there!
Three missiles inbound, accelerating fast. Impact in eight
seconds!"

"Clearing out," Iruuk replied.

"Hey!" Mayu shouted over comms.

"Get out means 'get out,'" Iruuk said.

"But you didn't have to throw me through the door," she
replied.

One of the missiles disappeared as a low boom sounded well
past Minn-Chu. "Knocked one down," Breaker said, straining.
"Two down!"

"Dammit! Heads up!" Breaker shouted an instant before the
final missile made it past him and struck the grounded drop
ship. A massive plume of flames and debris erupted, turning
rain into a cloud of steam.

"My team got out," Iruuk announced. "Maybe a hundred
watts of shield energy left between us, but we're all safe. I got
one crate of drives. The shop those soldiers were stripping is
destroyed. That was the real target, I think."

"I was able to pull the ship's core navigational log, I think,"
Mayu added.

"You think?" Jake asked as the Raven approached the scene,
descending between buildings.

"I'm connecting to it now, decrypting," Nigel said. "It looks
like the right module, but we won't know anything for a couple
minutes, Sir."

Minh-Chu locked onto the fourth drop ship they'd encountered again and resumed his chase. "I'm wishing I loaded something a little less lethal. They're focusing most of their shield energy aft. I'm going to have to hit them hard." A turret flipped around then and started its volley by striking the nose of Minh-Chu's fighter several times before he was able to get out of its sights.

"Stop letting them hit you, Ronin," Pixie said as she ripped at the drop ship's aft section with her guns, and launched a trio of missiles before the gunner started firing at her. After they scored several hits on her shields, she slipped out of the ship's firing arc.

Minh-Chu took advantage of the opening, launching three missiles from both of his launchers as he increased throttle. "I was just giving them a fair chance. Sometimes I forget that there's no point to be fair in warfare."

"My turn?" Pixie asked. She was surprisingly eager to take the drop ship out.

It was encouraging, but he didn't think she'd get a chance at another turn. Minh-Chu's fighter outpaced the enemy easily. He kept his main thrusters pointed parallel to its flight path as he rotated the body of his own ship like a turret. As he flew by, he locked on with missiles at close range, opened up with all four of his heavy guns, and then launched at the dorsal side of the vessel. "Sorry, Jake," he said as his rounds burst through the lesser shielding along the top of the ship, striking the bare hull before the three missiles he followed that up with burst through the armour into the main cabin.

The drop ship flew straight for a few seconds before levelling out, then starting a corkscrewing course to the ground, its thrusters still accelerating. "Oh, I don't think there'll be much left of that in a few seconds," Minh-Chu groaned. "Don't worry, it's not going to hit anywhere near anything or anyone we care about. Looks like the impact will be about fifty-five kilometres from the south shore of that lake."

"That is a nice kill," Pixie said, following it with an appreciative whistle.

"Good thing we won't need that ship intact. I got into the Nav Log Module from the one we found down here," Nigel said. "What do you want to know about Drop Ship Three?"

"How many are in its group?" Minh-Chu asked.

"Four drop ships, three scouts," Nigel replied. "The scout ships are already off-world. Two made it into a wormhole."

"Where are they from?" Jake asked.

"The Rixe, under the command of Order of Eden and Citadel Captain Vollis Mikan," Nigel replied, sounding proud at having the answer. "They were to rendezvous with the Rixe in the Rose System after finishing a thorough reconnoitring mission here. I have the exact coordinates right here in their mission data."

# NINETEEN

A Single Casualty

THE CLEVER DREAM, Raven, and the Errand all finished packing everything they needed into their holds and then rushed back to the Triton. Captain Blake and Captain Marda must have had experience with looting in a hurry, because they sent everything with cargo space down to the planet to speed up the effort when they were told the mission would be wrapping up in an hour instead of eight or more. All but Green Group covered their efforts while ships made frantic trips between the surface and the two Advanced Destroyers.

Minh-Chu's Green Group were the first to retire from the field. As he waited for the hangar crew to move his fighter to the service area, Minh-Chu looked at images of what happened to the Toy Factory. Other than an empty supply warehouse and one manufacturing line that looked like it got attacked by a rabid scrap cutter droid, the place was in great condition. Someone might come along, re-stock the raw materials, turn on the water pumps and start producing whatever they liked.

There wasn't one moment where Minh-Chu wasn't aware of where Alice was, or what was happening to her. When they travelled back to the Triton she was taken from the Clever Dream to the Triton's Medical Bay. Once there she was 'treated' and Minh-Chu didn't have the heart to look into the specifics. Then, as he was starting the debriefing for Samurai Squadron, she was placed in a suspension tank. That's when her status changed to green, stating that she was being kept unconscious but stable.

Minh-Chu and Ashley stole a moment before the debriefing started in a side chamber overlooking the launch bay. "I can't believe it," she told him as they embraced. There weren't many tears, and the ones that rolled down her cheeks were quickly brushed away. "I know, she puts herself at risk, but it happened so fast. Tammy says that she saved the rest of her team. They would have done anything to try to get that thing off of her before it went off, but..." she shook her head before going on. "Do you think that soldier knew what she was doing when she launched the rocket? That they were going after the squad leader?"

"I think the word is out on us," Minh-Chu replied, holding his fiancé's hand. "Our enemies know that we Haven Fleet soldiers will do anything for each other. They turned Alice into bait."

"But we aren't..." Ashley started, glancing down at Minh-Chu's armour before going on. "We still look too much like members of the Fleet, so they treat us like them."

"Yeah, and they're right to. Half of Alice's team didn't really know her, but they were willing to give their lives to save her. I know, I watched that happen while I was checking scans. Snooping is a bad habit, but sometimes she feels like my daughter too." Minh-Chu's throat threatened to close, but he cleared it and shook his head.

"I know," came Ashley's sympathetic response as she drew him into an embrace. "Do we have to debrief?" she asked after a while. "Now?"

"We should get it over with right away. If we don't keep things as professional as we can, our discipline will fall apart and people will start dying," he replied with more force than intended. He added; "That doesn't mean I won't keep it short."

Ashley blew her nose into a tissue, then regarded him. "You don't have to be strong for everyone, you know. No one expects you to be Jake."

"I'll just keep it together for now, we can fall apart later," Minh-Chu replied. "In the absence of real fortitude, a stiff upper lip can hold a tide of tears. At least for a little while."

"A British expression?" Ashley asked, cocking her head.

"We've been watching too many old Brit Townie Dramas, it's rubbing off," he replied.

A minute later Ashley was in the front row of the Ready Room and he was facing every pilot who flew in the action, even Carnie, which was a surprise. He was solemn and completely focused. Breaker stood up and asked; "Everyone here is wondering about Captain Valent's condition but is afraid to ask." He glanced down at the seat in front of him where Carnie was holding himself together, refusing to look over his shoulder.

"She's not back on her feet yet, but she's stable," Minh-Chu replied. "Don't worry, Alice has turned survival and recovery into an art form."

There was a collective sigh with the exception of Carnie, who stared at the floor for a moment, looking helpless before turning his gaze back up at his Wing Commander. All his attention was on the debriefing, as though that was what he was leaning on to keep him upright. "All right, let's get started," Minh-Chu said, bringing up footage from Carnie's Operations Recorder, advancing to the moment before Breaker launched a pair of Javelin Torpedoes into the side of a building and then letting it play. There was a spectacular explosion and Minh-Chu had to slow the footage down so they could see Breaker's fighter get hit by the blast wave that sent him through the skyscraper next to their target. After a couple of playbacks, Minh-Chu said; "Now you'll never shake your callsign, Breaker. Not only did you render your brand new Archangel fighter unspaceworthy, but you clearly proved the developer who wrote the warning about firing Javelins in an atmosphere right. I know, the warning is only two sentences long, but they're very important sentences and I want everyone to have them memorized before the next briefing. If you can't sing 'em, you don't know 'em." The last part of those instructions was something his first Sergeant would say back when serving with Freeground Infantry. He hadn't thought about him in as long as he could remember but was grateful for the impression he made. What he said next was entirely his own. "Oh, and all starfighter simulations will be set to atmospheric for the next two weeks."

That was a good note to start the debriefing on. For the next forty-nine minutes, most of the pilots were focused on learning from the action. When it was time to check on the rest of the debriefings that were taking place around the ship, he saw that his was the longest and that Jake hadn't attended any of them. He understood why, he had to check in on his old friend, but first, he followed Carnie, who looked stoic. He didn't say a word until they arrived in Medical.

It was a clean space with self-sterilizing surfaces everywhere. The size of a small hospital with more beds than Minh-Chu could count, the whole place was surrounded by two-metre-thick bulkheads. There were vault-like sections of the Triton, and that was one of them. Theodore met them as a small orderly droid with a thin stalk body and an oval head that was made to look so friendly that it was almost cheery led them to the Critical Care Bay. "Alice is stable and safe. She will recover. Jake is already there, how are you, Noah?" Theodore said as soon as he fell in beside Carnie.

"I'm fine, can I see her?" Noah asked.

"You may not want to. In fact, I advise against it. There is a procedure underway," Theodore said. The android was proving that he had the full range of human emotions with an expression and tone that was so sympathetic that Minh-Chu wanted to take the warning.

"I need to see her, Theo," Noah replied, his voice narrowing to a croak. "And keep telling me she'll be okay, man."

"I will, but..." Theodore tapped his command and control unit, his fingers entering a message and sending it so fast that they were a blur. "I've told Zac to activate a partial barrier. It shouldn't be so bad, but you should prepare yourself."

They continued on into the room, which looked like the last place Minh-Chu ever wanted to find anyone he loved. There were suspension tubes filled with blue-green gel that was almost completely clear. To one side there were surgical beds and several droids waiting for patients with the worst injuries. At the other end was a red and white door that Minh-Chu had seen the other side of when he used the ship's transit tube. He'd gone past it whenever he took a ride from the lower hangars to the quarters he shared with Ashley.

Alice was in the middle tube, floating in neutral buoyancy. Most of the tube walls were blacked out except for her head and shoulders. Jake was there talking to the lead Medical Technician, Zac while two other members of the staff monitored Alice at medical stations. In the background they were saying; "The Nanobots are finishing on her ribs now. We're almost ready to start tissue reconstruction. How are we doing with thoracic?"

"Bio-printing heads are in position. I hope she enjoys her new lungs, she'll breathe better than anyone we know in about ten minutes," the tech replied.

Minh-Chu hoped that he would see this as an interesting experience, finding out how Alice was being put back together. A realization that he'd come to trust the word of people in the medical field perhaps too much, especially when they told him someone he cared about was stable. Stable didn't mean fully recovered, and it especially didn't mean that someone would survive if something went wrong and the systems that were keeping them alive failed. He did his best to shake the tension and rising anxiety that thought brought on. Instead, he focused on Jake, Ashley and Noah.

"Why isn't she already okay? Doesn't she have the recovery meds and the..." Noah didn't finish the question before his knees failed him and he nearly dropped all the way to the floor. Minh-Chu was quick enough to get his arm around him, and

Jake turned in time to catch the rest of his weight then guide him to the chair.

Minh-Chu would never forget how Jake's expression was stern, harder than he'd ever seen at first. Then, as he turned and saw Carnie on his way to the floor, he was filled with sympathy, as though seeing the young man start to fall apart was enough to bring all of Alice's father's pain to the surface. "We've got her, she'll be all right. The bomb was just more powerful than we thought."

"So..." an orderly bot handed Noah a bottle of water and he drew on the straw, stemming the tide of tears for the moment.

Zac, tall, in a white and blue medical suit, came over and glanced at Jake, who nodded. "All right, I can tell you what's going on. First, she'll be all right. I'm sure that's what everyone's been telling you because it's what I've told everyone who asks."

"Okay," Noah replied, taking a deep breath and letting it out.

"The reason why she's in there instead of out here telling me she's ready to get back to work is that grenade was some kind of resonance bomb. Anyone who gets within about five metres of it would suffer a varying degree of fissure damage from a blast wave that causes more than normal trauma to living tissue. In short, it is made to tear biological life up."

"It was attached to her," Ashley said, a tear escaping her lid.

Minh-Chu put his arm around her and she leaned on him. "Go on," Jake urged.

"There's the obvious damage to her torso, a missing arm and most of her left leg. Most of her organs were nearly destroyed and there were hundreds of tears in her heart and lungs. The emergency medical recovery system built into her breastbone was damaged as well, but it was able to repair her pulmonary functions just enough for her to get into stasis. We're rebuilding her lungs now, printing her brand-new ones. The good news is that her helmet was able to almost completely protect her head. There are some minor micro-fissures in her brain, but we don't think her memories or personality will be affected. When she wakes up she'll be the same person you knew before."

"Okay," Noah replied. "How long will she be in there?"

Minh-Chu looked over his shoulder and regretted it immediately. Alice drifted up just enough for him to see the rough stump where her left shoulder once was. He'd seen that kind of thing before, but he wasn't ready to witness that kind of trauma on someone he loved like family. He made sure to give Zac all his attention in the following moments as he replied; "She's in, she's in a deep dream state and not feeling a thing. We're not going to rush her reconstruction or recovery. Her body will be rebuilt by the end of tomorrow. After that, I want to give her at least another three days for her brain to rewire itself a little. Like I said, she'll be the same person when she wakes up, but there was some damage and the dream state she's in is part of her recovery. I've already gotten in touch with Quan. He's on his way to help with that part."

"Why does she need help?" Noah asked.

"He's coming to make sure everything's okay, it's precautionary," Jake replied.

"I've never worked with an empath," Zac said, nodding his agreement. "I haven't gotten to that part of my training yet."

"I'd like to take a shift later. People should be sitting with her," Ashley said, looking at the tank.

"She might not know you're there, but I'll start a sign-up sheet and forward it to you," Zac said to Jake.

"I'll be here, as long as that's okay," Noah said, looking towards Minh-Chu.

"Your head is going to be here no matter where your body is, so you should pop a cot down and settle in," Minh-Chu replied. "I'll bring some snacks and hang out."

"Only two visitors at a time, please," an orderly bot said as it passed by.

"FC-Nine's right. Time for a couple of you to go do something else. We've got this," Zac said with gentle finality.

"Thanks, Doc," Noah said.

"If you want to thank anyone, thank her squad. If they didn't get her into stasis within a minute of the blast, then she wouldn't be in there," Zac said, adding; "Oh, and I'm still just a Med Tech. I'll be studying for another three years before you can call me a doctor. That's if it stays quiet in here. If things pick up that'll extend to nine, but I'll get there either way. I can go without sleep for a decade or so."

"Not medically. Studies have shown that a well-rested student is more effective in learning and creative thinking," Theodore explained.

"I know, just lightening the mood."

"Ah, right. I suppose I'll go then, but add me to the visitor list," Theodore said.

"No need. You actually are a doctor only without the hands-on training, so you're sticking around for as long as you can. We're a bunch of technicians who know how all this works. I want you here just in case something interesting comes up," Zac told him.

"Then I'll stay until she's awake," Theodore told him. "I really don't need sleep."

"I wish you knew how much I envy you right now," Zac said, shaking his head.

"We'll be back," Minh-Chu said, slipping his hand into Ashley's.

"Maybe expand the visitor maximum so we can be with her soon? There are going to be a lot of people who want to see her."

"Maybe when reconstruction is over," Zac said.

"All right, we're going to the Pilot's Den to get something to eat," Minh-Chu said, eliciting a mildly surprised look from Ashley, it was an expression that only she had when he surprised her with something, especially when he was thinking one step ahead of her. Lips pursed a little bit, dark eyes wide open and watching him, waiting to hear what he'd say next. "You're going to say you're not hungry, but everyone's gotta eat."

"Okay. Maybe we can update people there too," she replied.

"Well, with the permission of Alice's family," Zac said to Jake before returning his full attention to the progress his fellow technicians were making. The tissue around Alice's lungs were being printed.

"Tell them what's going on," Jake said. "I've got messages from a hundred-nine people who probably never met her but have a burning need to know how she's doing."

"Forward them to me," Ashley said as she gave him a hug and then started to leave with Minh-Chu.

# TWENTY

An Empty Seat At The Table

WHEN THE TRITON made a minor course change, Minh-Chu and Ashley were intrigued. Even when they were delivering fresh sushi she made herself to the family room in Sickbay, their curiosity lingered. Before Minh-Chu was about to take a moment to call Jake so he could ask about it, he and a number of officers were called to a secure meeting room beneath the bridge. He and Ashley started making their way there, meeting Iruuk in the transit tube a few stops away from Medical. The young Nafalli was uncharacteristically quiet and serious. "Hello," he said just like someone who didn't know what else to say.

"How are you?" Ashley asked, stepping towards him for a hug.

Anyone who was fortunate enough to know enough Nafalli people were aware that they loved contact. Embraces were like a language, families and young members of their society slept in shared beds, and couples almost always looked forward to the time of day when they could lounge together. Iruuk took Ashley into his arms, Minh-Chu joined her, and he squeezed the pair a little with a sigh before letting them go. As the transit car moved down the tube at a great speed, then slowed and raised a few decks, he replied; "I'm okay. I keep thinking about what happened, going through it second by second in my head."

"Then you know there was nothing you could have done," Minh-Chu said, looking up into the young man's big blue eyes. "She chose to keep everyone away so they would be safe."

"I should have seen that enemy officer. She was behaving differently, and I could have noticed it on my tactical display. I've looked at it over and over, and it looks like she singled Alice out really quickly. How? I mean, we were all behaving the same way except for me. I was more dangerous than anyone, the grenade should have been shot at me," Iruuk said. "I'm not bragging or anything, just saying that I was a more strategic choice."

"I've looked the events over too," Ashley said. "I think the enemy commander ordered all her soldiers to concentrate on you while she tried to distract everyone else."

Minh-Chu hadn't reviewed the tactical logs and was surprised that Ashley had. She had infantry training, which was required for all officers in Haven Fleet and in Jake's new group, but she wasn't generally interested in after-action reviews for events on the ground. "That lines up with what I saw as it happened," he agreed.

"Well, I'll learn from this. I won't make the same mistake again," Iruuk said as the transit car slowed to a stop.

"There's only so much any of us can do in any situation. No

one can expect more from you than your best, and you were great down there," Ashley reassured.

"I can be better," Iruuk said.

"Challenging yourself is admirable, but taking the blame for something your enemy did is unwise," Minh-Chu told him as Alaka joined them from a corridor to their left. "Alice wouldn't want you to blame yourself, so concentrate on doing your job and accepting what's happened."

"The good news is that she'll be all right," Ashley added, stroking his furry arm. "Have you seen her yet?"

"No, I haven't had time," he replied. "I will later."

The lights were dimmed. The walls were darkly tinted and glossy, making the room seem much larger than it was. Around a long table were Captain Stephanie Vega, Jake, and Liara in person. Perfect holographic images of Captain Yawen Blake and Captain Sel Marda were there as well. "So, what's happening?" Minh-Chu asked as he, Ashley, Iruuk and Alaka took their places in front of their seats. No one else there was seated, so they stayed on their feet.

"We're not going after the Rixe," Jake replied.

"We're going to arrive in the Rose System before it does, so there's an opportunity on the table," Captain Vega explained. "We have other things to cover first though, Liara?"

"The Intelligence team has finished looking through all the data storage we managed to save from the drop ship and there's mixed news. We're fairly certain that two of the smallest drives have files from Rogue on them, and there's an indication in one piece of metadata that makes it clear that these files were intended for Alice. There's really no doubt. Anyone can see it, as if Rogue made sure that whoever found the files would guess that they're valuable and that Alice would pay for them," Liara said, showing an older image of Alice with a halo of basic data that would point whoever saw it to the Haven System and how to reach her on the Stellarnet or Crewcast Network.

"We won't be able to unlock whatever she left for Alice until she's awake," Jake said, stony-faced. His voice was just as flat. "So we're moving on for now."

"Thank you, Liara," Captain Vega said. "Jake?"

"Right, the next thing. We left a Haven Node hidden in orbit around Tabrus. It was activated two hours ago, and I've already had a conversation with the new founders of New Zero. Anyone not running Order of Eden allied colours is allowed to visit the city and they're working on getting an orbital port up and running. Siren Technologies is moving into and refurbishing several stations up there. They have no qualms about taking advantage of all the empty spots they can. I see the practicality in it," Jake said.

"They could tell you thought they were corporate vultures," Captain Vega said, it looked like she approved. "It put them on the back foot since they obviously looked you up."

"Well, after doing some negotiating for us and the Rebel Captains, I put them in touch with the Haven Government, and our British Allies are taking an interest in the situation."

In response to a nod from Jake, Liara explained; "They want to work with Haven Fleet to help with orbital defences around Tabrus, especially near their port above New Zero. What they'll get in return is yet to be determined, but negotiations are underway. They'll probably carve out a large portion of Tabrus for a military base that'll be shared by the

British Alliance, Haven Fleet and their allies. We'll know within the week. We brought this to them, so we'll be welcome."

"Don't negotiations like that usually take weeks?" asked Captain Marda's hologram.

"Usually, but Jake's approach sped things up," Liara replied.

"What did you do, you devilishly clever man?" Minh-Chu asked cheekily.

"I told them that the Haven Node was under my control, and that I could turn it off if they didn't cooperate with our allies. When I talked to Oz about it, I told them to make a deal so good that New Zero wouldn't care about my threat."

Minh-Chu wondered about the other part of that conversation, the one Jake wasn't talking about, when he obviously told Oz about what happened to Alice. He suspected that there was another call that he wasn't mentioning to Ayan. His attention was called back to the present as Alaka said; "Haven Nation didn't want to distribute comm nodes with strings attached."

"I've been reminding him," Captain Vega said. "Even though I agree that we should have tighter control of the Nodes."

"Right. We won't control the technology forever, even with anti-tampering systems built in," Jake said. "So I'm going to use zero latency multi-lightyear communications for leverage whenever I can."

Minh-Chu wasn't comfortable with that. Haven was already using the network to watch for Order of Eden and Citadel communications, using access to extort cooperation didn't seem quite right, but he decided to think about that more before talking to Jake about it. He looked towards Captain Blake as she remarked; "Well, at least it's one more place that's free of the Order for now."

"That's the point at the moment. The Siren Corporation intends on taking control of as much of Tabrus as they can, but they're stretched thin. They're afraid that independent factions and small organizations will take small towns and chunks of the larger cities for themselves, eventually going to war with each other as settlements become city-states. The prospect of allies who can help them gain control of more territory sounded pretty good," Jake said. "All right, let's move on. The Rixe won't be in the Rose System when we arrive, so we're going after another target. Haven Fleet has been interrogating the Order spy we found aboard the Triton before we left our home solar system along with his crew. We've confirmed that he has a contact at Gold Haf Station in the Rose System. Not only that, but the Order has a number of shops and a travel office aboard that serve as a front for a small base of operations. They've been watching the Rose System carefully, coordinating a network of spies and processing all the information that they're gathering there. The Rose System is a major trade hub for several solar systems and is recovering faster than most, so they've been trying to take it over without disrupting its economy ever since their fleet suffered major losses in the Iyagda System."

"Gold Haf is a civilian station, a major spaceport," Ashley said. "There are going to be a lot of civilians there. We'll have to be careful."

Jake nodded. "The Triton will stay hidden in the outer solar system. We'll offload all the parts and supplies needed for the Bitter End onto the Hammer and the Renegade then they'll move on. Meanwhile, we'll load five fighters onto the Errand, which we'll use as transportation to Gold Haf. This is going to be a covert mission. We'll be dressed like passengers and crewmembers who are on leave. The fighters and their pilots will provide cover if we need firepower. I want you along for this, Ash. You and Tammy will be well-to-do passengers who are looking to party in the Rose System. Everyone will be looking at you and your servant, which will be played by..." he looked towards Minh-Chu.

He was thrilled by the prospect of playing manservant to his fiancé and her twin, but had fun feigning differently. "I'll be carrying bags and serving those two?"

"No one will be looking at you while you carry gear and equipment that'll be built into and hidden in their luggage. The security isn't great there, but I expect the Order to have scanners hidden everywhere. Ashley and Tammy will be staying in the high-end suites next to the section where the Order's operations are hidden."

"Okay, I'll do it for the good of the mission," Minh-Chu sighed exaggeratedly.

"Don't worry, we'll be kind to the help," Ashley reassured him to the amusement of everyone else in the room.

"All right, let's work the rest of the plan out then get some rack time," Jake said, bringing holographic schematics of Gold Haf Station, the Rose Solar System and planet Garos up so they hovered above the table.

"Good luck, everyone," Captain Blake said.

"Aye. I wish I was along for this one," Captain Marda added before both of their holograms faded out.

# TWENTY-ONE

Gold Haf Station

THERE WAS nothing special about the Errand other than a few power and shield upgrades. Most of the bulkheads lacked the panels that would normally hide cable runs and piping that was coloured according to what was flowing or strung through them. That was the appeal to Minh-Chu. It was an old-fashioned ship without frills, a former Customs Corvette once owned by an ally of the Order of Eden, the Sendega Corporation. He enjoyed seeing how neatly organized the cables and devices that would normally be hidden were.

His mind wasn't focused on his surroundings, however. He was carrying a large backpack with a pair of sizeable trunks on wheels standing up beside him. They belonged to Ashley and Tammy, who would be going by those first names. The false documents and backgrounds that were made for them by the

Triton's Intelligence and Fabrication Teams said their last names were Sego and there was a social media account to back up their past travels. Through a manipulation of the Haven Nodes and a database near British Alliance Territory, that false account looked like it was made there and that it was started shortly after the Fourth Fall. Civilian records dating back much longer were there as well, and it would be difficult to check anything using systems other than the Haven Nodes which had already been strung all the way into the heart of British Alliance territory. It helped that there were over thirty people who looked exactly like them. Haven Intelligence estimated that half of them knew they were fabricants, the others most likely had no idea. Either way, they could hide who they were without making any physical changes. Being manufactured had its advantages.

Minh-Chu's story was similar, only more sparse and he was in the background of many of their holograms and still images, always helping out or delivering something to the sisters. There was also a suggestion in some of them that he had or still was dating at least one of the sisters, which was explained to him as a way to cover up any over-familiarity between him and Ashley. As for his civilian background, it was intentionally spotty the further back you looked, but everything lined up with the name he was taking; Mars Param. He had to wear a Second Skin mask, which changed the shape of his jaw, cheekbones, nose and forehead enough to make him unrecognizable as his more notorious visage.

He sat down between Ashley and Tammy, on the edge of his seat since his backpack took most of the space behind him. They watched through the square porthole as the Errand closed in on Gold Haf Station. In the distance behind it, was Garos. They could barely make out the swirling brown and green clouds hanging thickly in its atmosphere in tumultuous swirls. "People live down there?" asked Ashley.

"That's what the briefing notes said," Tammy replied. "I've heard of mines on worlds like that, where the rain could burn you to the bone, and there were acid lakes."

"You know, I signed up for the Freeground Military thinking that I'd get to see some exciting places, but I didn't see anything interesting until I met Jake," Minh-Chu commented, aware that the ladies to his left and right were paying rapt attention.

"I saw a lot of amazing places after I started flying for him on the Samson," Ashley said. "You never knew where you were going next back then."

"I have a feeling those days are coming back around," Minh-Chu said as Jake entered the room in full armour. The horizontal slats that covered his body only made him look more imposing. "Are we still a go?"

"We are. There's an Order of Eden Heavy Cruiser in orbit, The Locon. You might run into some of the crew. We've confirmed that Darren Farmer is on the station as well. He's throwing a party for the officers on leave from the Heavy Cruiser."

"How did they confirm he was here?" Minh-Chu asked.

"Did they call him up?" Ashley added. She could tell that Minh-Chu was trying to get her old Captain to lighten up a little.

"Close," he replied, still so stoic that he seemed stony. "We sent him some junk mail that made it past his filter and he

checked one message from his office," Jake explained as he activated a seal check on his armour. The slats clicked, raised
lowered, and shifted from the neck down.

"Which message did he check?" Ashley asked.

"It was an ad for personal virility conditioning. If he ever
turns up in New Liverpool looking with that fake coupon for a
treatment, he might suspect something," Jake said before closing
his helmet.

"New Liverpool? That's over a thousand lightyears away,"
Ashley snickered. "It'll be a while."

"That's the point. I'll be outside. Happy hunting," Jake said
before leaving the port side debarkation room.

That was the only part of the ship that was freshly painted
and properly panelled. Jake was headed to another airlock,
where he and two people he hand-picked for the mission would
leave the Errand as it moved through a sensor dead spot. Minh-
Chu looked through the transparent section of the hull across
from him and shook his head. The armour plating had been
recently upgraded, and the edges of its panels looked like a field
of rectangular puzzle pieces. From their vantage point, he could
see one cannon that was obviously meant to break up asteroids
that were too large for its shields to handle or strike slow-moving
ships. There were thick pylons coming off of a cylindrical centre
that each had balls on the end, as far as the overall shape went.
"This place is a few hundred years old, but someone's put some
real money into it."

"Not long ago, either," Ashley said, pointing at the surface
of the station. "That plating pattern is Oro-Com, I've seen it
before."

"Oro-Com?" Tammy asked.

"They used to build and refurbish space stations and ground bases before The Fall. I guess they're running again?"

"This had to be done after the Fall. Our records show a whole different surface," Minh-Chu remarked.

"You two really are huge spacer geeks, huh?" Tammy asked. "I don't mean that in a bad way. I could probably learn a lot."

"Well, I was born on a space station," Minh-Chu said as he noticed more modern defences as the Errand passed an anti-ship satellite armed with a pair of pulse cannons.

"I've been in space for years now," Ashley said. "I love spending time on solid ground when I can though."

The trio watched as the Errand made its final docking manoeuvre. The mooring clamps latched and drew the ship to the station gently before the airlock cycled. A flat holographic image was projected through the doors showing a flythrough of the interior of a shopping area and the airlock speakers started playing audio to match the message. "Welcome to Garos Orbital Space," an androgynous voice said. "Please leave all but Class Four personal defence devices on your ship. If you cannot leave your devices on the vessel you have arrived in, then you may use the lockup to your left as you enter the station. All trade must be finalized using the Haf-Net unless you are registered with an organization with clearance to perform commerce on the station. Please declare the purpose of your visit as you enter the inner airlock. Your property, intentions and records are subject to assessment before you are allowed to enter. Please review the Law Document we have uploaded to your personal devices at your convenience. Your ignorance is not a defence. Please watch your step and enjoy your stay." The hologram disappeared after holding on the image of Garos with a gleaming star to its left which represented the station.

"Here we go," Ashley said as she led the way through the airlock. She and her sister were as graceful in high heels as Minh-Chu was in his casual but comfortable high-top shoes. The swirling black and grey pattern on Ashley's dress moved in slow coordination with the yellow and red decorating Tammy's. The undersuits they wore beneath were made to look like the fashionable, fitted safety garb that a lot of people started wearing under more revealing dresses, especially when they were off-world. They looked fantastic, and he saw how they would draw attention. Meanwhile, he was in a similarly fitted undersuit with long blue shorts and a tight shirt overtop that was a shade of green that reminded him of the colour of baby food after Laura burped it up on him a couple of months before.

Once they passed through into the station side the door closed behind them and a raspy, electronic voice demanded; "State the purpose of your visit while security conducts a scan."

"Pleasure, if that's possible here. We took a flight to this dump because it was cheaper than going directly to Rodus," Tammy replied dismissively.

The room's lights flashed green and the inner doors opened. A voice that sounded like the epitome of boredom was heard over the speakers saying; "You are clear, and the accommodations your party reserved are available immediately. Enjoy your stay on Gold Haf Station and avoid any areas marked with a red or yellow stripe across the deck. Gold Haf Concierge service is available upon request."

The floor in front of the airlock had wear marks from countless travellers' feet, and Minh-Chu immediately found the transit car that would take them to their rooms. The chests were heavier than he expected, so he led the way. There were several airlocks leading into the semi-circular outer hub, and in its centre was a pillar with advertisements scrolling up and down its length. In one of the advertisements, a grinning racer on a slender hoverbike rushed over a finish line as a spectator was suddenly bathed in a waterfall of platinum pips, slips and coins. Another ad replaced it wherein a young man was playing three hands of Blackjack at once. He tapped the first one and the attractive human dealer gave him a face card, exactly what he didn't want since it raised his total of twelve to twenty-two. Then his excitement rose as he got a total of twenty-one on the next hand, twenty on his third, and the dealer busted with twenty-five. "Live dealers and old-school games with real cards in Rusher Casino. Ten shuttles daily! Buy ten thousand credits and we'll give you ten thousand free once a day!"

"Oh, my God, is everything here about gambling?" asked Tammy as another animation of a family watching some kind of sleek four-legged animals race along a track played.

Minh-Chu glanced across the pillar and saw smaller adverts for spas, stores and finally one for immortality pass between the gambling ads. "Looks like they bought most of the space. Would you like me to reserve a table for you somewhere?" he asked.

"We're not here to gamble. Let's check out the room," Ashley said, putting her arm around Tammy's waist and following Minh-Chu to the transit car. "Maybe there are some rich mining executives hanging out in the lounge or something."

They assumed that everything they said was being monitored so the station could milk them for every credit or platinum coin they had. Liara and the rest of the Intelligence crew aboard the Triton assumed that there were organisations paying for data for other purposes. Someone from her department would be speaking to them using their subdermal communicators if they had advice that would get them close to Order of Eden Officers, he guessed.

The transit car was clean, the seats looked new, and it moved down the tunnel smoothly for only thirty seconds or so before they arrived at their destination. Minh-Chu followed Ashley and Tammy as they left the car and he was surprised by the sight of a giant red and violet geode that was in the centre of a large concourse. Lights from above and hidden within it cast vibrant light through and around it onto the circular pedestrian walk. Opposite the massive geological sample were shop fronts for clothing, shoes, at least two spas, gaming stores, and a few that Minh-Chu would have to get a closer look at to determine their purposes. The Spacerwares shop was darkened, and the sign was half taken down, spelling out RWARES instead. "Hello, ladies," said a man with a velvety, low voice to their right. He walked with practiced confidence and had a smile that could be used to reflect incoming laser fire.

"Those are some really white teeth. There's no way you grew them yourself," Minh-Chu snarked in his Mars voice, which was higher, more nasal. The tall dark and gleaming man ignored him completely.

Ashley and Tammy turned towards him. "Hi there," they said at the same time.

"Oh, I've got goosebumps," the tall, dark-haired man said. His grey and green uniform was perfectly pressed and tailored to his fashionable form. There was an insignia on his shoulder - one hollow bar - that Minh-Chu didn't immediately recognize.

"You two just elevated the class of the whole station, if you don't mind me saying."

"It's been known to happen," Tammy said, looking him up and down before locking eyes with him.

"Don't worry, I'll drag it back down," Minh-Chu snickered, mostly to himself, but he did catch a glance from Ashley that served as a warning. If he kept it up he knew he could make her crack up. His performance was already threatening to tickle her funnybone.

Ashley concentrated on the man in uniform. "Did I do something wrong, Officer?"

"Oh, I'm not with the station. I'm just wondering if you'd like to go to a function that we're holding later on. All the best and brightest are going to be there. I mean, that's unless you're here as traders."

"No, we're on our way to our room. It was cheaper to come here and stay a night before going on to..." Tammy was interrupted by Ashley, who elbowed her lightly.

She continued, changing the course of the conversation. "Well, we didn't really come this way to save money, we have plenty of that. We wanted to meet the real people of the Rose System; the people who run mining and development companies. They're the ones really making good things happen, right?"

"Of course," the man, who looked like he was probably in his early twenties, replied. "You ladies are upfront about what you want, I can appreciate that. Listen, I don't hang out on the concourse to chat ladies. I'm with the Order of Eden. We're into everything you were just talking about, and we're throwing a huge bash tonight for officers from a major ship that just pulled in. These things happen all the time here, and part of my job is to make sure that there are interesting people there like you, so I can give you two tickets, three if you need to bring the help along. These'll cover everything while you're there - drinks, food, entertainment, and fifty thousand credits at the tables. If you want to hear about what's going on in the solar system and meet the movers and shakers, then that's..."

As he went on to describe other activities and luxuries that would be on offer at the party, a blonde woman about Minh-Chu's height tapped him on the shoulder. Her hair cascaded over the shoulders of her uniform, which was open down the front, revealing just enough of her silky blouse and the shape of her inner cleavage as it strained to escape her jacket. "Hi," she chirped. She was standing and speaking so she could remain out of Ashley and Tammy's notice as much as possible, and it was working. "I know this is probably rude, but you're probably not serving those two because you want to, huh?"

It was his job to play along if they came across recruiters, so he did. "I would rather dig runoff ditches in a recycling yard," he replied in a whisper.

"You're probably way in debt or something? Or maybe they're your older sisters?" she asked in a sympathetic whisper.

"Well, I had a crush on Ash when we were kids and I guess I stayed under her spell after that. Then I got some gambling debt and, well, they bailed me out and I'm working for them now. I had no idea it would be like this, but don't tell them I said that," Minh-Chu said in a hush with as little confidence as he could manage. It was a good backstory, he approved the moment it was offered to him.

There was so much sympathy in the female Order of Eden representative's eyes that he almost felt bad for her as she said;

"You know, I was in debt too, then the Order paid everyone off so I could start levelling my life up. Now all I do is talk to travellers all day and I have so much time to myself that I don't know what to do with it all. What's your name?"

"I'm Mars," Minh-Chu replied. He didn't have to pretend to be interested because he was curious about what she'd say next. Making her think his curiosity ran deeper was easy. "What do I have to do? They're really nice in public, but they make me do all kinds of..." he hesitated, sending her an awkward look before whispering; "...things. And they used to make me sleep under the stairs." What those 'things' they made him do were, he hadn't made up yet, but he suspected that it conjured some terrible mental images in the imagination of his audience of one.

"Oh, I can help, here's my Ident. My name's Lyda. I don't give that out to anyone. Just come to the Welcome Centre when they're not looking, or come to the party. We can talk, okay? You don't have to live like this. You can level up."

"Mars!" Ashley called out, an edge to her voice that he'd rarely heard before. "Stop bothering her and show us to our room."

"Sorry, I'm coming," Minh-Chu said as he sent a nod over his shoulder at Lyda while he pulled the two trunks behind him. "I think it's this way."

A FEW MINUTES LATER, after they'd entered the room and activated a small ball-shaped anti-surveillance device that blocked all recording in the suite, Ashley slipped into Minh-Chu's arms. "Sorry, that felt completely wrong," she said.

"It wasn't just a little fun?" Minh-Chu teased, giving her a kiss on the cheek. "I mean, we haven't role-played in a while."

"Wow, too much information," Tammy laughed as she walked up to the transparent section of the hull overlooking the planet in the distance.

"Oh, our role-play was nothing like that," Ashley reassured her. "That was quick, though. I thought we'd have to visit the Order Welcome Centre before anyone like that would talk to us."

"I guess they're desperate," Minh-Chu said with a shrug.

"I overheard what the other one was saying to you," Tammy said with a smirk. "Well, enough to know that she was pretty good at getting to the point without scaring you off. And you're a good actor, by the way. I was starting to believe you were our poor manservant."

"Thank you, I do my best work in space," Minh-Chu replied with a bow as Ashley moved to one of the trunks. "When's the party, and am I invited?"

"It's in three hours. They're throwing it one level down in the Grand Gallery. Pretty stupid, if you look at it from a strategic point of view." Tammy was definitely the more tactically minded of the sisters. That and a few other very minor differences that most people wouldn't notice was how Minh-Chu could usually tell them apart. Sometimes it took a little concentration. He hoped he'd get better at it over time, especially since he was sure that their quickly blossoming relationship as sisters would last.

"How do you mean?" Ashley asked.

"Well, there are two airlocks and a lot of smaller interior doors leading right into the Gallery. If the map Jake showed us during the briefing is right, then it's a great place to hold a party with VIP guests because they don't have to go through the whole hospitality area to get there, but I would hate to work security there because the main area is way too open and there are so many nooks and crannies everywhere," she replied, her hands creating an outline of the space in the air in front of her then pointing at the edges. If she was assisted by holography, Minh-Chu was sure that she would have created a nearly to-scale image with rooms and exits along the sides of the space.

"Good for us though," Ashley said, pulling a dress out of the trunk and holding it against herself. "I wonder who we'll get a chance to make off with?"

"Make sure you change into the right dress," Tammy said, nodding at the trick trunks.

"This is going to be a great party." Minh-Chu wondered where Jake was exactly. It was easy to imagine that he was crawling around the outside, refining the plan they'd already set in motion.

# TWENTY-TWO

The Enticing Message

IN A COCKPIT or at the helm of a ship, Minh-Chu felt like he was in control of his destiny. The controls were at his fingertips, and the press of a button could make all the difference. As he, Ashley and Tammy made their way down a few short hallways, he knew that appearing at the party would expose all three of them to all kinds of risks. It would be the opposite of control, but they were going there with a specific purpose.

This was the biggest information-gathering mission that he had ever been on. The mask that hid his identity and the invisible film on his skin that gave him fake DNA was also recording every kind of signal, sound, and photon of light and even gathered things like smell and other free-floating DNA-laden material. It did so passively, and was a recent development from

Haven Fleet Sciences. Ashley and Tammy were both wearing the same, and none of them could feel it.

The metal hallways were painted soft pastel colours, but he didn't find that soothing. Everything looked too nondescript and clean. It was like walking through a pristine pre-fab base with no design features or portholes. The Triton's corridors were clean too, but they were designed to be practical and attractive, with colours and shapes that made people feel like they were in a space that was not only safe but permanent. You could be persuaded that the Triton was an enduring fixture in the universe, its destruction was inconceivable. The hotel was no such place, and Minh-Chu had to fight his nervousness as they came around a corner only to join a large crowd of people who were headed to the party.

He saw miners who did their best to clean up. In front of them were three spacers who were dressed in thin formal suits. Two of them had scars that, to someone who didn't know better, might look like burns, but he could see that they were from momentary exposure to space. Everyone was dressed for a party, and there were just as many people there who didn't look rough at all. In fact, they were just as well dressed and healthy as Ashley, who drew a few eyes with her twin at her side as they passed.

Minh-Chu was ignored as he walked behind them, staying close. "We see hundreds of people in the corridors ahead and moving in behind you. Your stats show heightened stress. Are you all right, Minh?" asked Liara's voice in his ear. The subdermal receiver would scan as skin, but he still had to whisper for them to hear his response, or at least mouth the words so they could read his lips using the changing shape of his mask. Either type of response could draw attention, so he was relieved when she said; "If you're okay, say nothing. If you need to get out of there, then say something to Ash."

He didn't say a word, but took a deep breath and then let it out slowly. "We're going to get separated," he told Ashley. "People are trying to get between us now, we don't match, even though I'm wearing the finest jacket from the case."

She half turned towards him. "We'll be okay."

"I know. We need to set a rendezvous," he whispered.

"Count the doors from the left and say a number?" she asked.

"I'll call it," he agreed. Then they came to a large pair of doors. This was the hotel's Grand Gallery, and it didn't compare to the ones in the Triton for size, but it was larger than the ballrooms in the Bitter End. There were hundreds of people in there, and more pouring in by the second. In the centre was a raised dais that was sectioned off by a gilded green barricade that looked like some kind of garden fence. He could see Order of Eden officers lounging in grey at the foot of a stage. "I see twenty-eight officers from the Locon, but the Vice-Admiral is not here," Jake's voice said in Minh-Chu's ear. "Ashley, Tammy, get up on that dais in the middle if you can without drawing too much attention."

Ashley went to work on that right away, turning to Tammy and saying; "I love the VIP Lounge, I love how it's in the middle of the whole place. We have to get there."

"Uh-huh, it looks like they have their own bar and waiters, and I love the uniforms," Tammy agreed.

"Well, you're in luck," said the young, well-coiffed man who greeted them when they entered the station's Main Trade Concourse. "How would you like to meet some of the most important people in the solar system? I can introduce you."

"Okay," Ashley and Tammy replied at the same time, giddy. They were getting good at that.

Before they took a single step towards the VIP, there was a tap on Minh-Chu's shoulder and he turned. "Oh, hi," he said as he laid eyes on Lyda, who, unlike her male counterpart, was still in uniform.

She leaned in close and whispered to him, her lips almost grazing his ear. "Do you still want to be free?"

When she leaned back and made eye contact with him, he nodded, aware that if he were really Mars, or himself when he was a young man, there was no way he would resist going with this woman. If this was one of the ways that the Order lured people into their organization, then it was probably pretty effective. A dashing young man with connections for people who were attracted to that kind of thing, and a lovely young woman who offered freedom to any number of other people. He wondered how many other types of attractive people they used, and how well they were paid. Then, as they were walking to a section of seats that overlooked the stage in the middle of the large room, weaving between dozens of people, she answered that question. "I feel like I have to be honest with you, Mars," she said, gesturing to a seat.

"About what?" he asked.

"If you decide to join us, I get a pay bonus. It's so I keep in touch with you, not that I need to get paid for that, I can tell that you're the kind of person I could get along with. I was a servant too. I was in so much debt that I couldn't imagine paying it off and being free in my lifetime. I'm here because I'm liberated. I believe that I can help you in the same way I was. I love introducing people to this. The little bump I get for showing how you can save yourself by levelling up isn't the point. I'll understand if you don't believe me."

The most convincing thing about that moment had nothing to do with her words. It was the shine of absolute belief in her eyes. The disclosure she was making was an opportunity for her to show earnestness and to relate to him. He took a moment to glance around and saw that there were several people watching her, and many other similarly dressed officers leading people to their seats. Before his silence grew too thick, he regarded her and said; "You can really help? It'll take me about fifteen years to pay off what I owe with service to those two unless I can get one of them to marry me, or something," he scoffed at the end. For a moment he forgot that Ashley was his fiancé and it actually seemed unlikely. When they started to get to know each other romantically, it was just like that. She was so kind, beautiful, and smarter than anyone gave her credit for back then that he couldn't believe that she was interested in him at all. He was transported back to the way it felt during the early days when he was sure she'd lose interest, and Minh-Chu supposed that that uncertainty showed on his altered face then.

"Oh, I can, don't worry," Lyda said, patting his knee.

"I've been to fifteen sessions," a young woman said from the row of seats behind. "Once Lyda took me to one of these I was locked in and I'm levelling up this week, transferring to a nice office on Rodus. I'll only have one roommate in the apartment they're setting me up in."

"Sessions?" Minh-Chu asked, glancing towards the stage and dais in the middle of the large space, which reminded him of an auditorium, only with much broader tiers in rings around the outer edges.

"Oh, we don't just pay your debt and make sure your body is okay with a place to live and all that stuff," Lyda said. "The Order will teach you how to address all your problems. They make sure that you're ready to live a maximized life, and that you're given the best opportunities for work that we can find for you. Larissa is going to be working in Robotic Logistics on Rodus, where she'll help rebuild the ruined sections of the planet."

"I'm going to be serving aboard the Locon, I wish I could say more, but it's classified," an older gentleman whispered. "I was requested after only five sessions over five days in the Elevation Program," a gentleman in a fresh Order of Eden uniform said. Then he nodded towards Lyda and said; "It's all thanks to her, she deserves every bonus."

"Thank you, Francis. Next time we meet, I'll be taking orders from you," Lyda said, invoking a trickle of laughter from most of the people around them. All her attention was on Minh-Chu then. "The Order can't promise that everyone gets a fantastic job, that's not realistic considering how many people will be joining soon. You're at the front of the line though, so you have a much better chance of getting something good right away. Even if you don't, you'll only have to work a basic boring job for a little while, because you're getting into this so early. There will be thousands of people in line behind you but only a dozen, or fifty ahead of you while thousands of jobs of all kinds in the Rose System, especially on Rodus, will be opening up, and..." Lyda stopped as spirited music with an optimistic tone began to play. The stage at the centre of the space below lit up. In a space next to it filled with sofas and booths with tables between them, he could see Ashley and Tammy, who were taking their seats. He counted the exits to the left of the one they'd come in through until he saw one that he was sure they could get to if there was trouble, then he said; "Do you think I could get a job after five sessions?"

"Five," said Liara. "I'm taking that as the door you want to use if you have to retreat. I'll pass that on if you don't say another number in the next ten seconds."

"Well, each session is about three hours long, and then you have to pass a test or take it again, but everyone is different, so it's possible. This is important though, I'd like to listen," Nysa said, regarding the stage.

A well-built man in a dark green suit of Order of Eden Knight armour raised out of the middle of the stage, his helmet withdrawn. It irked Minh-Chu that the flexible plates looked so much like the advanced armour that Haven Soldiers used. The slats weren't horizontally drawn across the wearer's body, but in more conventional shapes that flowed with his form, but he couldn't ignore the similarities. The figure on stage was all smiles, a drink in his hand, and he regarded the VIP area around him. "Fellow Officers, I salute you!" he raised his drink and took a sip before regarding the tiers where people were standing and sitting. "Guests! Future soldiers! Applicants and everyone who has come to embark on an incredible journey: Welcome to a gathering that you'll never forget. I hear there have been three of these every week on this station, but none of them has been so well attended or led by an actual Order of Eden crew. I have had the honour of serving aboard the Locon, a Heavy Cruiser built in the heart of Order Territory. The journey here was challenging, in fact, we almost didn't make it out of the Cefa System, where terrorists attacked the fleet. We lost some good people, but I couldn't be happier to be here now. The Rose System is filled with people who need our help, and I'm proud to announce that the Messenger is on her way here. It's a base ship with Eve, our living Goddess, aboard."

Jake was in his ear then. "This is where the Messenger is going to set up? Rodus is about to be overwhelmed."

Minh-Chu shook his head and faked amazement for the benefit of the people around him. He concentrated on the stage as the speaker went on. "I am Leader Bion, and I'm happy to announce that the Order of Eden has chosen the Rose System as our official home in the Cluster. This is where we'll reach out to the other ninety-seven nearby stars, linking up with bases we've already established and helping the billions of people who need our aid. The message is spreading right now. There are fifteen events just like this one taking place across the Rose System, where we're making our pledge to offer freedom, purpose, immortality and peace to all of you and every human being in this solar system, and then the entire Cluster. I know, for some of you, this is a send-off, you'll be taking transports tomorrow morning that'll take you to your new jobs, to a brighter future that you're helping us build. I salute you, and welcome everyone who is just about to take their first step on an incredible journey." He raised his drink to the tiers around him, the people in the seating area surrounding his stage began to applaud and everyone in the rest of the space followed.

Then he did something that Minh-Chu had seen Eve do in recorded speeches; Leader Bion looked at all the people, turning slowly as he stared in awe. The longer people applauded, the longer he kept it up, and when a section of the audience, who numbered over a thousand, felt like they were being seen, they surged, cheering back. When he looked in Minh-Chu's general direction, he could feel the energy of the crowd rise. He did too, but in his case, it was as if he was momentarily afraid that Bion would detect that he was a fraud, a spy to be bashed by the people surrounding him. It was irrational, but Minh-Chu did the best thing he could; he got to his feet and smashed his palms together, using his conspicuous applause to force his way through his anxiety in a performance of appreciation that had everyone who saw him get to their feet, including Lyda, who regarded him with a surprised smile before turning her full attention back to the stage.

The exuberance spread like a tide that rose to his left and right until everyone who was seated was standing. By the time the roar of appreciation started to wane, Minh-Chu's palms hurt, and that's when Bion downed whatever was left in his cup and tossed it far from the stage. "That's what humanity needs!" he cried out. "A lust for progress! A roar in unity that tells every-thing else to get out of our way! Humanity can never be defeated! We will come back stronger, smarter, and ready to embrace our fate as superior immortals!" he raised his arms in the air, inspiring another round of applause. As he let them down, the audience quieted.

"He has everyone in the palm of his hand," Jake said, and

Minh-Chu could hear that, wherever he was, his old friend was speaking through clenched teeth.

Leader Bion went on. "So, why would anyone need more than the comfort of a good life, a place in the universe, and a purpose to make everything better for their relations and loved ones? Why would you need something like the open Stellarnet that's already corrupting and twisting humanity in the Rose System? Is using the Haven Nodes worth sacrificing the promise of immortality and peace for all our kind?" A holographic scroll of fighting in the streets, flaming buildings and several hate sites that proclaimed that humanity had to be destroyed scrolled beside him in a large hologram then. There was footage of an Order Destroyer in its last moments as the Merciless finished it off, and then it faded away as the hull burst and warped. It was replaced with Jacob Valent standing in court, admitting to his crimes. "The Haven Nodes belong to him and his people," the Leader said, pointing at the image, which was twice as tall. "A war criminal responsible for the deaths of millions of innocent people. Civilians can't use them, can't trust them, and that's why the Order of Eden is offering you a secure network called The Order Network. It's just as fast and completely secure, and we've made sure that it's available wherever there's a Haven Node, so we are in full competition."

A small light flashed on the cuff of every Order of Eden uniform in the room, and it took a great deal of effort for Minh-Chu to keep a straight face as Lyda tapped it, activating a small display on her sleeve and swiped on ACTIVATE CONNECTION. A status screen said; SCANNING BIOMETRICS... CONFIRMING ACCOUNT... SENDING DEVICE ID 800634133795122 TO LOCAL MAIN TERMINAL...

IDENT    LEMBRUN003926312    RECOGNIZED...
MAKING    FIRST    CONNECTION...    SUCCESS!
WELCOME TO THE ORDER NETWORK, LYDA
EMBRUN!

"Wait, did we just get the biometric login credentials for
three people around Minh-Chu?" Liara asked in his ear.

"Oh, yes, how do I get one of those?" Minh-Chu asked Lyda
as he glanced around and saw two other people logging in for
the first time. No one suspected that he was starting his question
by answering Liara.

"You'll have one tonight if you follow me to the office after
this," Lyda told him, putting her hand on his wrist. "I can have
you logged in as a civilian and you'll never have to pay network
access fees again."

"Don't react to what I'm about to say, Minh," Liara warned
through his subdermal implant. "Ashley and Tammy just got
the credentials, a full biometric read and DNA profile by sitting
between a couple of officers each."

Minh-Chu did react, grinning at Lyda, who had no idea
what he was smiling about. Then his arms, back and chest
started to feel warm. Too warm.

Lyda's glad expression quickly turned to one of alarm.
"Your jacket's smoking,"

Realizing that he'd taken the wrong garment from one of
the trunks they left leaning against the outer hull inside their
room and that he was seconds away from being incinerated on
the spot, Minh-Chu yanked the fancy suit jacket off.
"Everyone back!" people around him stepped away, over-
turning folding chairs and bumping into each other as the
jacket burst into a bright, white flame then went out, leaving a

shallow burned divot in the floor. Guards were starting to move in from the aisles. He thought quickly and turned towards Lyda. "You see what they do? That practical joke could have killed me! You have to get me away from those sisters!"

To his relief, Lyda took him seriously and held her hand up, halting the guards. "You're right. Come with me, there's a hallway that leads right to our offices. I'll get you processed. You'll be free in an hour."

Liara was talking to him through his dermal implant then. "She's removing you from the event because you're causing a disruption. I know it's off mission, but we want you to go with her. The information you gather about the intake process could be important. Get as much data as you can before it's time to get out."

Minh-Chu followed Lyda, who marched him down the aisle, through a dark door into a bright hallway. He knew that the trunks in their room - which were filled with clothes made of a combustible material that would only be detectable the instant before it went off - were burning a hole through the hull of the station. The trunks were a special design too. They would seal to the holes that they made and provide a barrier so the cabin wouldn't decompress and alert the station using a basic energy field. "We're on our way in," Jake said. "The hull of the station is pretty flimsy, considering."

"Minh was wearing the wrong jacket. He nearly burned up," Liara replied to him over their secure channel. "Good hunting, and Minh? We all had a big laugh once we were sure you weren't about to burn alive or get captured."

Minh-Chu snickered at that, drawing the attention of his

escort. He covered by saying; "I can't believe I'm about to be free from those two. I can't thank you enough."

"That's what I'm here to do, help people," Lyda replied.

He took in everything as he passed down the narrow hallway. It looked like service access, and he mentally plotted the best path to the egress spot so he could do his best to get there when the time came.

# TWENTY-THREE

Up Close

AS MINH-CHU PASSED through the second black door - a bare hatchway with no adornment - he got a feeling that he might not be able to leave. When the lights came on in the next room he set eyes on a large silver form hanging from the middle of the ceiling. It was made of three long, slender spikes that joined in the middle so it looked like a human figure with its arms upraised. A simple circle was suspended between the shoulders, signifying a head. "You like it? The leadership just passed the symbol down to us to celebrate the expansion. I hear the entire Order is adopting it." Lyda looked so proud, there was more than the light of delusion in her eyes.

As he stared back at her, Minh-Chu wished he knew what he could say to shake her out of it. He told her; "This is much bigger than any of us." It was the most honest thing he could say without breaking his cover. This was the recruiting office. There were doors along the walls spaced out every three metres. The centre of the room was filled with groups of cubicles and there were several silver-skinned androids along the far end near the main doors that let out to the concourse. They were styled to look like the figure hanging over everything in the room, trying to greet people as they passed.

"That's what's so amazing. I know I'm making a difference in the galaxy, even though I'm just a part of something so big. I'm spreading a powerful message about humanity and bringing people in so we can complete our first mission in the Cluster."

"What's the first mission?"

"We have to show all the inferior species their places and take control of this wild space. I know, it seems impossible, there are ninety-eight solar systems and all kinds of places between, but you'll see. Let's get you set up. I'll enter your information so we can protect you from your debtors. Then I can start your first session. I bet you'll be able to start levelling up tonight."

Jake's voice was in Minh-Chu's ear then. "Ashley and Tammy are already on their way out. They excused themselves as soon as Bion's show ended. Get ready to move, Ronin. The sensors on the station aren't detecting us. They're not good enough to see through our stealth. We're on our way."

Minh-Chu followed Lyda to her desk, where an oval terminal projected the three-pointed symbol above it. As she sat down and pulled a stool out from under her desk, he gave in to the temptation to verbally provoke her, just a little. "I've had good friends who weren't human."

"Oh, there's nothing wrong with having a pet or two, but just because a dog wags its tail at you and it's always friendly doesn't mean it should be in charge of anything," she replied with a chuckle.

"Let her log in, we need to record the process and check the credentials," Liara said in his ear as he sat down.

Lyda waved her hand over the small console. The simple icon floating above it spun, and a holographic picture of her face appeared, then it changed into a group of icons including a money symbol, a cartoon crowd, a tiny old-fashioned screen, and others that he didn't have time to see before she tapped an icon that looked like a certificate decorated with a golden seal. Liara's voice announced; "We've got it. Your second skin suit picked up how it authenticated her and it has her DNA. She's not a low rank recruiter. You could be in more danger than you think. She's Level Five. It was right on her display when she logged in. There are only twenty-one levels, and what we've seen so far says that there are only three level fives in that whole office."

The level ranking detail was new to Minh-Chu, but from the looks of the office, there were at least thirty desks, and who knew what was behind all those doors. There could be inter-view rooms, training equipment, quarters or hallways that led to other offices. As a blank digital form appeared in her cubicle, so did a number of personal images of her with a group of friends her own age in uniform, in an open group hug with everyone grinning at the recorder. Opposite it was an image of Lyda when she was younger between who Minh-Chu guessed were her parents. "They look like good people," Minh-Chu said.

"Oh, that's my Mom and Dad. I miss them every day. They were killed in their sleep by Issyrian pirates who shouldn't have been allowed to have our technology in the first place." She stared at that image for a moment then shook her head. "I'm sorry, this is about you, this is your moment."

"The team is here, we are ready to extract you," Minh-Chu heard Jake say through his subdermal communicator. "Make the call."

If it wasn't for his training as a soldier, Minh-Chu knew that he would have faltered at that moment. Instead, he braced himself for the last phase of the mission to begin. At the last instant, Minh-Chu indulged his curiosity. "What do you think of Haven? They say they're trying to save people."

"They're liars," she whirled on him, turning in her seat. Her eyes stared into his with so much hate that it felt as though her stare could burn through him. "They're contaminating the galaxy with aliens and people who pretend to be human but aren't. They're too stupid to understand that humanity needs to follow a path or other species will take over and turn us into slaves. Leader Lucius Wheeler should have killed them all when he had the chance, but he was betrayed before he could. I admire him. He tried to show everyone on Tamber, that's the moon around Kambis where the Havenites started to organize, the path to progress, but they were already too corrupt to follow him. Now that place is a training ground for terrorists and where they build monstrous machines from stolen technology that they give to aliens that barely understand how to use it. The owners of the Haven System are so greedy that they send as many of those non-humans as they can trick to go fight for them while the Valents and their friends stay home where they're surrounded by servants who are completely brain-washed," Lyda turned away, squeezed her balled fists, then relaxed. A moment later, she apologized. "Don't worry, though, we'll teach you about that in the first two sessions, you'll see the difference between reality and propega..."

Minh-Chu pulled a stunner from under his waistband and pressed it to the back of her neck. Lyda slumped in her chair and he made sure she slipped to the floor instead of falling over. He didn't know if he stunned her then because she was perfectly distracted, or if he couldn't stand to hear anymore. Everything Lyda said seemed so upside down and wrong that he found himself struggling to find the words that could open her mind enough so she could question what she knew. It wasn't his place, it wasn't the time, and he was too frustrated.

"That is a true believer," Jake said over the secure channel.

Liara added; "According to her personal message log, she's leaving this post in a week to join the fleet as an officer. She's already completed their Boot Camp and a curriculum that an Academy Apex Program graduate would find intimidating. Haven Fleet Intelligence is going to go crazy over the course materials we're downloading."

"Well, I hope she comes to her senses before we have to fight her," Minh-Chu replied as he straightened. A droid's flat, circular head was turning towards him, looking overtop the cubicles. He looked around, pretending to be mystified, then regarded the droid, shrugged and said; "Where'd Lyda go?" hoping that the robot's sensors were too primitive to detect her as she lay half under her desk with several rows of cubicles between them. When it started moving from the front door and down one of the aisles, he knew that wasn't so. "Time to go."

One of the doors to his left opened and Minh-Chu saw the inside of a simple interview room with a table and two chairs. "Get in, I don't want you to disappear from plain sight," Jake said.

He ran in and closed the hatch. He couldn't see his armour, but felt it drop onto his back. It was heavy as it closed around him like a living thing, engulfing him in a familiar embrace. The synthetic muscle layer kicked in and took the weight off, then his display activated and he could see as though he wasn't wearing a helmet. He could see that his stealth systems were running, and there was no sign that the station detected him. "My armour checks out. I'm good to go," Minh-Chu said as he opened the hatch and gingerly stepped past the android, who looked inside the interview room, searching every corner of the cube-shaped white space.

"The path to the escape pods is marked on your map. I'm moving on to the other objective. The main data lines. There are thousands of people on this station that think it's safe to ally with the Order and even more who are just doing their job in orbit. I'm going to show them they're wrong."

"Don't do anything you'll regret," Minh-Chu said, watching Jake's marker move towards the Commerce Concourse at a run.

"It'll just be a message unless they retaliate," Jake replied.

There was a high chance that they would, but Minh-Chu was sure that the Locon would move in to defend the station. It was the best way to make sure that it was far away from the Rixe's arrival point. He spotted Ashley and Tammy's names in the squad list. "Everything okay, Ash? Tammy?"

"We're okay. Agameg delivered our armour and we're headed to the lifeboats now," Tammy replied.

"You okay, Ronin? You sound down," Ashley asked.

"I'm all right. I just saw the face of the new Order of Eden. I have a feeling that things are about to get a lot worse," Minh-Chu replied, unable to forget Lyda's pure hate.

# TWENTY-FOUR

Sight

THE WAY ALICE was handled by the containment system could have been impersonal, even cold. As Noah watched the tube she was suspended in tilt as it emptied with her unconscious form inside, the process seemed gentle instead. Zac and two other medical technicians watched status displays as the tube wall she was resting in changed shape, reforming into a bed, its core inflating as it softened as a mattress by the time it was horizontal. When the process was finished, he would have never guessed that the fully transparent bed, mattress, and rails were once the tube that she was suspended in.

"There's no washing cycle," Zac said as he laid a sheet on top of Alice's resting form, adjusting it so it came up to her chin. He handled her like his own daughter, it was touching. "The last of the gel is a restorative that'll be completely absorbed by her hair and skin. She'll thank us for it later."

"I remember," Noah said, sitting down on a chair that one of the technicians placed by the bed. "When I nearly lost my arm."

"Right, I have been trying to remember where we met before without checking your file," Zac said. "Sorry, it's a kind of absent-minded professor thing I've been struggling with since I doubled down on my medical training."

"Your people did a good job on me, no worries, Man," Noah said, unsure of whether to touch her hand or not. The mattress was dry already. "I wasn't sure which one it was the other day. Can't feel a difference."

"Glad to hear Fleet Medical took care of you," Zac said as he ran a scanner down the length of Alice's form. "She's doing really well. The last phase of recovery is almost finished. A few extra hours in suspension saved her weeks of physiotherapy. She'll wake up feeling almost completely like herself. Now we just have to give her time for her brain to recover."

"That's something I don't understand. If there was damage, then there's probably memory loss and maybe a change in personality, right? I mean, that's what we were taught about TBI's," Noah asked.

"Right. We made sure that her brain has been restored to its physical state from the scan her helmet took moments before the bomb went off. We're helping her re-establish the same thought patterns and memories by using the neural scan data to guide her redevelopment. It's not quite like duplicating a data chip, because we're just providing a pattern, she's filling in most of the blanks herself. If we used the framework method, then we'd just be reprinting her brain then imposing a copy of the last scan on it. It wouldn't be much different than her dying and getting remade. I mean, I like the idea that we can get recreated, but I see it as a last resort. Trying this is like continuing her life instead of giving up on her."

"I get it now," Noah said, looking at her peaceful face as a technician slipped a pillow under her head.

"Quan is on his way already, he's going to make sure..."

Alice started grinding her teeth and groaning in her sleep as a nearby display turned red. "What's that?"

"That's not normal activity," one of the technicians said. "She's not dreaming, something else is going on."

"You're right, there's neural activity I don't recognize. Call Quan now," Zac said, pulling up another holographic display and running a quick diagnostic. "This is out of our expertise."

"What's happening?" Noah asked as Alice started to kick, her brow deeply furrowed, hands clenched into fists.

"It's a seizure," a technician said as she looked at Alice.

"No, look at the readout, this is nothing like a seizure," Zac told him hurriedly. A hologram of Quan in meditation robes appeared. "It's Alice, I'm seeing readings I don't understand."

"I'm looking at the readouts now. This is telepathic, but this isn't interference. She's sensing something. What's going on outside the ship?" asked Quan's image.

"We haven't contacted the bridge yet, I'm looping them in. How close are you?" Zac asked as one of the technicians contacted the bridge.

"We're a little over twenty hours away from the Shattered End," Quan replied. "I can request that we re-route if you think it's required."

"That depends, what exactly is this telling you? What is this pattern? It repeats with odd variations between," Zac asked, highlighting part of the neural readout.

Quan looked at something to his left, probably at a display that was in the room with him. Then, after swiping at a holographic interface for a while he replied; "She's threatened, hiding. The repeating pattern shows that she's making an effort to do something else at the same time. Something Alice is being very careful with, that's why it looks so minimal. She's good at hiding her sensitivity from other telepaths. That tells me she has the sense that she's being hunted."

"By what?" Captain Vega asked as she appeared at the foot of the bed as a hologram.

Noah guessed what the worst answer could be. A Geist, the synthetically designed and grown telepathic beings that guided the crews of some large Sol System vessels. Their existence wasn't well known, but Noah remembered that Alice's empathic sense was given to her during an attack by one.

Not having an encounter with one himself, Noah guessed that any Geist must be extremely dangerous, considering the effect they could have on someone. Not all of them were bad, though, since the Triton used to have one and, even though Noah was sure he would never trust one, that Geist was helpful according to what Alice told him about it. Captain Vega avoided making the assumption that Alice was feeling one nearby, and so was Zac. Quan hesitated, looking at something on his end then finally regarding everyone in the room. "Whatever she's sensing is something she wants to warn us about, but you're keeping her in a sleep state, so she can't."

"I can bring her out of it," Zac said, focusing on another status display.

"Please do," Captain Vega said. "We just detected three major wormhole exit points outside the solar system. Whatever made them is on its way here, and they were high-powered. If she has something to tell us, I need to know what it is."

"I wouldn't advise that," Quan said. "Her mind is probably still healing. If her current treatment works, there may be no need to try to re-write her memories from an engram backup. We don't want to do that. Give me another minute to examine these scans. Keep sending me the live feed."

Then, like a second voice in Noah's head, he heard Alice. It wasn't exactly the same voice that he'd heard aurally, but purer in a way, as though the version he'd heard was filtered and distorted by air before. "Is everyone in the squad okay?"

"Yes," Noah whispered.

"Am I okay?"

"All in one piece," he replied, taking her hand.

"I feel that. Thank you for staying with me. Tell Stephanie that there are three Geists and two telepaths. They don't know I can sense them. I'm going to close my senses off before they can find me."

Noah regarded her unconscious form. She was relaxing quickly. "She says that there are three Geists and two telepaths in the solar system."

"Can she tell us exactly where?" Captain Vega asked.

"One minute. She's in my head, it's weird," Noah said with a chuckle. It also felt good. She was alarmed, but in a playful mood at the same time. "Do you feel all right?"

"I..." came the response in his head. "I am so aware of you. Everything else is getting closed off, it's the only way I can make sure the others don't sense me. Wait, I'm keeping you from something. Flying. You should be at your ready station but you're worried about me. I can feel your love. It's wonderful. I want to stay connected to you, but I'm tired. You should go, do your duty. I only need sleep, and I can do that alone. I'd like to leave you with something."

As Noah listened to her words in his mind he could feel a glow warm him from the inside, something wonderful and nearly overwhelming. It reminded him of how he felt about her in the best of moments, but he knew it was coming from Alice, that she was showing him not just how much she loved him, but how it felt. Someone in the room asked; "What is that?" pointing at a display.

"They're resonating. Alice has telepathically connected with Noah. They're sharing thoughts and feelings at the same time," Quan said, in awe. "There's no sign of the resistance or harm that there used to be when she used her gift for telepathy before. It's safe for her to do this right now. Maybe it's because something changed, or perhaps she's highly focused and relaxed at the same time."

"I'm sorry to break the moment, but I need more information," Captain Vega said.

The sensation of becoming tired made Noah slump in his seat, still holding her hand and Alice spoke in his mind softly. "I'm going to rest now. I have to shut everything out, including you. Here is what I see. All the telepaths I see are from the Sol System. They are Citadel."

The connection faded along with the feeling that she was inside his head but it left a very strong sensation behind, a clear mental picture. As quickly as he could, Noah brought up a tactical map of the solar system, centred the view on the Triton, then drew five lines leading away from it. "There are three Citadel ships with Geists. Two more ships with human telepaths aboard. I can't tell you which ones are closest, and which direction they are from the ship. This is how she sees other telepaths?"

"Yes, that's exactly what it's like," Quan said. "She's changing. I don't know what she'll be like at the other end of her recovery."

"Transfer that map to the bridge," Captain Vega said. "Three of those are close to the station. Warn the team there, immediately."

Noah sent his map to the bridge and nodded. "I have to get to my fighter."

"I don't think you're ready to fly," Zac said.

"I've never been more clear-headed. I don't have time for tests and scans," Noah said, kissing the back of Alice's hand and putting it down at her side. He tapped his command and control unit, connecting to the Flight Deck. "Slick, there are enemy ships on their way into the system. Two of them will come close to the Triton. I'm ready to fly, put me in a fighter."

"One second, let me check your..." Slick started saying, then he exclaimed; "Holy crap, I've never seen lower stress levels. Yeah, you're good. Could use a shower, but you're flying solo, so you're clear to sit down in your cockpit. I'll have your fighter loaded into a punter in ten minutes or less."

# TWENTY-FIVE

Leaping Into the Dark

THE CIVILIAN SECURITY outside the relatively small area of the station that was controlled by the Order of Eden was good, but not as daunting as any military installation that Minh-Chu had experienced in the past. As he passed unseen and unheard between pairs of human guards who were on patrol near the lifeboat stations, he had to remind himself that this wasn't a military base. The lightly armoured police in white and blue uniforms only had sidearms, and every second one had an aid kit slung over their shoulder. It seemed that the security personnel were just as well equipped for a medical emergency as they were for a crime.

Minh-Chu stopped at a corner, letting a pair of them pass. As they sauntered he listened to the woman regard her partner.

"You know, I really didn't think that Order bunch would trick so many people with their big shindig."

"I hear they just reached a signup milestone for the station, they won't stop talking about it on their local channel. Five hundred new joiners, just today," said the man, who was carrying the medical pack.

"Wow, there are a lot of suckers out here," his partner said, shaking her head.

"I've got debt and dreams, you know," he said with a shrug. "I make good dosh walking around, waiting for trouble here, but I perked up when they got here and started telling us about how they can wipe my loans out and get me years closer to buying a touring ship."

"You served in the Orbital Guard. They'd send you out fighting somewhere right away. Better to pay the debt off the slow way. It might speed up if you stop collecting that tile game," she replied.

"This has nothing to do with Gatherer Tiles. I'm just saying the Order's offer is tempting, you know? Imagine getting in with a group like that, sticking around until you get your hands on the immortal tech. I'd have all the time in the 'verse to just do whatever I want. Imagine..."

The conversation trailed off, and Minh-Chu's heart felt lighter as Ashley and Tammy joined him. They were still cloaked in their armour, but he could see them on his tactical display. "Whatcha doin?" Ashley asked, touching his shoulder.

"Listening to the natives. My faith in humanity just grew back a little," Minh-Chu replied.

"The Life Boats and the airlocks are over here," Tammy said, pointing at the security door a few metres down the hallway. "I like this station, by the way. Too bad about the Order people."

"I know. Maybe we can liberate it," he said as he followed her and Ashley

"There are hundreds of stations of every shape and size in the Rose System," Jake said over their comm channel. "Remmy just cracked into the Administration Controls. This place is exactly what we were told it was. Other than the spaces the Order is leasing, and that isn't much, this place is neutral ground. Give us a minute, we'll open the airlock so security isn't alerted."

Ashley asked the question that passed through Minh-Chu's mind. "Who was telling you about this place?"

"It was in a leak on the Stellarnet from Scanlon, if you can believe it. That's where the schedule for the Order's recruitment centre came from, though we verified it against what we were able to find once we arrived in the solar system," Jake replied.

"I bet that's how you knew the Locon was here too, right?" Ashley asked.

"It was, but that's the part we trusted the least. We aren't trusting everything in Scanlon's leak, even the secure parts that we had passwords for, but everything we've seen has been right. That's why we're not going after the so-called spymaster on the station. He's only as powerful as his data, and we have that." Minh-Chu would swear to anyone that he could hear Jake smiling as he finished the statement.

"Pardon me, we didn't have to come here?" Minh-Chu asked.

"We did. It was the only way to confirm the list of Order

Operatives we have, and I bet you three learned plenty about how the Order plans to recruit people in the solar system."

"Did I ever," Ashley replied as the outer airlock door opened. "They offered Tammy and me a big loan to clear our debts and to pay for a really cushy life if we signed up to go on a special retreat. They called it the Level One Life and kept telling us that it would get us on the path to levelling up."

"That was being advertised on Rodus, according to Easy and Dame's reports," Agameg said on the channel. "Maybe the Level One Life recruitment drive there and here are the same?"

"I wouldn't be surprised," Minh-Chu said, remembering images of the signs in the city of Panda. "When I watched their reports, it looked like they were trying to introduce the wealthiest people to the Order lifestyle. This is dangerous. It seems like they have something for everyone. If there's one thing I know about cults, it's that anyone can fall into one, especially people who think they're too smart to get tricked. The Order has been working on this for a while."

"Ever since they named themselves, starting in Regent Galactic and Vindyne territories," Jake agreed.

"I hate to admit it, but I'm grateful that they don't want Issyrians. My people can be gullible when they first start living on dry land," Agameg said mournfully.

"They would have had me if I didn't know better already," Tammy admitted.

"Well, I've seen the sights, met some people, and I think it's time to go," Minh-Chu said. The lights in the long room came on to reveal a row of large four-person, oval-shaped escape pods that looked older than Minh-Chu, but in brand-new condition. They were clean and status panels hanging above them showed that each one was ready for launch. "You know, my opinion of this place just got better. It looks like they've got a decent maintenance staff."

"He grew up on a space station," Ashley explained to Tammy.

"Oh, I guess you'd pay a lot of attention to this safety stuff," Tammy said as the inner airlock door slid open.

"You'd be surprised. Most people don't think about the lifeboats until they're in a hurry to leave," Minh-Chu said as he checked on the status of Green Group. He could see that Breaker and Pixie were right outside, their fighters clinging to the hull of the station just outside the airlock. There were two empty ones along, ready for him and Ashley. "Hey, Breaker, how do you like being an invisible fly on the wall?"

"You know, this was a lot more exciting in simulated missions because there was always a point where things went wrong. I'm not saying that would be better, but..." Breaker trailed off, leaving the rest unsaid.

"Thanks for stopping a few words short of completely jinxing us," Pixie grumbled from the seat of her fighter.

"Let's not talk about what's not happening, or what could happen, okay?" Easy said from where he was flying near the station. "I'm the one scouting for trouble here."

As Minh-Chu passed through the outer airlock door behind Ashley and Tammy, he looked out at the planet far below. It seemed brighter than any should, but he knew that the light of the star was shining on its atmosphere. They were in the shadow side of the station, its hull seemed like the darkest place in the solar system. "You know, I never got used to leaving a nice, warm pressurised station behind. Spacewalks really aren't my thing."

"I love 'em. It's like giving nature the finger every time you survive a nice long tumble in space," Pixie said.

"If you're tumbling during a spacewalk, then something has gone completely wrong," Minh-Chu chuckled.

"The finger?" Tammy asked.

"Oh, a rude gesture that goes way back in human history," Ashley explained.

"My tutors must have skipped that chapter. Rude gestures and foul language," Tammy said as they walked along the surface of the station's hull towards their fighters.

No one could see them or the fighting machines affixed to the outside of Gold Haf. The only reason why they knew where to go was the outline displayed on the inside of their helmets. Jake and Remmy emerged from the airlock behind him. "Are you sure we're not kidnapping anyone? I feel like we're forgetting something," Remmy said.

"No, we've got what we need, and the Triton is still downloading," Jake replied.

Minh-Chu checked on the position of the Errand. It had used the shadow of the station as cover from the Locon Heavy Cruiser's sensors to drop off the fighters in its hold and was far away, following a Navnet course out of the Solar System. "All right, you're where you should be. Everything is working out."

Ashley was getting into the front seat of her fighter while Tammy was dropping into the back. "When will I get to fly an Archangel?"

"After you finish six months of training and simulations.

You don't even have your general flight license yet," Ashley replied. "You're in my back seat until then."

"There are worse ways to get around," Tammy sighed.

As Minh-Chu's canopy closed over him, his fighter's systems linked to his armour. He shuddered as the neural link asserted itself and he mentally connected to his ship as though it was an extension of his body. He lifted off and hovered along the surface of the station until he was in position above Jake, Agameg and Remmy. Next, he opened the lower compartment doors. "You guys should have plenty of room in there since you didn't pick up a couple of unwilling passengers."

The crew module that connected to the underside and flared out into a spot with seating for five added a lot to the profile of his fighter, increasing its hull size nearly three times. It also replaced his lower turret and a missile magazine. "We're in, closing the hatch," Jake said.

"Yeah, and there's plenty of room to stretch out," Remmy added. "I love a boring mission. It means everything went right, people did their jobs, and I don't have to lose an arm, a leg, or both."

"How are you feeling, by the way?" asked Ashley.

"Better. The Fleet Sciences folks say that my condition's stable, finally, but I'm starting to think they don't know what to expect next with this whole superhuman rebuild thing. I still feel like a science project, but I have some pretty serious abs going on now, so I think it balances out. Thanks for asking. Oh, and I was wondering..."

"There's a priority transmission coming in from the Triton," Jake said as it appeared on Minh-Chu's communications system. It took nine minutes to reach them.

"Captain Vega to Green Group. We've been able to verify that there are two Destroyer Class Citadel ships between the Triton and you. We're moving to a new position using the asteroid belt for cover and we're sending you the navigational data. Each one has a Geist or telepath aboard. We are not engaging. I'm marking the last known locations of a Zhan Class Carrier that's also been detected on the other side of the system. There's a lot of room to move out there, but be careful."

"Great, we're surrounded, but not too surrounded," Pixie said.

"I'm just glad this solar system is huge. If we play this right, no one will ever know we were here, and we won't even need cloaking once we're far enough away from the Locon."

"Speaking of which, follow my lead," Minh-Chu said as his fighter skimmed the surface of Gold Haf Station's hull. "I'm going to get as much of the station between us and that heavy cruiser as we can. Then we'll follow the plan: boost hard, get away from it then open a wormhole outta here."

As the small fighter group made their way, Jake spoke to him on a private channel. "Alice is back in one piece. Zac says she's as healthy as ever, but she just had a telepathic moment with Carnie."

"I thought she couldn't do that." It wasn't the first time that Jake confided in him about Alice. He was mostly kept in the loop about her and the whole family.

"Zac's run all the scans five times. There's no damage, but she's still healing. He doesn't know what she'll be capable of when she wakes up. Well, all the way up."

Minh-Chu was about to ask; 'all the way up?' but decided that those extra details weren't as important. "I'm glad she's all in one piece. I bet she'll be up and making trouble before we're ready."

"I hope so. The Rebel Captains need her," Jake replied.

*You'll need her more,* Minh-Chu thought. The station was behind Green Group, and there was no sign that anyone from the Order detected them. "Start boost in five seconds. We want to get a hundred thousand klicks between us and the station before we open a wormhole."

They passed a cargo ship hauling a long train of containers. By the time the counter ticked down to zero, it was out of the way of their thrusters. The rumble of the ion engines was a relief as Green Group started to put more distance between them and the Heavy Cruiser. He was reminded of something his father once said. *A good parent is only as happy as their most sullen child.* "She's going to be all right, Jake."

Before he could say anything, a warning tone sounded in Minh-Chu's helmet and he evaded. "Engaging ECM," he said as he activated his electronic countermeasures, sending targeting scrambling signals and laser flashes in the direction of the two fighters that were trying to get a missile lock on him.

"They were hiding behind one of those old asteroid drilling rigs," Breaker said. "Keep playing bait, we'll go after them."

"One of them is trying to go head to head with me. Huge mistake," Easy said. "Missile lock, firing five M-Nines, jamming his incoming and breaking off."

What Easy didn't announce was that he scored a quick series of hits on the enemy fighter that was trying to close the gap between them with all four of his guns, then launched his missiles. The pair of heavier ones that the enemy launched at him missed as the approaching craft was forced to launch countermeasure decoy spikes and seek cover from Easy's shots. It was always a mistake to go head-to-head with an Archangel.

"We have five fighters within engagement range," Minh-Chu said after turning his scanners up all the way, sending a pulse that would reveal cloaked ships in all directions then checking the readings. "I'm the least manoeuvrable, so I'm turning my generators up all the way and pushing my shields. You guys are going to have to clear the sky."

"I'll fly close cover," Pixie announced. "It's about time we get to see what Swift can do in a real dogfight."

# TWENTY-SIX

Two Directions

RONIN WAS MOVING AS QUICKLY as he could away from Gold Haf Station. With the extra weight on board, he was forced to use his afterburners constantly. If he had to make too many manoeuvres, fuel would be a problem, then he'd be down to normal thrust. Three tones merged into a dreaded harmony in his helmet. "Missile locks on me from three sources, using decoy drones," he called out to his fellow pilots as he launched a set of five drones the size of his palm that would pretend to be his fighter as they flew off in different directions.

"Five? Those things take expensive materials," Jake said from below.

The tones disappeared. It worked. "Don't get cheap on me now, Hitman. There's no substitute for quality countermeasures."

"Nice shot, Easy!" Pixie said over their secure channel. One of the two fighters chasing after Swift spun out of control as Easy's rounds ripped through its cockpit.

Pixie was flying backwards, trying to get missile locks on any fighter that came within practical range where enemy fighters had a lower chance of dodging or countering missiles and bullet hits. Fitful blasts from her cannons kept the three that were trying to keep up with them from following in a straight line for more than an instant.

"Spotted, new vessel hiding behind that group of asteroids," Swift announced, marking a sixty-three-metre-long ship that had an outrigged frame to either side bristling with emitter rods. "It's not coming up on Regent Galactic's list of vessels."

"That's because it's Vindyne. A fighter transport," Jake replied darkly.

Their escape route would lead them right past it. "This is not as straightforward as it should have been. The intelligence didn't include any of this support." He looked at the asteroid group it was hiding behind. There were hundreds of large bodies of rock lined up, ready to be mined. Low-value, leftover stone and dust were being driven towards designated points by robots that gathered it up as it was ejected by the rigs. It was a perfect hiding place for fighters and ships under a hundred metres long.

Then, over the main Navnet channel, he heard a voice declare; "This is Orico Mining Operation Two Three Five to the fighters on approach. Please avoid our rigs and other equipment. We have nothing to do with your trouble and do not want to be killed in the crossfire."

"Hey, have you noticed that there's a tiny carrier hanging

out near your stuff? I mean, there's your problem," Minh-Chu replied as the tactical map in his head alerted him that ten enemy fighters launched from the tiny carrier. "We'll finish what they start if they get in the way."

"Sorry, lead incoming fighter. That's not part of our claim. Talk to Regent Galactic about whatever's waiting for you behind A-Thirty-Five-Zero-Zero-Six-Three," the operator replied.

On the encrypted Green Squadron channel, Easy said; "Holy crap, he's not talking about the ship we spotted. There's another one closer in. He just pointed out another one of those baby carriers. It's running silent, no significant emissions. Just waiting for us to go by. Its bays are half empty, so there are at least five more fighters on patrol out here."

Minh-Chu considered the situation as he watched the sensor data running through his mind's eye. Breaker and Swift had both attracted the attention of one of the fighters originally after them. What their pursuers seemed to fail to realize was that they were being led around by their quarry on purpose. Breaker and Swift finished their gradual curve, taking a few minor hits on their rear shields, then crossed each other's path so they were able to get a missile lock and full barrage with their guns on each other's chaser.

The Order of Eden fighters were each blasted by short-range missile hits, then ripped to pieces by gunfire. As the still decompressing hulls of their enemies spun towards the gravity well of the planet in the distance, Swift and Breaker turned and hit their afterburners so they would catch up to Ronin and Pixie.

"Going for a lock on Fighter Alpha Four," Swift announced, pinging one of the fighters that were after Ronin.

"I have a lock on Five," Breaker said. "Firing five M-Nines. Let's finish this one off."

"I've been pecking at them for ten minutes," Pixie said. "Okay, more like three."

"Firing three M-Nines at Alpha Four and switching to guns," Swift announced.

Ronin watched as the two enemy fighters remaining in the fight launched countermeasures and tried to break out of the vice they'd put themselves in. With Pixie ahead of them, Breaker and Swift quickly approaching from behind they weren't able to get away. They were blasted to pieces in a hail of seeking missiles and gunfire.

An energy spike only a few kilometres behind them showed up on Ronin's tactical map. "There's a wormhole exit point right behind us," was all he had time to say. A trio of gunships, each fifteen metres long, armed with three turrets appeared behind them. Minh-Chu's fighter was jostled hard. He recovered from a spin. "They're already hitting me, going evasive. Start charging your wormhole drives."

"Three Order gunships making a precision jump through one wormhole? Where did they find their navigators?" Easy asked no one in particular.

"Sending scrambler drones, locking all my Res-Nukes in. Breaker, Easy, cover me," Swift said as her fighter flipped end over end and thrust towards the incoming gunships. All four of her cannons began to fire at the lead one as she fired her lateral thrusters in what looked like a random sequence, making her incredibly hard to hit.

Easy and Breaker were quick to join her, firing ten missiles at a time at the other gunships, every time they got a lock. They would be empty in no time, but they were getting close to their safe departure point. "All right, we're jumping early, as soon as the light show's over."

"Four nukes hot, firing one and two," Swift announced. A pair of Javelin Torpedoes armed with nuclear warheads flew free of her craft. Minh-Chu counted two seconds, the time it took for those launchers to reload. "Firing Three and Four," she announced as soon as his count was finished.

Swift, Breaker and Easy pulled up and started burning towards their exit point. All three pilots indicated that their wormhole generators were ready. Three of the nuclear Javelins were destroyed by the gunship's turret fire, then the fourth exploded in a bloom of white light.

One was still intact but damaged, the other two were destroyed and Minh-Chu thought the blast damaged his fighter somehow when a strange system notification appeared in the middle of his display: PASSENGER COMPARTMENT HATCH OPEN.

"Hitman?" Ronin asked as he checked the status of the cramped cabin below.

Three new contacts appeared next to his shuttle and were quickly moving towards the asteroid field. "Ronin. There's a lot going on here. We're going to find our way onto a ship. Tell Captain Vega to drop a Haven Node in orbit and to hide another one as a backup nearby. We'll signal for help if we need it. We won't."

"Oh, I'm going to get my ass kicked if I don't get you back to the Triton," Ronin said, not sure what else to say. The three dots showing the location of Agameg, Jake and Remmy started to move towards the heavily damaged gunship and then disappeared.

They were cloaked and probably using the lowest power mode their suits could maintain while keeping them alive. "Ask Vega about the plan. Take care of Alice," Jake said before he, Remmy and Agameg completely disconnected.

"What do we do here? We have ten fighters closing in," Easy asked.

"Jump. Now," Minh-Chu ordered. If it were anyone but Jake, he would doubt his survival, or even that there was a plan involved at all. He saw at least some of the opportunities his old friend did, however. There were ships built by Vindyne, from an incredible distance away. A major Order of Eden ship - the Heavy Cruiser Locon - in the area, and a significant recruitment centre in a combined civilian-industrial space station orbiting a planet rich with resources. The gunships conformed to a Citadel design. There were too many things lined up in one place.

Ronin's pilots followed orders, and he made sure they all jumped before he did. Having an empty crew compartment made him feel like he'd failed, and he didn't look forward to the conversation he'd be having later with Ayan.

# TWENTY-SEVEN

The Better Part of Valour

THE RETURN to the Triton was so routine after Ronin and his Green Group emerged from their wormholes that he had plenty of time to think. Slick's team used the Triton's Landing Guidance System to retrieve the fighters. The deck crew helped Minh-Chu out of his fighter. He thanked them, then went straight to the Squad Room. His pilots, including Ashley, were similarly pensive. It didn't take him long to realize that he wasn't the only one who felt like they'd lost more than they gained on their most recent mission.

Minh-Chu couldn't stop wondering what Jake wanted to accomplish at Gold Haf, on the planet it orbited, or perhaps the Locon. He couldn't shake the feeling that he was missing something. It took him a few minutes to look through the automatic reporting data from the mission they'd just flown. "We're going to go through the nuts and bolts of this action," Minh-Chu said, immediately catching the attention of all of Green Group. Breaker, Easy, Pixie, Swift and her sister Tammy stopped quietly talking to each other and stared at him. "The pilots will be called back later to review the high and low points of the mission. There were both, so we can learn a lot here. The first point of this debrief is secrecy."

The doors at the back of the room parted. Captain Stephanie Vega and one of her junior officers entered the room and sat behind the pilots. "Sorry to interrupt. I'm here to listen in."

"Welcome to the Squad Room," Minh-Chu replied. Then, addressing his pilots, he said; "We're going to keep what Jake, Agameg and Remmy did at the last minute to ourselves. This can't get out until we're ready for people to hear it, or until they're back with us."

Easy leaned forward in his seat. "Sorry, Ronin, but I've gotta ask; what are they hoping to achieve? Is it extended spy action?"

"Possibly," Minh-Chu replied.

"You can't tell us anything, can you?" Pixie asked, already disappointed.

"Other than; 'think about it all you want, but say nothing,' no."

"The further we get away from the Fleet, the more it seems like the Fleet," Tammy said with a little chuckle.

"That's not helpful," Captain Vega said, leaning around the back of Tammy's seat.

"Okay, on with the debrief, this will be quick," Minh-Chu said, and he went through the most important parts of the dogfight during their escape from Gold Haf. When it was over, Breaker asked; "Why didn't we bring a Comm Node? A little instant communication with the Triton might have been helpful."

"The Triton was never supposed to go anywhere near Gold Haf, so not really," Minh-Chu replied, then he decided to reveal something that so few people knew. "Okay, one more problem that's really two. No one is sure when or if someone other than Haven Fleet and the Triton will be able to locate Haven Comm Nodes. There's always a risk there."

"Why are those two problems?" Pixie asked.

"If someone figures out how to track signals back to their origin point, they'll get a map of the whole network. That's one problem. The other main problem is that they'll know which ones are aboard ships and which are relays near planets and stations. They'll be able to track whoever is using them, so it wouldn't take much work to figure out where the Triton, or other ships carrying nodes or quad drives are."

"Oh, that explains a lot, thanks," Pixie said, eyes wide as she dropped back into her seat.

"Haven Sciences is working on a solution for that, just so you know," Captain Vega added.

"So, any other questions for me? I have a feeling I'm about to have a serious conversation with the Captain."

"No, can't save you this time, boss," Pixie said as she slipped out of her seat.

"Before you run off, I'd like to congratulate you on a successful mission," Captain Vega said, rising to her feet and stepping into the aisle. "We got lucky. Hundreds of faces have been passively scanned, all of them officers, new recruits and enlisted members of the Order and their cult. We also verified the existence of a new leader, Bion. A new attempt at using our network for their encrypted communications was discovered as well, along with hundreds of credentials to access it. I can't tell you what intelligence led us there, but we've done incredible work, taking advantage of the opportunity. Thank you."

"You're welcome, Captain," Minh-Chu said, voicing the sentiment of the moment.

Everyone cleared out of the Squad Room except for Stephanie, Minh-Chu and Ashley. Normally there would be a few lingering who didn't want to go to the Pilot's Den or their quarters, but Minh-Chu had seen the deployment board. The rest of the Squadron was getting back from patrol duty after recovery. They would be debriefing with Slick in the Strategy Centre near the bridge.

When the doors closed, Stephanie leaned against one of the high-backed seats, relaxing her official composure. "So, I know a little more than you do. Jake wanted to start hunting and he's already working on his first target. As soon as Zac told him that Alice would recover, something clicked. It was as if the three years hadn't happened. The bounty hunter came back."

"So, the Jake you worked with," Minh-Chu replied.

"The hunter who had entire jobs figured out before we changed course to get there," Stephanie agreed. "Only this time, he is looking further and higher than I've ever seen. He told me this would happen. That he'd see something, no, many things coming together in one place. I didn't believe him until he showed me the Scanlon dump." she gestured to the middle of the room and it was filled with images. Order starship locations, officers, key people, navigational data for paradise worlds, political influence maps, studies on important public figures and profiles on enemies. Minh-Chu was surprised and amused to see his own face surface along with Ashley's. It was the picture they took right after getting engaged. Neither of them had ever looked happier.

"There's Gold Haf, right there. A whole section of the file," Ashley said, stepping to the front of the room and drawing the holographic icons towards her. "The arrival time of the Locon, and Bion. Minh, did you notice something? Did Bion seem familiar?"

"I really didn't get a chance to get a good look at him. A little," Minh-Chu replied.

"Take a closer look," Stephanie invited, enlarging the image.

Minh-Chu walked up to the hologram and shuddered. "This is life-size?"

"Exact height, exact dimensions," Stephanie replied.

"No, this can't be right," Ashley said.

Minh-Chu turned Bion's figure and looked up at it. "He looks a lot like Jake."

"It's a fast-grow. A doll. A fabricant someone in Citadel made," Ashley said. "They finished him three months ago. It says it's based on Jake's DNA with a lot of modifications. The engram set is custom, she didn't know whose memories they used."

"Scanlon only knew enough to say that Bion is dangerous and experimental. Her theory was that the Knight Program was failing because they didn't have the right leadership, and Dron ordered Citadel to create a charismatic figurehead using a proven template."

"Leave it to the Order to use the most complicated solution

to solve a simple problem. They must have known that he'd find out sometime, that it would mess with his head. Now I know why he didn't tell me anything about this. I would have locked that compartment up and done anything I could to stop him from going back." It was aggravating, but more worrying than anything Minh-Chu had heard in a while.

"I agree with you completely," Stephanie said. "I bet he would have found his way back to Gold Haf, no matter what you did."

"Poor Jake," Ashley said, leaning against Minh-Chu.

"This could be worse for the Order than it will be for him though. He used to have a way of getting himself into the middle of things and coming out on top. He saw other things happening around Gold Haf. Ships from Vindyne territory, the recruitment, Order and Citadel ships coming to this system, probably this planet. What about the Rixe?"

"There are too many unknowns for it to be a good target. If that ship has a full crew, it'll best us," Stephanie replied. "We don't have all the people we need, Shamus isn't running the Gunnery Deck, and we don't know what their fighter compliment is. It would be a crazy fight, but they would take us. That's something we can fix. I called Oz before Quan got on his way. You'll have another group of pilots, I'll have another fifty-five crewmembers who are capable of working on the Triton right away. It's not half the number I wanted, but it's a start."

"Are the pilots from my list?" Minh-Chu asked.

"Five are, the other two are volunteers. Both aces. We didn't have time to consult you on this round, but Jake told me to let you in on everything if he started his hunt suddenly. Did he say anything specific about what he saw? Why he made the leap other than Bion?"

"No. He told me to take care of Alice."

"Well, I know you weren't there when he left off Pandem, but this isn't the same. When he left then he thought he could prevent trouble by making a pickup on his own. I know he left on his own because he needed to clear his head. This time he's looking for a crack that runs all the way through the Order so he can show us how to break it right apart. He wants to bring Dron here or make him irrelevant."

"He should have let me in on it," Minh-Chu said, a little confused and hurt.

"That's what I told him. I also wanted Ash in on it, but he said something that sounded more like something you'd say; 'As long as he is where he's supposed to be, he'll know what to do.'"

"I never told him that, but you're right. It's something we both heard on Freeground when we were growing up." Minh-Chu sighed and looked at Ashley. "He's right, though. I can do a lot more leading a fighter squadron, and the Triton needs you."

"I know. I don't know if I'm made to be a fighter pilot," Ashley said. "I wasn't afraid until you were the one all those fighters were after, and you were the slowest. If you need me in a cockpit, I'll go, but I'm Stephanie's best pilot."

"It's up to you," Minh-Chu said, stroking her arm and taking her hand. It actually shouldn't have been. As Wing Commander, he had a say. As the Captain of the Triton, Stephanie was entitled to recruit the best pilot she could find for the job. For his own sanity, he wanted her on the Triton, and was happy that Ashley was leaning that way. "You might be the best pilot on the ship, so you should be flying the boat with the most passengers."

"I knew you'd see it that way," Ashley said.

"Thank the stars," Stephanie sighed. "I was afraid I'd have to trade for her."

"What would that offer look like?" Minh-Chu asked, earning an elbowing from Ashley.

"You'll never know," Stephanie said, smiling at first, but that diminished. "What was he like, right before he left?"

"Quiet. I thought he was being a good passenger," Minh-Chu replied. He looked towards the image of Bion. In it, he was sleeping in a maturation tube. Perhaps it was moments before they woke him up for the first time. He recalled Alice only hours ago in a tube of her own. He considered what Jake must have been thinking while he was waiting to escape, sitting in the crew compartment beneath a fighter. That must have been a rare, helpless moment. Minh-Chu was sure that Jake was probably thinking about Bion, and how he was made using his DNA. Even if it was modified, that must have felt like an insult, a violation. "What's on your mind?" Ashley asked.

"Jake couldn't leave it alone. It's like the Order and Citadel are personally taunting him with Bion," Minh-Chu replied. "Then again, imitation is the highest form of flattery."

"Maybe he wanted to see how similar Bion is. What if he could become family?" Ashley asked.

"I don't think that's what made him turn around," Stephanie countered. "Especially since he took my security officer and Remmy, who was finally ready to get back to work. I needed those two. When Jake said he was going to take the next opportunity to make a difference the moment he saw it, I didn't think it would happen the same day."

"What can I do? How can I help?" Minh-Chu asked. Ashley nodded her agreement.

It didn't look like Stephanie expected such a straightforward offer or any help at all. After a moment's hesitation, she replied; "You have your hands full with the squadron. Ash, you have officer training and Tammy was on the officer track before she joined us. I'd like you two to help me lead the ship security team. I'll still need you to supervise the helm staff too."

"Sure, I was getting way too much sleep anyway," Ashley replied. "I mean, I'll get to work with you and Tammy, so that'll be fun."

"I don't know about fun. There are still crewmembers who think that there are no rules because we're separated from the Fleet," Stephanie said.

"We'll help you keep things orderly, Captain," Ashley said, exaggerating her response with an official tone a little.

Minh-Chu's command and control unit vibrated and he could see that it was notifying him that the Triton was leaving the solar system using its quad drives. "We're on our way to the Shattered End?" he asked.

"We have a few things to take care of there, and I'm hoping that you can get an update on the status of the Rose system ready for the Rebel Captains. I hope Alice will be ready to present it by the time we get there, but I can't get a straight answer from anyone on her condition. Zac, Quan, no one will tell me when she'll be finished recovering, when she'll be awake."

"I'll tell the Captains what's up with the Rose System if I have to. By the way, how bad is it?" Minh-Chu asked.

"Not bad. Even if a base ship arrives, and the Order of Eden presence triples, there will be plenty of room to sneak around. It's a huge solar system. It will take thousands of ships to patrol it, never mind lock it down, and most of the governments don't want the Order there and they don't know what to make of Citadel. There are a lot of opportunities here for a ship like the Triton, especially if your Space Superiority Wing is in play. If you can get the Rebel Captains to cooperate in the Rose System too, then we'll be able to make a difference here."

"What about the British Alliance? Lorander? The Nafalli?" Ashley asked.

"The British Alliance are still busy with Tiy. Lorander is up to something, but Oz couldn't share. There's a lot of corporate secrecy there, but he told me that they're helping. We just don't get to know how yet."

"What about our furry friends?" Min-Chu asked. The Nafalli had thousands of warriors who were eager to rejoin the fight against the Order, and the Triton had room.

"Um, last I heard, the Elders are considering timing and transportation," Ashley answered.

"That's what I was told. They tried to get a Haven Fleet destroyer but were denied. They'll be coming some other way."

"But they are coming," Ashley said, nodding enthusiastically. "If you're looking for crewmembers, then you'll find a lot. They're not sending newbies."

"Is there any chance you can get me in touch with the Elders so I can coordinate and get an idea what kind of people we can expect? I have command and trade gaps to fill," Stephanie said.

"I bet I can get you in touch in a few hours," Ashley said. "They want to work with you, but they wanted to be very careful not to offend anyone in Haven Fleet."

"This is starting to look more like a real resistance," Minh-Chu said. "But have you told the Nafalli about Alice?"

"No," Ashley replied. "I wanted to tell them good news as soon as I had some."

"Why don't you tell them what happened?" Minh-Chu said, knowing the answer. After having young Nafalli crewmembers aboard the Clever Dream and taking care of them, teaching them, Alice was seen as a warrior and friend by the Nafalli.

"That's a bit manipulative," Ashley said. "It might get them moving faster, though. I'll do that as soon as we finish up."

"Speaking of, I want to know how you're doing before we go our separate ways," Minh-Chu asked Stephanie.

For the second time, it seemed like she was caught off guard. She straightened her uniform jacket, an unconscious act, and cleared her throat. "I'm in love with this ship again. I thought Jake would be in charge most of the time when we came back, but I was wrong. Now, where it goes and what it does is up to me. I look forward to being on the bridge, and there hasn't been a watch yet that didn't end with someone reminding me that I'd been working for twelve or more hours and it was time to go back to my quarters. I've never felt more at home, or more alive."

"So, what's the plan for the next few days, Captain?" Ashley asked.

That brought a little smile to Stephanie's lips that time.

"We're picking up a few allies, then I'm going to see if we can get some Rebel Captains to join us on a hunting trip in the Rose system. With or without them, we're not spending any more time in the Shattered End than we have to. I want the Triton back here so we can act on whatever Jake finds. In the meantime, we're going to conduct strike and fade hits on every viable target we can find."

# TWENTY-EIGHT

The Worry of Youth

THE KIND of quiet in the Recovery Section in Medical was a restful one. Minh-Chu and Ashley followed the faintly blinking line on the floor to the right room. It didn't take long, Alice was the only occupant and they put her close to the centre of the Medical Centre where everyone gathered to work behind a high circular counter. From there they could see and hear everything happening in the entire Centre, but the place was almost empty, so it looked like the five medical personnel, Zac included, were busy with tasks that didn't have much to do with whatever was going on in the Centre.

A robot, the one Minh-Chu recognized as Zac's medical assistant from its long, thin body and freshly repaired oval head, trundled in front of Ashley and Minh-Chu. She smiled at it for a moment, but that faded too quickly. "Are you all right?" Minh-Chu asked as they stopped short of Alice's door.

"It's not something I wanna talk about here," she replied.

"We don't have to go in right away, Iruuk is in there now. She's not alone," Minh-Chu said, watching her eyes lower.

The answer was coming, she only needed a moment to put it into words. When it did, a shrug was included. "I feel like I'm disappointing you, backing away from flying with the Squadron. You need pilots, and I rate high, but..."

"That's one of the reasons why you shouldn't be in my chain of command. Anything I do, anything you do could start feeling personal."

"I know," Ashley replied, and that was true. She'd been through as much officer training as he did. "I just thought I'd be more professional than this."

"So did I," Minh-Chu admitted. "I was more on edge during our last mission than I've been in years. I really didn't think things through when I borrowed you from the Triton and put you in the line of fire. Strange thing is, I wasn't as nervous about you going under cover. I guess I thought you'd be better at it than I was, and I was right. I even picked the wrong jacket from the trunk."

"I know, that's funny now, but I was afraid you'd burn up right in the middle of a bunch of Order wannabes," Ashley snickered.

"It's good to be quick when your brain misses a trick," Minh-Chu said with a smirk, but the moment of levity was fading fast. "Hey, the Triton needs you," Minh-Chu said reassuringly. "It makes sense for you and the ship."

"I know, it makes sense for us too. That's not the whole reason I'm in my head right now, though," Ashley said. "I saw one of those pilots I shot die. I was zoomed in, following my gun's line of fire when I made the shot. When I knew he was dead and I didn't feel anything. I'd never been so focused on anything, and when it was done I moved on to the next thing like I was sorting our holomovie playlist."

"It's compartmentalization," Minh-Chu said, stopping himself from reminding her that she learned about it, even trained to enhance it while she slowly trained as an officer while she was in the Fleet.

"I know, but I want to feel bad. Especially after what I saw on Gold Haf. I know the people around me in that audience weren't crazy, maybe a little gullible, but not stupid. They were just falling into the Order's indoctrination. Everyone there was ready to find something to believe in and try a new way of life, so the Order caught them before anything else did. That pilot might have been the same. A person who was just there to improve things for themselves or maybe their kids, or brothers, sisters, who knows? I can't get there, though, Minh. I can replay what I did to him in my head, and I have, but nothing comes."

"I want you to consider something. I don't know if it's the answer, I don't know if I have one, but just think about this, okay?"

"Okay," she said, looking up into his eyes.

"Some of us can weigh what we're defending against who we have to kill, and our enemies can come up really short. Someone who I shoot down could have been my friend if we met somewhere else, but they're trying to kill me or ruin something - maybe someone - I care about, so I can't let that happen. Being able to pull the trigger is a skill for most of us, and we know that the consequences of being passive can be horrible. That's what puts my guilt to bed most of the time. The rest is the Kill Capacity, and I don't know if I believe in that science yet."

"Fleet measures that, but I haven't looked at my results," Ashley said, but it seemed like she wasn't feeling any better. "I don't want to be in a cockpit again until I understand why I can kill someone like that and…"

"You are feeling something. I know it doesn't help right now, but you're thinking it through. If it really didn't matter to you, you wouldn't be talking about it at all," Minh-Chu said, knowing that there was nothing he could say that would fix it.

"That's true," Ashley said, concern returning then. "But there are other pilots who can lead the Triton's flight team. I don't want to leave you short for patrols or missions."

"I'll make something out of the new pilots. Besides, there's a good core group. That's half the battle," Minh-Chu replied. "You can make sure the Triton gets where it has to go without hitting anything. All our stuff is here."

Ashley relaxed a little, but he hoped she'd speak to someone more qualified if it kept bothering her. Quan or Theo would be happy to help, and they were who he could go to if he needed someone with professional training. "You know what would help?" she asked, brightening a little and tapping the tube under his arm. "I'd like to hear you play that."

"As you wish," he replied, quoting one of her favourite ancient films. They'd even played the full-dive virtual reality game version of it. "I'm rusty though, so there will be a few missed notes."

"Like I'd notice," she replied, rolling her eyes.

The nurse robot regarded them, its head panning up and down as if to question whether or not they'd be going in anytime soon. As they approached, it activated the door and it silently slid aside.

The room was large enough for two beds with room to spare, but it was set up with one. It looked more like a proper bedroom with a dresser, proper intelligent linens that kept her comfortably tucked in and a faux window that was showing the interior of the Botanical Gallery. The green agricultural tower with vines draping the sides was an appealing contrast to the blue and white decor of the room.

Iruuk was sitting in a seat that was too low for him, talking to Alice. "...barely hear it, but it's soothing. I could see how..." he turned around, his long, increasingly blonde snout pointing at them as his big blue eyes went wide. "I'm sorry, I didn't know who was coming next. It just said 'A' and 'M' on the signup."

"Well, I hope it's a good surprise, not an 'oh, it's you,' kind of disappointment thing," Minh-Chu replied.

"No, no, I'm sure she's happy you're here," Iruuk said, standing, filling the space beside Alice's bed with his considerable height. The knee of his prosthetic leg collided with the frame and he patted the side of the bed as if to shush it. "I'm still a little clumsy on this."

"I think you're really steady," Ashley said as she approached Alice's bed. She touched her hand. "Hello, Alice. I hope you don't mind if we hang out for a while."

Alice slumbered, her chest rising and falling regularly,

looking serene with a halo of red curls. "I'm sure she's happy you're here," Iruuk replied for her.

When he looked back to Minh-Chu, he could see the emerging worry on the young Nafalli's face. He put his collapsed guitar down and invited Iruuk outside. "We'll be right back."

"Okay, just us girls for a while then," Ashley said, sitting on the bed beside Alice.

"What were you talking to her about when we walked in?" Minh-Chu asked, curious, but more interested in starting the conversation smoothly.

"When... Oh, I was telling her about how there's a little white noise in this part of the ship. Most mammals find complete silence uncomfortable, so they generate a kind of undulating sound that even I can't hear unless I concentrate, but it's nice. I guess it's nice. I only noticed after I read about it."

"Running out of things to talk about?" Minh-Chu asked. "I'm guessing you've been here a while?"

"Well, no. I mean, yes; I've been here for a few hours, and no, I'm not running out of things to talk about. It's just that I'm trying to talk about anything other than, you know. Other than her father leaving, or the crazy things you and Ashley saw on the station, or what the Rebel Captains will say when they realize she's... I don't know what to say about that. Zac says she'll wake up when she's ready, but I don't know if I believe in what they're doing. Letting her fix herself using deep REM sleep? That's all this remapping thing is. The memories might be there, but she has to sort it all out, and that's how they think it'll happen. It doesn't sound exact. It doesn't sound like science.

I know it's neuroscience, but how can they know what will happen?"

"Or who she'll be when it's all said and done?" Minh-Chu knew he was asking the question he was afraid of.

"Yes," he said, his nose down, hand covering the top of his head, it sounded more like a low growl. "I don't want to say anything to her that'll foul up how she is when she comes back."

"So you've been avoiding talking about her father and Gold Haf," Minh-Chu finished for him, wondering how he found out that Jake didn't come back.

He nodded, letting his hand drop back to his side and his gaze rise back to Minh-Chu's. "I wouldn't want to hear that if I were her."

"Protecting her is important, you're a good friend," Minh-Chu said, stroking the tall Nafalli's furry forearm. "But maybe you're not giving her enough credit. Remember how strong she is. I've never met anyone who can endure what she has. The only problem with Alice is that she seems to invite change, to transform over and over. It's practically part of who she is. She looks a little different, even now. I know they say they put her back together the same way, but..."

"I know. No one is talking about it, but she looks a little different. I looked it up and Sol Medical journals call it Regenerative Plasticity. At least she still looks enough like herself, but I wonder what she'll think when she wakes up."

Worry creased his brow, and Minh-Chu decided to derail his train of thought before it took him to despair. "She'll wake up and see that her best friend is there with two old friends. Well, that's unless she comes to after Carnie takes over, or when Stephanie sits with her before her shift. There are so many people on that schedule that it looks like a manifest of half the ship." A question came to mind then. "Why didn't you want to tell her about what we saw on Gold Haf? Oh, and how do you know about that already?"

"I follow the status streams of all the missions while I work in the Sciences section. It's easy to hide an extra earpiece in here," he said, plucking at one of his pointed ears. "I was listening in to the report when you landed and saw that Jake, Remmy and Agameg didn't report in. Then an hour passed, and they still didn't appear back on the ship. I made a guess. Are they all right?"

"They're fine, and if you were guessing they went back to Gold Haf, then you were right. Just keep it to yourself," Minh-Chu replied.

"I will. Don't tell anyone about my earpiece, okay?"

"No worries," Minh-Chu replied. "I'd hide all kinds of things if I had your fur."

Iruuk huff-whuffed a short laugh. "You'd be a very small Nafalli."

"Yeah, you'd have to pass me off as your baby brother or something. Just wondering, though. Why not tell her about Gold Haf?"

"The cult things you saw are horrible. I don't understand how so many humans can gather around that. I know their promises are only true up to a point. I met people who had their debts purchased and were about to be forced into service. How can they not see that it'll happen to them? Indentureship is so obvious if you think about it. No, I wouldn't want to give her nightmares. Being trapped is terrifying."

"The people who were at the gathering on the station were

desperate. They didn't want to look too closely at the opportunity they were seeing. I've been trying not to think about it, but there are humans, probably tens of thousands of them, that went to the Haven System for the same reasons. Well, there could be half a million of them, for all I know. Opportunity, the promise of freedom from hardship, and the chance to make a fresh start are so attractive to people who are down to a thread of hope or less."

"Yes, but the Haven Nation makes sure everyone knows what they're getting into, and we don't force them to do anything unless they break the law," Iruuk said. "People can leave. They've been given money so they can leave and not be helpless at the next port."

"The Order tells their recruits very similar things along with other promises. They don't give them a chance to leave after a few meetings, I bet, but I was surprised at how similar the Order and Haven's pitch can sound if you strip out some of the details," Minh-Chu explained.

"I still don't understand how people don't see through it. I would," Iruuk said with an aggravated huff.

"Maybe because you know what a loving family is like, and what it is to be amongst friends like Alice and the crew of the Clever Dream. If you were alone, I bet you wouldn't be able to see it. That's what the people who designed the recruiting strategies they're using are taking advantage of. That's what makes them some of the worst humans in the galaxy. They use our need for community against us and give us common enemies so their followers won't listen to people like you. People who know what a real family looks like."

"Then it's as sad as it is dangerous," Iruuk said.

Minh-Chu nodded and patted Iruuk's arm. "You understand it as well as you have to. I don't think you'd give her nightmares if you talked about our adventure on Gold Haf. It wasn't as dangerous as it could have been, when you think about it."

"But Jake didn't come back," Iruuk said. "Are you sure something didn't go wrong? That they're all right?" Iruuk asked in a hushed whisper.

"They're up to no good, and that's good," Minh-Chu replied, tapping his lips with his finger, trying to get the Nafalli to stop talking about it. "I can't say any more."

"Oh, oh, that's good, as long as they're the ones doing the hunting," Iruuk said, smiling at last. "I still won't tell her Jake's not here, though."

"Well, you can't. It's classified," Minh-Chu said.

The nurse droid emerged from the room and Minh-Chu looked past it before the door closed, spotting Alice, who was sitting up. Ashley was busy filling a cup of water from the dispenser beside the bed. He grabbed Iruuk's arm and turned him. "Hey, Fur-Face," Alice croaked.

The Nafalli moved to the bed in three strides and gently hugged her. "Alice."

"I'm fine. Maybe better than ever. Just really hungry," Alice replied.

"We should get you something. There are two kitchens open. What can I go get?" Iruuk asked.

"I think that medical droid is going to take care of it," Ashley said as she handed Alice the cup. "It was the first thing she said when she nearly startled me out of my suit. I'm just getting my gab on, and she says; 'Ash?' I said; 'Yeah, hey! You're awake!' Then she smacked her lips and said; 'I'm hungry.'"

"Welcome back," Minh-Chu said, grinning so much that it almost hurt. "You just can't keep a Valent down." She was awake sooner than Zac said she would be, but from what Minh-Chu could see, she was acting like the Alice he'd come to know and love like a niece.

# AFTERWORD

Thank you very much for picking up and reading this one. I've been looking forward to writing a Star Fighter centric book or trilogy for years now, and now that the first one is out, I have to say that I only want to write the next two even more.

As with most Spinward Fringe books, this one was multi-layered. Minh-Chu provides our perspective for nearly every chapter as we watch him guide a number of his pilots through the events of this novel, continue his relationship with Ashley, navigate some of his old problems and take on a new challenge. He's a difficult character to write because he's more clever and wise than I am in many ways. Many of his decisions and dialogue required a lot more thought than you might expect.

Another thing that you might have found in this book is that the main character certainly knows less than usual. A lot of planning happens without his inclusion and that takes us to the big event at the end of the novel, when Jake, Agameg and Remmy stay behind to pursue a plan of action that Minh-Chu has been left out of. He's left guessing as he has to focus on doing the best thing for his pilots while he leaves his best friend behind.

I had to consider how loud his reaction would be to that for a while, especially since I had to write the ending of this book right after Jake's twist. In the end, I decided that Minh-Chu would turn his focus to the people he could help instead of holding people to account for leaving him out of some serious planning. He would focus on Alice and her friends, which includes his fiancé, Ashley. The fact that he was excluded from a lot of planning will come up later, when more of the people involved are back aboard the Triton.

The other layers of this book concerned the Rebel Captains and the Order's new recruitment drives. While completely separate, they were equally important parts of the story to come and sides of the same coin. You can expect a collision between these groups later on.

The idea of Bion possibly being a genetic relation to Jake came along late, and it was a gift because it could feed back into themes that have been running through the series for a long time. A component of all good Space Opera is family, whether it's a group of friends, a traditional band of relatives, or through science using stolen DNA. I can't say more, but how Jake navigates this situation will be interesting.

As you've probably noticed, this book is shorter than most of the Spinward Fringe novels, and there's a reason for that. Whenever I start a trilogy, I have a tendency to keep the first book short and impactful, with a few memorable moments like the party at the Bitter End, that are meant to set the stage for what's to come. The second book is usually a little longer, digging into the details and moving the story along while giving our characters something to work through. The third focuses on resolution and a final cast of characters who face a challenge that is partially new but largely an ultimate representation of what the whole trilogy has been building up to.

Since this is a trilogy that keeps a fighter squadron at the centre, you can imagine that there will be some interesting missions, new sights, and impactful events as we move through the story. I won't be abandoning Minh-Chu's perspective either. He'll be one of the strongest voices in the next two books, but Alice and Jake Valent will have their moments too.

So, thank you for reading, and strap in for the next book in the series because it's available now from your favourite retailer or on Ream Stories.

RL

Ream, where you can find my latest serialized stories and my entire library, including exclusives: http://www.reamstories.com/randolphlalonde

My Main Website: http://www.randolphlalonde.com